PAPER AVALANCHE

www.davidficklingbooks.com

Also by Lisa Williamson:

The Art of Being Normal
All About Mia
Malala (Yousafzai) – First Names Series

Co-written:
Floored

LISA WILLIAMSON

PAPER AVALANCHE

David Fickling Books
31 Beaumont Street
Oxford OX1 2NP, UK

Paper Avalanche
is a
DAVID FICKLING BOOK

First published in Great Britain by
David Fickling Books,
31 Beaumont Street,
Oxford, OX1 2NP

www.davidficklingbooks.com

Hardback edition published 2019
This edition published 2020

978-1-910989-97-5

1 3 5 7 9 10 8 6 4 2

Papers used by David Fickling Books are from well-managed forests and other responsible sources.

DAVID FICKLING BOOKS Reg. No. 8340307

A CIP catalogue record for this book is available from the British Library.

Typeset in Sabon by Falcon Oast Graphic Art Ltd.
Printed and bound in Great Britain by Clays Ltd, Elcograf S.p.A.

For Joyce, who always made me feel special
And Bella, who told me I could write

SUMMER

1

'Umami.'

I look up from my phone. Jamie Cannon, a boy from my year, is standing in front of me with his hands in his pockets. My heart, until now beating in a perfectly normal, healthy fashion, quickly morphs into a big fat thumping monster.

'Sorry, were you talking to me just then?' I ask, nervously tucking an invisible strand of hair behind my ear.

'Who else?' Jamie replies, smirking and pouring himself a cup of orange squash.

Annoyingly, he makes a valid point. We're the only two people at this end of the drama studio. Everyone else is gathered at the opposite end, caterwauling along to the *Hamilton* original cast recording. I've been camped out by the buffet table for the past twenty minutes now, filling the time by filling my face.

The drama club's production of *Grease* finished half an hour earlier and this is the official after-show party. The members of the cast, with their quiffs and perky ponytails, faces waxy with stage make-up, easily outnumber the black-clad backstage crew, of which I am one. I would have headed home straight after the curtain call, given the choice, but my backpack and jacket are locked in Ms Chetty's office and Ms Chetty has mislaid her keys, leaving me stranded until the caretaker turns up with the master.

'Umami,' Jamie repeats, nodding at the bowl of chilli heatwave flavour tortilla chips I've been ploughing my way through. 'That's what they call any addictive savoury flavour. It's why you've eaten forty-two Doritos in the past five minutes – they're covered in the stuff.'

'You've been watching me?' I ask, heat creeping up my neck.

'Maybe,' Jamie replies, a completely unself-conscious grin spreading across his face.

I swallow. Jamie and I are in the same year but have never really spoken before. This is unremarkable. Ostborough Academy is a big school, and I'm not exactly what you'd call a social butterfly. Plus Jamie is part of the 'popular' crew who hog the beanbags in the social area and say everything in loud booming voices, like they assume everyone in listening distance is automatically interested in what they have to say. This must be a dare. I glance over at the crowd gathered around the speakers, but no one is looking in our direction.

Jamie pours himself a second cup of squash and perches on the edge of the table like he's here to stay.

Out of the corner of my eye, I note he's about three inches taller than me and muscular, the fabric of his close-fitting white T-shirt straining across his chest and biceps. I can tell from the way he's folded his arms high across his chest so his muscles bulge like inflated water balloons – that he's ridiculously proud of them.

He drains his cup of squash, immediately pouring himself another one. 'You were on lights tonight, right?' he asks, wiping his mouth on the back of his hand. His upper lip is stained pale orange.

I nod.

'You into all that, then? Lighting and things?'

'I suppose.'

At Ostborough Academy, every student is required to participate in at least one extra-curricular activity. Operating the lights for school productions is both the least time-consuming and least socially demanding option available, and I've clung onto the role since Year Seven.

'You don't fancy being on stage?' Jamie asks, tossing an M&M in the air and catching it in his mouth.

I shake my head so hard my plait smacks me across the face.

Jamie starts to say something else, but my attention is stolen by the arrival of the caretaker.

'Excuse me,' I say, cutting off Jamie's sentence and heading for Ms Chetty's office.

'Wait, you're not going, are you?' Jamie asks, following me.

It's weird, but he almost sounds disappointed.

'Yep,' I reply, ducking under the caretaker's arm and scooping up my backpack and denim jacket.

'Are you getting a lift?'

'No, walking.'

'I'll walk with you,' Jamie says, reaching for his hoodie from the heap on the floor and tying it round his waist.

'Don't be mad, it's still really early,' I say, panic fizzing in my belly.

Hamilton has been replaced with the *Grease* soundtrack and the cast are re-enacting bits of the show they've literally just performed, hyper from Haribo and syrupy squash.

'I was going to go soon anyway,' Jamie says. 'I've got to be up at six. Paper round. Plus, I'd be a proper dickhead if I didn't. It's dark out.'

I try to argue, but it's no good. Jamie's mind is made up.

We walk down the corridor in silence, our trainers squeaking against the rubber floor. We're both wearing Converse. Jamie's are charcoal grey and obviously new, the laces brilliant white. Mine are ancient, the canary-yellow canvas faded and streaked with dirt. Despite my efforts not to, we keep falling into step with each other. It's all *very* discombobulating, like my universe has been shaken up like a snow globe and everything has landed back in slightly the wrong place and no one has noticed but me.

'So, where do you live, Ro Snow?' Jamie asks as we step out into the muggy July night.

Hearing him say my name out loud sounds weird. More than weird. Until tonight, Jamie has never even registered my existence, never mind indicated he knows my *full* name.

'Quite far,' I answer, leaping on my chance for an out.

'Right over the other side of town. Probably totally out of your way, actually.'

'Try me,' he says, folding his chunky arms across his chest.

'Er, Arcadia Avenue,' I say, mentally crossing my fingers. 'You won't know it. Like I said, it's a proper trek.'

Jamie takes out his phone and jabs at the screen a few times before holding it up so I can see. 'It's not that far,' he says. 'You were making it sound like you live in Timbuktu.'

I smile weakly.

'I can't believe Year Nine is nearly over,' Jamie comments as we cross the road. 'This term's gone well fast, don't you think?'

'I suppose so.'

'Got any plans for summer?'

'Nothing special.'

'I'll be in Florida for most of it. My grandparents live out there. You going away anywhere?'

'Not this summer.'

As if this summer is the exception and not the rule.

The journey veers between awkward silences and equally awkward small talk and I'm weak with relief by the time we turn into Arcadia Avenue.

'Well, bye then,' I say, hovering by the street sign. 'You can just leave me here.'

'Don't be mental,' Jamie says. 'I said I was walking you to your door and I'm gonna. What number are you again?'

'Er, fifty-six.'

I increase my pace, hoping Jamie will follow my lead but

he does the opposite, slowing down, his head swivelled in the direction of the houses on his right. Reluctantly, I reduce my pace to match, all the while hoping the crazy hammering in my chest doesn't sound as stupidly loud as it feels.

'Do you know who lives here?' Jamie asks, stopping in front of number 48.

'No, not really. Why?' I say, fiddling with the hem of my jacket and looking in the opposite direction.

'I just thought you would, being neighbours and everything.'

'Well, we're not exactly neighbours,' I say. 'It's not like I live next door or anything.'

'Lucky you. I bet they have rats and all sorts.'

I keep walking, hoping Jamie will notice and follow but he stays stubbornly where he is, gazing up at number 48 as if under some sort of spell.

The house is mostly hidden behind thick thorny bushes, old crisp packets and plastic bags impaled on the thorns, fluttering in the faint breeze. Rotting climbing ivy clings to the walls, obscuring almost all of the filthy windows, their frames scuffed and peeling. Although its leaves are brown and brittle, the ivy seems to multiply by the day, as if slowly choking the dirty, crumbling house to death.

'I wonder what it's like inside,' Jamie ponders, screwing up his face. 'Well skeezy, I bet.'

As if on cue, a mangy-looking cat shoots out from under the gate and scampers across the road.

'Can we keep going? I kind of just want to get home now.'

'OK,' Jamie says, reluctantly dragging his eyes away from the house.

We continue down the street in silence, the only real sound the soles of our trainers scuffing against the paving slabs.

Number 56 is in darkness.

Good.

'Bye then,' I say, reaching for the front gate.

Jamie moves in closer. He smells of sweat covered up with aftershave. I try to step backwards, but I have nowhere to go, the catch on the gate digging into my lower back.

'You're different, Ro Snow. Did you know that?' Jamie says. 'Good different,' he adds quickly when I don't say anything. 'What I mean is, it's a compliment.'

He grins. He clearly has no idea that 'different' (the good *or* bad kind) is the very *last* thing I want to be.

I fumble for the catch with my left hand.

Before I can register what's happening, Jamie has wrapped both arms around my waist, his open mouth looming towards my very much closed one.

'Er, what do you think you're doing?' I say, pushing him away.

'What's wrong?' he asks, staggering to regain his balance, his face slack with confusion. 'I thought we were getting along. Didn't you?'

'I wasn't really thinking about it, to be honest,' I say, digging into the front pocket of my backpack for my keys.

'Oh . . . Well, can I use your loo at least?'

'No!' I cry, the keys slipping from my hand.

Jamie's eyes widen in alarm.

'What I mean is, you can't,' I stammer. 'We're . . . we're having our bathroom retiled at the moment.'

'I wasn't planning on pissing on the tiles.'

'Very funny. Look, the whole bathroom is out of action, OK?'

Jamie frowns. 'If you don't want me to come in, then just say so. You don't have to lie.'

'I'm not. God, do you really think I'd bother lying about something so mundane?' I crouch down to pick up my keys.

'But I really need a wee,' Jamie whines.

I stand up. 'For God's sake, can't you just go in the bushes or something?'

'Hey, don't have a go at me,' Jamie says, holding up both hands. 'We were having a nice time until you started making weird shit up.'

'It's not my problem you find the concept of my bathroom being retiled so bloody exotic!'

He shakes his head. 'You're a weird girl, you know that, Ro Snow?'

Downgraded from 'different' to 'weird' in a matter of minutes. It's clearly a very fine line.

'Well, that's rich, coming from the boy who spent most of the evening monitoring my Doritos intake,' I snap. 'Because that's not creepy at all.'

Jamie's eyes narrow into a glare. I return it with a glare of my own. He looks away first.

'Seriously, I'm going in now,' I say.

Jamie doesn't say anything, his shoulders hunched over like a sulky toddler as he pushes a pebble back and forth with his foot.

'Night then,' I add.

'Night,' he mutters, sticking his hands in his pockets and striding back up the street.

I sigh, ease open the front gate and walk up the path. I wait until I'm at the top before sneaking a look over my shoulder. Jamie has increased his pace and is already several houses away. Instead of using the front door, I go round the side of the house, the security light flicking on as I pass beneath it. I press my back against the wall, the bricks rough and cool against my splayed hands. I close my eyes and silently count down from sixty. About halfway through, the security light snaps off, plunging me into reassuring darkness for the rest of my countdown.

'Three, two, one, zero,' I whisper.

I creep back down the front path and look both ways, relieved to note the street is quiet and empty.

I take a brisk left in the direction I've just come from.

Towards number 48 Arcadia Avenue.

Towards home.

2

A rustling in the overgrowth.

Rats.

I saw a pack of them in the back garden just the other morning, scampering about leisurely, bold as brass. They were fat, with well-fed rounded bellies and tails as thick and pink as the strawberry cables you can buy for 30p from the corner shop. I'm certain they're in the house too. I haven't spotted one yet, but I've seen the droppings – skinny black pellets – and I can hear the scrabbling of their tiny sharp claws at night.

With a shiver, I push open the creaking gate. Faded red paint flakes off on my sweaty hands, the prickly shards sticking to my palms. I follow the path round the side of the house, weeds tickling my ankles and ivy tangling in my hair. The front door hasn't been used since I was tiny. I've never even seen a key for it. Not that a key would make much difference, seeing as the doorway is totally blocked from the inside anyhow. It's painted the same shade of red as the front gate. Sometimes I like to close my eyes and imagine what it looked like when it was freshly painted – shiny and bright. Above the door there's a stained-glass panel of a sunburst, each of its panes, once brilliant shades of orange and yellow, now covered with a thick layer of grime. The letter box is sealed with layers of peeling gaffer tape accompanied by a handwritten note in a dirt-splattered plastic sleeve, attached to the door with rusting drawing pins, instructing the postman to go round the back.

I unlock the back door and push it open as far as it will go. As I squeeze into the kitchen, the familiar smell of home hits, filling up my lungs and nostrils with its stale, dusty, rotten, chemical scent. It's the same scent that seems to cling to my clothes and hair, no matter how many times I wash them, and forces me to keep a miniature bottle of Febreze at the bottom of my school bag.

I grope for the light switch with my left hand. The fluorescent strip lights take a few seconds to flicker on, buzzing angrily like a disturbed beehive. During this thin slice of time I sometimes fantasize that while I've been out, some sort of miracle has occurred, and the lights will turn on to illuminate the sort of sleek, orderly kitchen you see in the pages of the IKEA catalogue. It never does though, no matter how hard I wish for it. Instead, it's the same old chaos – overflowing cupboards, a kitchen table groaning under piles of rubbish and an endless supply of dirty dishes stacked in the sink.

I inch across the overly bright kitchen, navigating the

boxes and bags and gravity-defying piles of papers, climbing and squeezing, ducking and contorting like I'm a contestant on *The Cube*.

I imagine a parallel universe where I invited Jamie in. Just the thought makes me want to shrivel up with embarrassment. And fear. Because it's not just about him thinking I'm weird or disgusting. It's about him telling an adult. And that adult making a well-meaning call to Social Services. And Social Services coming to take me away. And then what would happen? Because as bad as the house is, it would be a hundred times worse if I wasn't around. How long would Bonnie last without me? I dread to think.

I shudder and continue into the hallway. It's similarly packed, the flowery wallpaper almost entirely hidden from view. A string of fairy lights winds round the bannister – a remnant of a time when my mum and I actually celebrated Christmas properly, with presents, and a real tree, and turkey for lunch. I've been waiting for them to run out of juice for years now, but they stubbornly hang on, their bulbs emitting the weariest of rainbow glows as I pass.

There was a time when I could walk down the hallway more or less normally, but over the years, as more and more junk has been piled up against either wall, the floor space has become narrower and narrower, forcing me to edge along it sideways, like a crab. According to the internet, the 'experts' call these narrow passages 'goat paths', because they resemble the well-trodden trails goats follow on mountainsides. Only whereas the goats are treading on grass and dirt, I'm treading on paper – mounds and mounds of it, the surface slippery and bumpy beneath my feet. It's been so long since I last saw the hallway carpet, I can't remember for certain what colour it is.

My mum, Bonnie, doesn't really discriminate when it comes to her 'collecting', but it's definitely paper that dominates – newspapers, battered paperbacks, leaflets, catalogues, bills, receipts, handwritten letters, postcards, travel brochures, shopping lists, old telephone books, calendars and diaries from years gone by, notebooks filled with empty pages, recipes and vouchers clipped from the pages of magazines, envelopes separated from their original contents, old train tickets. And greetings cards. Hundreds and hundreds of unsent greetings cards – birthday cards, Christmas cards, congratulations cards, thank you cards, get well soon cards – each one of them blank inside.

Sometimes, I try to ignore the mess, not to let it get to me. Or I try telling myself that it could be worse, that Bonnie could be what is known as a 'dirty' hoarder and the house could be full of used sanitary towels and human excrement, so aren't I actually quite lucky? Occasionally my pep talks work. Not tonight though. Tonight, every single scrap of paper makes me want to scream at the top of my lungs, until my voice is hoarse and my throat red raw.

I brace myself and push open the living-room door. Bonnie is sitting in the one available spot – a floral armchair with a broken footrest and lumpy seat cushion, the fabric discoloured from years of occupation. A large glass of red wine is balanced precariously on the stack of old newspapers acting as a makeshift side table.

Bonnie.

Never Mum or Mummy or Mother.

Just Bonnie.

We look nothing like each other. While Bonnie is tanned (albeit out of a bottle) and blonde and comic-book curvy, I'm pale and mousy and straight-up-and-down. The only feature that's vaguely similar is our eyes – big and rain-cloud grey and exactly the same shape, drooping down ever so slightly at the sides.

'Sad eyes,' my gran (my dad's mum) once remarked with more than a hint of disapproval. 'Just like your mother's.'

I spent ages in the mirror after that, smiling inanely at my reflection in an attempt to fight what nature had given me. But it was no good. My gran was right. Even with the biggest, toothiest grin on my face, my eyes can't help but tell a different story.

Bonnie is wearing one of her stage outfits – a low-cut red sequinned dress with a split up the right thigh. From afar, it looks great, but up close it's difficult to miss the loose threads and numerous sequinless patches. Her shoes, a pair of matching glittery heels that she has to respray before every gig, lie abandoned on the floor, the soles scored with scissors to prevent her from slipping on stage. The red clashes with her brassy blonde hair, hard and crunchy to the touch from all the backcombing and hairspray she subjects it to before each gig.

I don't know for sure, but I'd hazard a confident guess that when Jamie imagined the sort of person who might live in place like this, he wasn't picturing Bonnie.

My eyes fall on the half-smoked cigarette smouldering in an ashtray on Bonnie's lap.

'You do know that if that goes over, this whole place would go up in flames,' I say. This entire house is one massive fire hazard – a big fat bonfire just waiting for a match.

'Sorry?' Bonnie says, her eyes flickering with annoyance at the interruption.

Both the television and radio are blaring – 'Sweet Talking Guy' by The Chiffons battling to be heard over an episode of a reality TV show I don't know the name of.

I swear under my breath as I search for the radio, eventually locating it nestled amongst the pile of junk covering the sofa. I turn it off, and repeat what I just said.

'Don't get at me, Ro, not tonight,' Bonnie says, lifting the cigarette to her lips and taking a hungry drag.

'Why? What happened? I thought you had a gig,' I say, looking for somewhere to put the radio before giving up and tossing it back where I found it.

'Ha!' Bonnie says, stubbing out the cigarette.

On the TV, a group of bronzed and bejewelled women are gesticulating wildly as they screech at each other. Bonnie appears enthralled, but it makes my head hurt.

'Can you turn that down a bit?' I ask, pointing at the screen.

Bonnie sighs, lifting the remote like it's made from lead and reducing the volume by a few notches.

'What happened to your gig?' I ask, finally able to hear myself properly.

'It was cancelled,' Bonnie replies, peeling off her false

eyelashes, each of them thick with layers of old glue. Discarded on the arm of her chair, they look like a pair of dead spiders.

'Why?' I ask.

'Oh, booking cockup at their end. Bloody bastards rang me when I was halfway up the pissing M1 and told me not to bother turning up.'

'Are they still paying you?'

She tuts. 'I wish.'

'But that's not fair.'

'Tell me about it.'

'Have you spoken to Pip? What did he say?'

Bonnie removes her chandelier earrings, draping them next to her eyelashes. The cheap glass catches the light.

'Bonnie, did you hear me? Have you spoken to Pip? It's his job to sort out stuff like this.'

'Pip's not working for me any more,' Bonnie says, not quite meeting my eye as she massages her red earlobes.

'Why not?'

'I sacked him.'

'You sacked your manager?' I splutter. 'When?'

'Just after Easter.'

All I can do is stare. She sacked Pip over three months ago and didn't think to say anything. Even now she's acting like it's no big deal, humming as she reaches for her wine.

'Why didn't you tell me?' I ask.

She breaks off from her humming. 'Because I knew you'd only go and make a big deal out of it.'

'What happened?'

'We had a falling out.'

'Over what?'

'He was rude about my set. And I can't work with someone who has no faith in me. It stifles my creativity.'

'But we're skint!'

Over the past few months I've opened our bank statements and watched our balance steadily fall. Now I know why.

'Oh, don't be dramatic. We're fine,' Bonnie says.

'We're not "fine"!' I cry. 'We've been overdrawn for ages now. I keep telling you, but you never listen!'

Bonnie closes her eyes and rubs the bridge of her nose. 'Please don't get at me, Ro, not tonight. I've just driven halfway to Manchester and back for sweet F.A. I'm tired and I'm fed-up and all I want to do is have a glass of wine and watch a bit of telly and forget about the whole bloody fiasco for a few hours. Is that really too much to ask?'

'Yes! We've got a load of bills coming out of the account next week. If we don't top up it up we'll be even *more* in the red!'

'So, we go a bit further into the overdraft. Isn't that what they're for?'

'How would you even know? You haven't opened a bank statement in about five years.'

'Attitude!' Bonnie cries, pointing an accusing finger towards my face.

I shake my head. 'Attitude' is Bonnie's go-to reprimand when she has no other defence left.

'Look, I never asked you to deal with the banking,' she says.

My eyes bulge. *Is she for real?*

'Fine. I'll stop doing it then. Just don't come whining to me when the bailiffs come knocking. Which they will, if you have anything to do with it.'

Bonnie responds by picking up the remote control and turning up the volume to maximum.

'Nice!' I yell over the racket. 'Really mature, Bonnie!'

Bonnie pretends not to hear, her gaze fixed stubbornly on the TV screen.

'Oh, grow up!' I snap.

I stamp out of the room, acutely aware of how topsy-turvy this all is. I'm the child, not Bonnie. And yet every one of our exchanges these days seems to slip into this messed-up dynamic.

You're a weird girl, you know that, Ro Snow? Jamie's words echo in my ears as I stomp up the stairs.

Jamie Cannon, you have no idea.

3

On the landing, I pause to catch my breath. I need to calm down. I close my eyes and count to ten and will the pent-up anger to vacate my body. When I open my eyes again, although I still feel furious, my breathing has at least calmed down a bit and my hands are just trembling now instead of full-on shaking.

I take a long deep exhalation and concentrate on plotting my route to the bathroom, ploughing all my energy into planning exactly where I'm going to place my feet. Bonnie acquires new items almost constantly so the most direct path changes on a daily basis. Tonight, I have to navi-gate a large box containing a deluxe foot spa (unopened), a piñata in the shape of a donkey, a broken record player and at least ten stuffed black bin bags, as well as the usual piles of paper. When I was a little kid, I used to think all people lived like this, that everyone's house resembled a dangerous playground, filled with obstacles and booby traps, requiring you to be on constant alert in order to make it safely from A to B. It was only after a run of playdates and birthday parties at other kids' houses that I twigged that *I* was the odd one out. I specifically remember going to the loo at Georgia Purnell's house and the creeping unease I felt when I realized it took me just ten seconds to walk from her living room to the bathroom, rather than the full minute it took me at home.

As Jamie suspected, the bathroom is not being retiled. The bathtub is piled so high with stuff I can't even *see* the tiles. I haven't had a bath since I was about five or six. I shower in the cramped plastic cubicle in the corner of the room instead, one of the few spaces in the house that Bonnie hasn't yet colonized. I sometimes wondered if my favourite bath toy, a wind-up Nemo, is still in the tub, buried for ever under years' worth of rubbish, still smiling his sweet hopeful smile as he patiently waits to be found.

I brush my teeth and wash my face, still wearing my backpack on my shoulders, then pick my way back across the landing to my bedroom.

I pause outside the door. A hand-painted wooden sign declaring it as 'Ro's Room' hangs on a small plastic hook at chest height, just as it has done for as long as I can remember. I trace my name with my index finger.

Ro's Room.

My bedroom.

My sanctuary.

I reach into my backpack, take out my keys and unlock the door.

The lock is relatively new. I added it two years ago, after I'd finally had enough of Bonnie sneaking her crap into my room while I was at school.

I step inside and instantly feel calmer.

Around the same time I fixed the lock, I used that year's birthday money from my dad to paint my entire room white. My bed linen is also white, topped with squishy cushions in coordinating shades of pebble grey and duck-egg blue, and a soft fleecy throw. My desk and bedside table are clear and the walls bare apart from the full-length mirror that hangs to the right of my bedroom door. There's no clutter, no mess, no fuss – my room is the calm at the centre of a raging storm.

I go into autopilot – changing into my pyjamas, spraying my pillow with lavender-scented sleep spray, and climbing into bed. I usually read for a bit, but tonight all I want to do is sleep. I turn off my lamp and lie on my back, the duvet tucked under my arms. Bonnie has turned the radio back on, Sixties pop floating up the stairs. God knows when she'll turn it off and go to sleep. Bonnie is a night owl, staying up until the early hours and dozing until lunch.

I retrieve my earplugs from the top drawer of my bedside chest and shove them in my ears. It takes me for ever to drop off, and when I do, I dream the dream I've dreamed at least one hundred times before.

Being buried alive under piles and piles of paper.

4

On my way to breakfast, I stop to peer around the slightly ajar living-room door. Bonnie's snoring away in her armchair, her head lolling forward to expose her naturally dark roots, a crocheted blanket crumpled around her ankles.

I sigh and creep over to her, picking up the blanket and draping it loosely over her knees. Her snoring is soft, pretty almost. She looks different when she's asleep – younger, sweeter – her face relaxed and free from its usual thick layer of stage make-up.

As I watch her doze, the lingering anger from last night begins to fade a little. I haven't a clue how she manages to get a decent night's sleep in this horrible lumpy old chair. I wish I could scoop her up and carry her to her bedroom, but, even if it was physically possible for me to get her upstairs, there'd be no point. There's a reason Bonnie's sleeping down here and not in her bedroom.

I tuck the blanket round her knees and press my mouth

to her cheek. Her skin is cool and soft against my lips.

'See you later,' I whisper.

Bonnie murmurs a sleepy reply and turns her head in the opposite direction.

I spend my Saturday mornings pushing leaflets advertising local takeaways and cleaning firms through letter boxes. The headquarters, where I pick up my leaflets, are located above a pet shop on the high street. On reflection, 'headquarters' is probably far too grand a description for the higgledy-piggledy collection of rooms.

'Morning, Ro,' Eric calls when I arrive.

I stick my head behind his office door where he's sitting behind his paperwork-laden desk. 'Morning,' I reply.

'Just a few more days at school now, isn't it?'

'Yeah, we break up on Wednesday,' I say. 'Cup of tea?'

'You read my mind.'

I smile and swipe his Avengers mug from the debris and head into the narrow kitchen, the squawk of birds from the pet shop below just audible over the boiling kettle. I'm rifling in the box of tea bags when Jodie stumbles in. She's wearing a crop top with huge pompoms sewn onto each shoulder, leggings covered with lightning bolts and a battered pair of gold Reeboks.

'Are you making tea?' she asks.

'Well spotted. Do you want one?'

'Yes. A million times yes, you little beauty.'

She collapses into a chair, resting her forehead on the tea-stained Formica table. Her choppy bleached-blonde hair flops forward, forming a curtain around her face.

'Out last night by any chance?' I ask, teasingly, plopping a tea bag into each of the assembled mugs.

She groans. 'No shit, Sherlock. Student night down at the George. Three sugars please.'

I spoon three heaped teaspoons of sugar into Jodie's mug before pushing it under her nose.

'Thanks, babe,' she says, groping for it with shaking fingers. 'You're an angel without any wings.'

'You should really eat something too. Want me to pop out to the cafe before we have to head off? Get you a bacon sandwich or something?'

Jodie shakes her head hard. 'I can't, Ro. I'll spew, I swear.'

'It'll make you feel better. You need to replace the salts you've lost.'

Jodie peers up at me between strands of knotty hair. Her eyelashes are thick and crusty with day-old mascara. 'You're far too bloody wise for your age, Ro, do you know that?' she says, pausing to take a long slurp of tea. 'I'm twenty, you're fourteen. I should be guiding you through your disgusting hangover, not the other way round.'

'Have a biscuit at least,' I say, ignoring her and pulling the lid off the ancient Quality Street tin that houses the communal biscuit supply. 'Iron.'

Jodie laughs and reaches for a custard cream. 'You'll make a great mum one day, Ro,' she says, dunking it in her tea. 'Do you know that?'

'I don't know about that,' I say, turning away and tending to Eric's tea.

*

Ten minutes later, I head out into the sunshine. My delivery patch is near the park, where the streets are wide and tree-lined and the houses big and sprawling with driveways large enough for at least four cars.

I like my job. I like the fresh air, even on the days when it's freezing cold or tipping down with rain. I like the peace and quiet and being up and about when most people are still lazing in bed. I like peering in through the windows of the houses I leaflet and admiring the spacious living rooms, drinking in the fancy wallpaper and matching scatter cushions and framed art on the walls and fantasizing about the orderly lives the owners must lead.

Today, though, despite the glorious sunshine and cornflower-blue sky, I'm distracted, and even my very favourite stops on the route (the Georgian villa with the sunshine-yellow door, the row of art deco semis with their elegant curved windows, the Victorian house on the corner with its very own turret) can't get me back on track. I just can't stop my stupid brain from replaying the events of last night, all the very worst sound bites from my conversation with Jamie making me want to slide between the cracks in the pavement. I lurch between feeling mad at Jamie for being so pushy about walking me home, and mad at myself for giving in so easily. I let my guard down and it backfired. *Horribly.*

There's no use in dwelling on it though. I need to move on and learn from it. And that means never, ever putting myself in a situation like that again.

*

I'm almost home when I notice a large red lorry with 'Addis & Son Removals' on the side parked up outside 46 Arcadia Avenue.

Number 46 has stood empty since its former occupant, an elderly man called Terry, moved into a care home just after Christmas. I liked Terry. A lot of people would have a problem living next door to a house like ours, but Terry never had a bad word to say. He even let me borrow his toolbox and lawnmower whenever I asked and gave me a chocolate egg every Easter and a Cadbury's selection box every Christmas. I was sad to see him go, but mostly scared of who would take his place, well aware that not everyone would be as forgiving. Lots of people have been round to have a look, but the 'For Rent' sign has remained up and the house has continued to sit empty.

Until now.

I approach with caution, slipping behind the cluster of bushes that separate my front garden from number 46's, and peer through the foliage. I watch as the removal men unload an assortment of mismatched furniture, cardboard boxes and black bin liners from the half-empty van. I'm struck by just how little stuff there is. I wonder how many vans' worth of junk my own house contains. Two? Three? Five? More?

A few minutes later, a black SUV with a dented bumper pulls up behind the van. A man and two boys get out, one around ten years old, the other around my age. All three have the same shock of inky black hair and olive skin. All three look utterly miserable.

The man opens the boot of the car and removes a large,

clearly very heavy suitcase. It lands on the driveway with a thud. Sighing, he extends its handle and wheels it towards the front door. The younger boy follows, the Arsenal Football Club backpack he's carrying in his hand trailing on the floor behind him. The older boy reaches for a black sports bag and hauls it over his shoulder. The strap's too long and it bangs against his lower thigh as he makes his way up the driveway. In his other hand he carries a guitar case covered with stickers. He's basketball-player tall and dressed all in black apart from a pair of grubby white hi-tops. His features are sharp and delicate at the same time, and make him look like he belongs in the past, in a frock coat perhaps, reciting poetry.

I can't take my eyes off him.

The boy pauses outside the front door and glances over his shoulder. I hold my breath, terrified I've been spotted. But the boy's gaze fails to settle on any spot in particular before returning to face the exterior of number 46. He looks it up and down through lank strands of black hair, before shaking his head and disappearing inside, the door falling shut behind him with a dull clunk.

Bonnie's in the back garden, marooned on a rusty sun-lounger in the centre of the overgrown lawn. Without access to Terry's lawnmower, the grass has grown so high it looks like she's floating on a carpet of green. The back door is open and the radio's on – Adele lamenting 'Someone Like You'.

It isn't quite warm enough for sunbathing, but Bonnie is

wearing an itsy-bitsy red bikini at least two sizes too small for her anyway, her boobs barely contained within its flimsy Lycra triangles.

'Bonnie,' I say. 'Bonnie. Are you awake?'

'Mmmmmm,' Bonnie says, rolling onto her stomach and tucking her bikini bottoms between her bum cheeks.

'Did you see? Some new people have moved in next door.'

'Have they?' she murmurs sleepily, resting her head on her forearms.

'A man and two kids.'

'No woman?'

'I didn't see one.'

'Hmmmmm.'

'Anyway,' I continue. 'We should probably put in a bit of extra effort to get our place in order.'

'Why?'

'They might not be as relaxed about things as Terry was.'

'What things?' Bonnie asks.

My insides twist with annoyance. 'What do you think? Living next door to us. To *this*.' I gesture towards the house.

'I don't see what the problem is,' Bonnie says.

'Of course *you* don't.'

Bonnie props herself up on her elbows, and peers at me over her shoulder, through heart-shaped rimmed sunglasses.

'You're clothed, aren't you?' she says. 'Fed? I mean, I know the house is a bit busy, but the way you act sometimes, you'd think I'd installed razor blades on the stairs or something.'

'But what if they say something?'

'Who?'

'The new neighbours!'

'Who on earth to?' Bonnie asks, incredulous.

'You know who. Social Services.'

Just saying it out loud makes my palms prickle with nervous sweat.

'Oh, don't be daft,' Bonnie scoffs. 'What could they do?'

What could they do? For starters, send me to live with Dad and Melanie, leaving Bonnie all alone. I once went away on holiday to the Isle of Wight with Dad, and when I got back, the house was such a mess I couldn't even open the back door properly. If that could happen after just a few days, what state would the house be in after a couple of weeks? A month? A year? An image of Bonnie buried under a mountain of her own belongings, just her feet poking out, invades my brain.

A lump forms in my throat and I can feel tears gathering. I try to blink them away before Bonnie notices. I needn't have worried though – she's already flopped back on her belly, her face buried in her forearms.

'You really are like your father sometimes,' she says in a muffled voice. 'He was always worrying about something or other. There's no need to get in a tizz. They're only renting. You'll see – they'll probably be gone in a few months.'

Her phone, abandoned in the grass, vibrates into life, the screen flashing as a tinny rendition of 'I Will Survive' by Gloria Gaynor crackles from its tiny speaker.

I bend down to pick it up, noting the unidentified number before passing it to Bonnie.

'Hello, Bonnie Snow!' Bonnie says in an extra-theatrical version of her usual voice.

Even though the divorce went through over six years ago, she still refuses to reclaim her maiden name.

'Saturday the eleventh? Just give me one moment while I consult my diary,' she trills.

She holds her phone to her chest.

'See,' she says, grinning triumphantly. 'Who needs a manager, eh?'

She springs off the sunlounger and sashays into the house, her hips swaying in time with the music, leaving me alone on the patio, chewing on my thumbnail and worrying.

Always worrying.

5

The last day of term falls on Wednesday. As is tradition, normal lessons are abandoned in favour of games and quizzes and DVDs.

In English, Mrs Merry announces we're going to be playing literary charades. She nominates two captains and asks them to choose teams.

I'm second to last to be picked.

This is not unusual. It's the same in PE, whether we're playing netball or hockey or rounders. I don't mind. It's never done in a cruel way. I just don't think people notice me until something forces them to, or I'm literally the only person standing in front of them.

When it's my turn to mime, I let a girl called Zahra go up in my place. No one notices. The other team wins by a mile anyway – twenty-one points to eight.

At 3.30 p.m., instead of ripping off my tie and tearing out of the gates like almost everyone else, I take my time, calmly clearing out my locker as the school empties out around me. I get their euphoria, but I don't share it. For them, the summer holidays mean freedom; for me, it's more like a prison sentence.

A few metres away, three girls from my year are making plans go to Shake It Off, the milkshake bar on the high street.

One of them, Alice, went to my primary school. We used to play together sometimes, and I went to a couple of her birthday parties. Since moving up to senior school though, we haven't really spoken.

'Hurry up, Sof,' she says. 'If we don't get a move on, we'll miss out on a booth.'

Her friend Sofia is trying to stuff her PE kit into her already stuffed backpack.

'Do you want to put anything in my bag?' Shazna, the third girl, offers.

'I think I'm gonna have to,' Sofia says.

I watch as they divide up Sofia's PE kit, giggling over her stinky trainers and debating which flavour milkshake to order ('I'm going to have Oreo!' 'But you always have Oreo!' 'So? You always have Toblerone!').

I imagine them suddenly noticing me, and asking me to join them. Then the four of us huddled in a booth, elbows touching, laughing and joking and making plans for the summer.

'Finally!' Alice says, jolting me from my fantasy.

Immediately, I feel stupid for even letting my brain go there. Alice probably doesn't even remember my name. And it's not like I could actually say yes, even if they did ask me. It's too risky.

Sofia's PE kit successfully distributed, they link arms and head for the exit, oblivious to my eyes on their backs.

By the time I step out into the sunshine, the crowds have dispersed and my footsteps echo on the concrete as I make my way towards the gates.

Instead of my usual route home, I find myself heading for the high street. A long queue snakes out the door of Shake It Off. From my vantage point on the other side of the road, I can see Alice, Sofia and Shazna sitting in the window; they got their booth after all. They're laughing at something Shazna just said. I watch as they shift along the plastic seating to make room for some other people from our year.

Alice's head swivels in my direction, and for a split second our eyes lock. Panic floods my chest. With fumbling fingers, I pull my phone out of my blazer pocket and pretend to answer it.

'Hello?' I say.

My voice is shaking even though there's no way Alice can possibly hear me or know I'm faking it.

As I walk away, my phone still pressed to my ear, I sneak a glance over my shoulder. Alice isn't looking at me any more.

No one is.

6

'Where's the tank?' I ask as I climb into Dad's car on Sunday morning.

As usual, he's parked several doors down, firmly out of sight of his former home. Instead of his ridiculous and entirely unnecessary four-by-four, he's behind the wheel of Melanie's car, a shiny red Mini with plastic eyelashes attached to the headlamps and a 'Princess on Board' sticker displayed in the back window.

'Mel needed the big car to pick up the cake,' Dad replies, pulling out into the road. 'That for Izzy?' He nods at the plastic bag on my lap.

'No, Princess Charlotte,' I say, rolling my eyes.

'Rosie,' he says in a warning voice.

The name on my birth certificate is Rosie but I've been known as Ro for as long as I can remember. Dad (and by extension, Melanie and Izzy) are the only people who insist on calling me Rosie, or, even worse, Rosebud. I'm so not a Rosebud, it's unreal.

'Sorry,' I say. 'It was just kind of a stupid question.'

'Stupid or not, I could do without the attitude.'

'Where are we going?' I ask after a few minutes of loaded silence.

Instead of heading out of Ostborough and towards Claybridge, the nearby town where Dad lives, we're driving in the complete opposite direction.

'The trampoline park, of course.'

'What trampoline park?'

'There's more than one?'

'Wait, I don't understand. I thought Izzy was having a pizza-making party at your house.'

'She is. After the trampoline park.'

'You didn't tell me about the trampolining. You only told me about the pizza.'

Now it makes sense why Dad's wearing a tracksuit instead of the usual chinos and shirts Melanie lays out for him at the weekend, like he's a little kid.

'I don't have a change of clothes with me,' I say.

Dad glances over at my outfit. I'm wearing one of the few dresses I own (a loose denim sundress) and a pair of black rubber flip-flops. I only put the dress on in the first place to stop Melanie from lamenting that I don't 'make enough of my figure', the way she usually does when I turn up in my normal weekend uniform of jeans and baggy shirt.

'Well, I don't know what you want me to do about it,' he says. 'We can't turn back now. Mel'll go spare if the guests start arriving before we do.'

'God forbid,' I mutter, closing my eyes and resting my head against the window.

Melanie and Izzy are already there when we arrive, waiting just inside the foyer. Izzy has an oversized '10 Today' badge pinned to her pink sequinned hoodie, her gleaming blonde hair pulled into a neat ponytail.

'There you are!' Melanie says.

She waves us over, the Pandora charm bracelet she wears on her left wrist jangling, every charm polished within a millimetre of its life. Everything about Melanie Snow is spotless, from her French-manicured nails to her bouncy blonde bob. Even in tracksuit and trainers, she looks pristine.

'Now, Rosie, don't you look a sight for sore eyes. A dress! Finally! Although it could do with cinching in a bit.'

I brace myself as Melanie steps forward, wrapping her hands round my waist, her fingers pinching my skin.

'There!' she says. 'Much better! Perhaps we can find you a belt when we get back to the house . . .'

'Are you going to trampoline wearing that?' Izzy asks, looking me up and down and pulling a face. 'Everyone will be able to see your knickers.'

'I'm just going to watch,' I say.

'Don't be ridiculous, it's Izzy's birthday!' Melanie says. 'Plus, we've paid for you.'

She stalks over to the Reception desk, pushing to the front of the queue and returning less than a minute later brandishing a pair of baggy red shorts.

'From the lost property box,' she says, handing them to me.

'I married a genius!' Dad says, kissing Melanie on the forehead. 'Say thank you, Rosie.'

I stare down at the shorts in my hands. They're huge. 'Are you serious?' I ask.

Melanie tuts. 'Oh, don't be such a drama queen. Just tie the drawstring nice and tight and you'll be fine!'

If Dad notices the look of horror on my face, he doesn't acknowledge it. But then he's used to ignoring things that make him feel uncomfortable, even when they're right under his nose.

I manage three bounces before the shorts are around my ankles, sending Izzy and her gruesome little mates into mass hysterics.

'We can see your pants! We can see your pants!' they chant as I pull them up, struggling to tuck my dress into the waistband.

'Oh, for heaven's sake, Rosie,' Melanie says, bouncing over and tying the drawstring so tightly I might as well be wearing a corset. 'You're not even trying to make them work.'

Cue sniggers from a group of girls around my age on the next trampoline. My face flames.

'Forget it,' I say, pushing Melanie away.

'Rosie?' Dad calls after me as I head down the padded steps towards the changing rooms.

'Oh, she's just having one of her strops,' I hear Melanie say. 'Leave her.'

*

I wriggle out of the shorts and return them to Reception before going to the café where I'm 3p short of enough money to buy a bag of crisps. I ask for a glass of tap water and sit down with an abandoned copy of yesterday's paper.

On page 11 there's a story that makes my blood run cold. An elderly woman's body has been found buried under her belongings in a cottage in Wales, the post mortem suggesting she'd been dead for over four years. Her daughter was also found on the property, weak and severely dehydrated. Every word makes my stomach turn over.

I'm still thinking about the story when Dad and I pull up outside the house he shares with Melanie and Izzy. It's not even 2 p.m. but it feels like light years later.

On the drive over, I was tempted to ask him to drop me at home so I can check on Bonnie, but I knew he'd only make a fuss if I did. He hates it when I try to pull out of anything relating to Melanie or Izzy.

'They're my family, Rosie, and by extension, that makes them your family too,' he's fond of saying.

They feel like a family, all right – just not mine. And I can't fake it, no matter how much Dad tries to guilt-trip me into it.

I can't pretend I feel at home in their house either – a symmetrical new build with double-glazing and cream carpeting and a kitchen full of shiny white appliances. All of Izzy's toys, of which there seems to be an endless supply, are kept in an elaborate shelving system in her playroom just off the living room. I'm used to it by now, but every so often the unfairness of it all hits so hard it takes my breath away.

In the end, I settle for sending Bonnie a text.

Just checking in. Everything OK? Rx

The front door is festooned with pink balloons, a shiny silver birthday banner stuck diagonally across it. Melanie has changed out of her tracksuit and into a floral dress and pink apron, every inch the Stepford Wife of Dad's dreams, and is assembling the pizza ingredients while the kids tear around the garden.

'I thought you might like to sit with Izzy and her friends, Rosie,' Melanie says, pointing out a seat round the extended dining table.

She dresses it up as a friendly suggestion, but the subtext is quite clear: you're sitting with the kids, no arguments.

Behind Melanie hangs a wooden plaque listing the 'Snow Family Rules' – things like 'hug lots' and 'laugh out loud' and 'dream big'.

God, I hate that plaque. Cheesy crap. Sometimes I fantasize about smashing it into a dozen pieces. Or graffiti-ing all over it – BULLSHIT, in big angry red letters. I wonder what would happen if I did. Melanie would definitely cry. She cried when someone helped themselves to her rhododendrons. And Dad would go ballistic, accuse me of being rude and ungrateful and tell me off for upsetting poor delicate Melanie.

While Izzy is opening her presents, I sneak upstairs and use the bathroom before slipping into the guest room for a quick lie-down.

Although Dad and Melanie insist on referring to it as

mine, apart from a single drawer containing spare sets of underwear, socks, pyjamas and school uniform, there's barely any evidence of my monthly occupation. The room is dominated by Melanie's epic collection of Disney snow globes – 27 at last count – and her massage stuff. She's training to be a massage therapist and when I'm not here she uses this as her treatment room, her fold-up massage table tucked away in the corner and a selection of oils and a stack of fluffy chocolate brown towels stored neatly on a shelf above the bed. Usually the stench of massage oil keeps me awake, but today I fall asleep practically the instant my head hits the pillow.

'Rosie, Rosie, wake up.'

I open my eyes. Dad is bent over me, his left hand shaking my shoulder.

'What time is it?' I ask, rubbing crispy flakes of sleep from the inner corners of my eyes.

'Gone six. The party's over. You missed Izzy cutting her cake.'

He's clearly annoyed about it, his mouth set in a straight line and his arms folded across his chest.

Irritation flares in my chest. 'It's not like it's her wedding,' I say.

Dad lets out a sigh. 'Please don't talk like that, Rosie.'

'Like what?'

'Like that. Full of attitude. It doesn't suit you.'

Oh, yes it does. It suits me perfectly actually.

'I'm going to need to drive you back in a bit,' he says.

'OK,' I reply, sitting up too quickly, the blood rushing to my head as I grope for my abandoned flip-flops with my toes.

'Before I do though,' Dad says, his eyes focused on the snow globes above my head, 'I need to talk to you about our plans for half term.'

'I've been doing some research actually, Dad,' I say. 'And I really want to go to the Natural History Museum. They have this really cool wildlife photography exhibition on.'

Dad hesitates, raking his hands through his wiry, dirty-dishwater brown hair – pretty much the only physical trait I inherited from him. That's when I know our annual October half-term trip to London – literally the only time I get Dad to myself – is officially off.

'I'm really sorry, Rosebud, but we're going to have to postpone,' he says. 'It's mine and Mel's anniversary in November, and you know what a special place Disney is for us' – he nods up at the snow globes – 'well, we thought it would be nice to do a trip with Izzy and, the thing is, half term is our only real option.'

'But you've been to Disney loads of times.'

The mantelpiece downstairs is littered with photos of the three of them cuddling up to Mickey and Minnie in the Florida sunshine.

'Not to the one in Paris.'

'Right.'

'I would have offered for you to come along too, but I know how you hate all that stuff.' He glances up at the snow globes again and rolls his eyes. I can tell he's trying to be conspiratorial with me, but I'm not in the mood to play along.

Dad reaches out and smooths down my slept-on hair. I just about resist the urge to slap his hand away. I'll only be accused of 'attitude' again if I do.

'I'm sorry,' he says. 'We'll go another time . . .'

'Whatever.'

Dad sighs. 'Please don't be a brat about this, Rosie.'

'What about Izzy? She's been behaving like a massive brat all day!'

'It's her birthday. And please don't call her a brat.'

'Why not? You just called me one. Or is it one rule for me and a different rule for Izzy? Or is that a stupid question?'

There's an anger-charged pause. I can practically see it crackling in the air.

'I'm not getting into this now,' Dad says briskly. 'Meet me downstairs in ten minutes. It's time I dropped you home.'

I wait until he's closed the door behind him before letting the furious tears fall.

7

'Ro, is that you?' Bonnie calls as I make my way through the kitchen.

Of course it is, I want to yell. *Who else is it going to be?*

'Ro?' Bonnie repeats in a slightly shriller tone.

'Yes, it's me,' I yell back.

'Can you come in here, please?'

I sigh. All I want to do is go upstairs, watch YouTube and stuff my face with the fat slice of birthday cake Melanie pressed into my hand as I was leaving.

'Ro!' Bonnie calls out again. 'Did you hear me?'

'Yes!' I shout back. 'Just give me a second, will you?'

I pick my way through the kitchen and hallway and push open the living-room door.

'Look what's on,' Bonnie says, her eyes shining. 'Our favourite.'

I look at the TV. The opening credits of *The Sound of Music* are frozen on the screen.

'It started a bit ago,' Bonnie says. 'So I put it on and paused it for you.'

'I'm not sure I'm in the mood,' I begin.

Bonnie's face sags with disappointment.

'It's just that it's quite a long film,' I add.

'It's only half seven,' Bonnie points out. 'It's not like you've got anything to get up for in the morning, is it? And I thought we could make a night of it and order Chinese or a pizza or something. Or I could nip out to the chippy?'

She looks so hopeful, her hands wedged under her thighs, her lips pressed together in anticipation of my answer.

I glance back at the TV. It's ages since I last watched *The Sound of Music*. We have the DVD somewhere although I wouldn't have a clue where to start looking for it. When I was little, we'd sing along with all the songs, Bonnie doing the Maria bits while I multi-tasked as all seven of the von Trapp children. Cue a jolt of nostalgia so potent it makes my eyes water.

'Oh, go on,' Bonnie says, her voice warm and encouraging. 'It's been ages since we watched telly together.'

I think of the article about the mother and daughter in Wales.

'OK, then,' I find myself saying. 'Let's get fish and chips though. It's cheaper.'

'Whatever you like,' Bonnie says, jumping up out of her chair.

While she's gone, I carve a space out for myself in front of Bonnie's chair. As I push aside a heap of old newspapers, my eyes fall on this week's TV magazine. *The Sound of Music* is circled in red pen. The start time was 3 p.m. Hours ago. Has Bonnie had the TV paused all this time? The thought makes me ache with sudden affection for her.

That's the thing about Bonnie. One minute she can make you so angry you want to chuck something at her head, the next she's breaking your heart.

She returns a few minutes later with a portion of cod and chips for us both, two slices each of thickly buttered bread, two battered sausages, two pickled onions, each almost the size of my fist, and two cans of fizzy drink. It's far too much food but Bonnie seems so excited I bite my tongue and don't comment on it.

'Ready?' she asks, once we're settled with our food on our laps.

'Ready.'

Bonnie presses play, and within seconds the room is flooded with the familiar score, making my heart swell.

Quickly, I'm sucked into the story I know so well, the chaotic living room with its bags and boxes and piles of rubbish slowly melting away. Although I can't quite bring myself to sing along the way I used to, I can't help but hum and tap my foot during the musical numbers.

As the von Trapp children warble 'So Long, Farewell', I set aside my tray and nestle into Bonnie's legs. Behind me, Bonnie wipes her greasy fingers on a length of kitchen roll and loosens my hair from its long plait.

'This OK?' she whispers.

I nod.

Bonnie begins to play with my hair, the way she used to

back in the days when we still watched television together on a nightly basis, raking her fingers through the length and massaging my scalp, somehow managing to be both firm and gentle at the same time. It's been so long since it last happened, I feel like I've just stepped out of a time machine – back to when Bonnie and I were a team; back when she made every day an adventure. Like the day she woke me up before dawn and drove us to Alton Towers so we were there when the gates opened, or the time we made a den in the living room and spent the entire weekend huddled inside it, living off crisps and pick 'n' mix. It feels like another life now, another Bonnie and Ro.

'How was the party?' Bonnie asks during one of the quieter scenes.

'Fine,' I say, my shoulders tensing slightly.

'It's just that you looked a bit upset when you first came in.'

'Did I?'

I'm surprised Bonnie noticed. She seems to spend most of her time completely blind to everything around her, me included.

'A bit, yes,' she says. 'Everything OK?'

I'm torn. Part of me wants to tell Bonnie about the cancelled half-term trip. I'm worried she'll gloat about it though (Bonnie – one, Dad – nil). Another bigger part of me just wants to forget the whole thing.

'It was just a bit full-on,' I say eventually. 'Lots of kids being loud and annoying . . . Which reminds me, I have cake. Do you want some?'

'Did Melanie make it?' Bonnie asks.

She says 'Melanie' in a spot-on imitation of Melanie's voice. Even though she's only met Melanie once, she has her babyish delivery down perfectly and I can't help but smile.

'No. She ordered it online, I think. From somewhere fancy.'

'I bet she did. Go on, then, let's have a taste.'

I retrieve the piece of cake from my bag, unwrapping it from its napkin and passing half to Bonnie.

I take a bite of my piece. It's annoyingly delicious – light and buttery, with just the right amount of sweetness.

'What do you think?' I ask.

'Bloody horrible,' Bonnie says. 'You?'

'Worst cake I've ever eaten.'

We burst out laughing, Bonnie's husky guffaws blending with my bubbling giggles. It's not especially funny, but laughing together feels so nice we keep the joke going for far longer than it really deserves. When it eventually dies out, Bonnie leans forward, looping her arms around my neck and kissing me on the top of my head, her breath warm and sugary. When she sits up, she leaves one hand resting on my right shoulder. After a few seconds, I reach up and place my left hand on top of hers. I hold on for the rest of the film, clinging onto the moment as tightly as I can.

8

The first few weeks of the summer holidays seem to last a lifetime. With no school to break up my day, the minutes creep by and the remaining weeks unfurl in front of me like an endless desert trek, the horizon bleak and unrelenting. Everyone knows the holidays are only worth getting excited about if you have friends and/or money, and I'm short on both. I try not to dwell on it – after all, there's nothing I can do about either thing – but it's hard not to feel down when there's literally nothing to look forward to.

To make matters worse, it's rained almost every day, confining me to the four walls of my bedroom or the local library. The only thing keeping me from going mad is the novelty of the new family new door.

It's strange having people on the other side of the wall again. Terry was a creature of habit, spending the majority of his time in his living room, listening to Radio 4. The new family, although not especially noisy, are unpredictable in their movements, and for the first few days I'm thrown by the sound of footsteps on the stairs and doors slamming and toasters popping and a washing machine whirring.

I keep tabs on them as best I can, on high alert for any indication they might be about to lodge a complaint of some sort. They haven't initiated any contact so far, but surely it's only a matter of time before they get sick of living next door to us and express their dissatisfaction. Mostly, though, they keep themselves to themselves and barely give our house a second glance. I still can't completely relax though, dedicating most of my available time to careful surveillance.

Two weeks in, I've pieced together the following details about our new neighbours:

1. Their surname is Hornby.

2. The younger boy is called Finn, the older boy Noah.

3. Mr Hornby drinks a lot of beer (Grolsch or Budweiser, according to the labels on the empty bottles in the communal recycling bin).

4. Mr Hornby sometimes goes out wearing a suit, always returning a few hours later, his tie loose, shoulders slumped. The rest of the time he watches football matches on a television set so huge you can probably see it from space.

5. They eat a lot of takeaways (mostly pizza, followed closely by Chinese, then Indian).

6. Noah occupies the room adjacent to mine (number 46 Arcadia Avenue has the exact same layout as number 48, only in mirror image).

7. Noah and his dad don't get on.

'Don't you dare walk away from me while I'm talking to you!' Mr Hornby is shouting.

'I'll do what I want,' Noah yells back. His voice, although muffled, is raw with anger.

'This is my house, and while you're under my roof, what I say goes,' Mr Hornby bellows.

His words are cut off by Noah slamming his bedroom door shut, so hard it makes my entire room shake.

It's a predictably wet Friday afternoon and I'm in my bedroom watching an old episode of *Blue Planet II* on my battered laptop. I press pause, freezing a pod of bottle-nose dolphins in mid-air, and scramble over to the wall. A few seconds later, the music kicks in – hardcore heavy metal. It never lasts for long. I know the drill by now – after a couple of songs, the volume will be turned down to an acceptable level and replaced with something a little less shouty, something with acoustic guitars and mournful lyrics and an air of tragedy.

I wait, ear pressed against the wall. I can hear the floor-boards creaking as Noah paces back and forth, and the squeak of his bed as he sits down. And then, the gentle thump of his head against the wall. I can picture him perfectly, his head tilted towards the ceiling, his long legs dangling off the edge of his bed. I shift my position so I'm mirroring him, the only thing separating us a wall that feels flimsy and impenetrable at the exact same time, Noah's pain and anger seeping through the layers of plasterboard and mingling with mine.

*

The following week the weather cheers up so I can venture outside, taking long walks around Ostborough Park or through the tangle of woods on the eastern edge of town.

As I walk, I think about Noah. I don't mean to. He just keeps popping into my brain, uninvited. I imagine bumping into him on the path and plan what I'd say and what he'd say back, the looks we'd give each other, the exact sound of our mingled laughter. Before I know it, I've scripted hours and hours of conversation in my head, complete with highly detailed stage directions.

A few times I see people I recognize from school. They're never alone. It's as if they only exist in groups. I pretend not to notice them and they do the same. Or perhaps there is no pretence and they just don't notice me to start with. Sometimes I can go an entire day without speaking a word out loud. Some days, I'm OK with that. Other days my thoughts are so loud inside my head I want to scream.

When she remembers, Bonnie asks me where I've been.

'To the park,' I say.

'Who with?'

'Just people.'

Most parents would want names and details, but Bonnie never digs; she just nods, seemingly satisfied with my obvious lie, and gets on with what she's doing. She disguises it well with her ever-changing roster of singer friends, but I get the feeling Bonnie's as big a loner as I am.

Between my jaunts to the park and woods, I continue to spy on the Hornbys. One Thursday I almost have a heart attack when someone knocks at the back door in the middle of the afternoon, certain it's going to be Mr Hornby ready to lodge his first complaint, or even worse, someone from Social Services with a lanyard and a clipboard, asking to speak to 'Mrs Bonnie Snow' in a stern voice. In the end though, it's just a delivery person, dropping off the fruits of Bonnie's latest Amazon spree. Ever since our evening in front of *The Sound of Music*, the atmosphere at home has been much more harmonious, but the sight of so many packages with Bonnie's name on them breaks the spell in one fell swoop, resulting in a row so furious I'm still shaking with rage about it two days later.

'You OK, babe?' Jodie asks before our shift on Saturday.

'I'm fine. Why?' I ask, giving the biscuit tin a shake before opening it and rescuing a broken chocolate bourbon from the dusty bottom.

'Oh, I dunno,' Jodie says, hauling herself on top of the fridge. Her skinny jeans have holes in them, exposing her knobbly pink knees. Someone had drawn a picture of a sunflower on her left one in black biro. 'You just haven't quite seemed yourself lately.'

'I'm OK,' I say automatically. 'Just a bit tired probably.'

'But it's the summer holidays. Aren't you having loads of lie-ins?'

'I'm not very good at lying in.'

This is true. Thanks to the lock on my door, Bonnie's hoard no longer encroaches on my space, but I still feel the weight of it all around me, and once I'm awake it's impossible to comfortably loll in bed knowing what lies on the other side of my door.

'I worry about you, you know,' Jodie says.

'Me? Why?' I ask, my heart fluttering the way it always seems to when people seem to take more than a passing interest in me.

'Oh, I don't know,' Jodie says. 'You just seem to carry the weight of the world on your shoulders sometimes. Don't you think, Moses?'

'Think about what?' Moses asks as he enters the kitchen, stretching and yawning, his T-shirt riding up to reveal his hairy belly.

Moses is a tall, skinny and impossibly cheerful man in his early thirties who juggles five different jobs in order to support his wife and four little kids.

'I was just saying that Ro seems to carry the weight of the world on her shoulders,' Jodie says. 'Which is fine if you're like fifty or something, but you're not fifty, Ro – your life is just beginning.'

All I can do is shrug. The truth is, I feel more like one *hundred* and fifty some days.

'I'll tell you what it is,' Moses says. 'Our Ro here is an old soul.'

'Thanks, Moses,' I say, shooting him a grateful smile.

'Old souls can still have a bit of fun every so often,' Jodie says.

'I have fun,' I say.

Jodie puts her hands on her hips as if to say 'Yeah, right'.

'I do!' I insist.

'When? Like, what do you get up to with your friends?'

'How do you mean?' I ask, stalling for time.

'You know, in your free time? Like after school and stuff.'

'Oh, you know, the usual,' I say. 'The cinema, ice skating, shopping . . .'

As I recite my fictional list, I try to remember the last time I did any of these things, my skin prickling at the realization I've never done any of them with anyone other than Bonnie or my dad.

'Listen, I'm not having a go at you,' Jodie says, her hand on her heart. 'All I'm trying to say is, life is short and there's only a limited amount of fun to be had. You need to make sure you get out there and take your fair share.'

'Noted,' I say, tipping the remainder of my tea into the sink and reaching for my trolley.

I know Jodie's only trying to be nice, but things just aren't that simple. I decided a long time ago that I couldn't risk getting close to anyone – the stakes are just too high. And even if I did change my mind, it's too late now. Everyone is taken.

After my shift, I dump my trolley back at the office before heading home, stopping off at the corner shop for an ice pop.

I'm at the bottom of our driveway when I realize it's leaking; sticky red liquid trickling on the pavement. I tip my head back, pouring what's left into my mouth, the slushy ice sliding down my throat.

'Hi.'

My head snaps back into position.

It's him.

Noah Hornby.

My breath catches in my throat.

He's standing about two metres away from me, wearing a pair of baggy black shorts and a faded black T-shirt. Up close I can make out details I've only been able to imagine up to this point – the sooty black lashes, the colour of his eyes (treacly brown), the little nick on his left eyebrow, the faint acne scars on his cheeks, the way I can perfectly imagine what his skull might look like if you were to peel all the skin away.

'You've got some on your top,' Noah says, pointing.

I look down. There are three dots of red on my grey T-shirt. It looks like blood.

'Oh, right. Thanks,' I say, rubbing the material together and making the stain at least three times worse.

I was a lot more articulate in the scripted version of this exchange.

'You live here, don't you?' Noah adds, nodding up at the house.

I want the pavement to swallow me up. I'm desperate to deny it, but how can I? I'm standing right outside the place.

'I've seen you coming and going,' Noah adds, removing the possibility anyway.

'Right,' I murmur.

On the one hand, I'm mortified that my efforts to slink in and out of the house without Noah seeing me have failed. On the other, I'm weirdly exhilarated to learn he's been interested enough to note my comings and goings.

'I live there with my mum,' I say, looking at my feet. 'What I mean is, it's her house.'

I want to expand, to make it absolutely clear I have nothing to do with the state of the place, but I don't know how to put it, or if he'll even believe me if I did.

'Do you have the bedroom at the back?' he asks.

'Er, yeah.'

'Me too.'

He opens his mouth to say something else but is cut off by an angry voice from inside the house calling his name.

'My dad,' he says, his face flushing. 'I'd better go.'

'OK.'

'I'm Noah, by the way,' he says as he backs away, the laces of his hi-tops trailing on the ground.

I know, I say silently.

'I'm Ro,' I say out loud.

'Ro,' Noah repeats, as if trying it out for size. 'Is that short for something? Rowan or Rowena?'

'Rosie,' I admit.

He cocks his head to one side. 'You don't look like a Rosie.'

I lift my chin slightly, pleased with his observation. 'I know.'

'Noah!' the voice rings out again.

Noah winces apologetically and swivels on his heels before jogging up his driveway and disappearing through the open front door, leaving me standing, slightly stunned on the pavement, sticky ice pop juice running down my wrists.

9

The Saturday before the new term starts, I return home from work to discover Noah standing outside number 46 wearing a T-shirt, lounge shorts and a pair of really quite ridiculous Gruffalo slippers.

It's been raining steadily all day, and even with my umbrella up my trainers and jeans are damp. From several metres away, I can tell that Noah is soaked to the skin.

Our eyes met and he raises his hand in greeting, his mouth stretching out into a grim version of a smile. I hesitate before heading up the driveway towards him.

'Hey,' he says.

'Hey,' I reply.

His hair is stuck to his forehead in clumps. Wet, it looks even darker than usual.

There are a few seconds of awkward silence.

'Nice slippers,' I blurt eventually.

Nice, Ro. Smooth.

'That wasn't a diss by the way,' I add quickly. 'I know it sounded like one, but it honestly wasn't. They're great slippers. I mean, who doesn't love *The Gruffalo*? I just had no idea they made them in adult sizes.'

Oh God, shut up, Ro.

'They were a present,' Noah says. 'From my gran.'

'Great present. Your gran clearly has amazing taste.'

There's another horrendously awkward pause.

'I'm locked out by the way,' Noah says. 'In case you thought I was just hanging out in the rain in my slippers for a laugh.'

'How come?' I ask. 'Don't you have keys?'

'I was taking the rubbish out and the door slammed shut behind me. It's the kind that locks automatically. I didn't know . . .'

His T-shirt has Luke Skywalker from *Star Wars* on it. The image is faded, Luke's features ghostly pale. It clings to Noah's skinny body, the white cotton almost translucent. Through it, I can make out his nipples and belly button and the outline of his ribs.

Oh God.

'Where's your dad?' I ask, dragging my gaze upwards.

'At the cinema with my little brother.'

'Do you know when they'll be back?'

'They left about hour ago, so at least another hour, maybe more if they stop somewhere for food afterwards . . .'

He shivers. The hairs on his arms are standing up on end, like rows of magnetized iron filings.

'Look,' he says. 'I feel really weird asking this but I don't suppose I could hang out at your house until they get back? I tried the people at number forty-four but there was no one home.'

His proposal makes me dizzy with panic. It's one thing acknowledging where I live, quite another actually inviting someone in. And not just anyone. Noah. Since Dad left, the only other person to cross the threshold apart from me and Bonnie was the plumber who came to fix the boiler a few years ago, and that had been quite traumatic enough, for all involved.

'I don't need entertaining or anything,' Noah adds. 'I mean, if you've got stuff to do. Excuse me a second.' He turns away and sneezes into the crook of his arm.

'Bless you,' I murmur.

He turns back to face me and sniffs apologetically. There's a perfect raindrop hanging off the tip of his nose.

I have no idea what to do. If I say no, he'll think I'm rude and heartless. But I can't possibly say yes. The idea of leading Noah through the house of horrors I call home is unthinkable. What if he tells his dad? And his dad brings it on himself to call Social Services . . .

Think, Ro, think.

An idea begins to formulate in my brain.

'OK,' I say unsteadily.

'Really?' he says eagerly. 'I mean, are you sure that's OK?'

'Sure. I mean, why not?'

'Wow, thank you.'

We walk round the side of the house in single file, the concrete paving slabs slick and shiny from the rain. I'm trembling. I really, really hope he can't tell.

I rest my backpack on the doorstep and open the front pocket, my quaking fingers brushing my keys as I pretend to search for them.

Here goes.

'Oh my God, you're not going to believe this,' I say. 'I haven't got my keys either!'

I cringe. I sound like I'm rehearsing a bit part in a very bad school play.

Luckily, my performance is upstaged by a flash of lightning slicing the sky in half, followed by an angry growl of thunder.

'Whoa,' Noah murmurs.

A gunmetal grey cloud swoops over our heads, shrouding the back garden in shadow, and within seconds hail begins to pelt down, clattering against the patio.

Time for phase two.

'The shed!' I yell. 'Quick!'

I lead the way across the overgrown lawn, hail bouncing off my umbrella and backpack.

The shed door is rusted shut and it takes two attempts for me to yank it open.

'In here,' I say.

Once upon a time, the shed was Dad's domain. It wasn't kitted out with anything particularly fancy – just a wooden workbench, an old armchair, a few books, a portable heater and a battery-operated light.

I slam the door shut behind us. We peer out through the misty Perspex window. The lawn is snowy with hail and the rain is coming down in sheets.

'End of the world weather,' Noah says, his left shoulder grazing my right one.

'Yeah,' I agree, the skin on my shoulder on fire.

As we continue to look out the window, I keep waiting for him to make a comment about the house but he doesn't. He must be thinking it though. How can be not be? It's right there in front of him.

'Um, sorry there's nowhere to sit,' I say, collapsing my umbrella and propping it in the corner. Dad took his chair and stuff when he left.

'The floor's fine,' Noah says, plopping down cross-legged on the knotty wooden boards. 'I'm just happy to be out of the rain.'

I sit down opposite him, my back against the wall, knees drawn up under my chin. I wondered if the shed might still smell of Dad, but all I'm getting is the heady scent of timber.

There's a long silence. Noah is looking up at the ceiling.

'What have they gone to see?' I ask.

'Sorry?'

'Your dad and F—' (I stop myself from using Finn's name just in time). 'Your dad and brother. At the cinema.'

'Oh. That new Pixar film. You know, the one about the mouse?'

I don't, but I nod anyway.

'You didn't want to go with them?' I ask.

Noah shakes his head hard, spraying droplets of water like a dog attempting to dry off. 'Er, do you mind if I take these off?' he asks, pointing at his sodden slippers.

'Oh, no, go for it.'

He smiles gratefully and removes them. His feet are skinny with long, bony toes and tan marks from where he's been wearing flip-flops.

'I've been in France,' he says, noticing me looking.

Great. Now he probably thinks I'm some kind of weird foot fetishist.

'Who with?' I ask, forcing my eyes upwards.

'My mum, my brother and one of my mum's mates,' Noah adds.

'Was it nice?'

'It was OK. I didn't really do much, just lazed around next to the pool while my mum and her friend drank half the wine in the Côte D'Azur.' He smiles a sad sort of smile.

Another silence descends. They're quickly becoming our speciality.

'Have you been away anywhere?' Noah asks after a few seconds, pulling his damp T-shirt away from his skin, distorting Luke Skywalker's face.

I shake my head.

'How come?'

'We just . . . didn't.'

Bonnie and I haven't been on a summer holiday since Dad lived with us. With no photos to help jog my memories, our trips to the seaside are vague and hazy, like I dreamed them.

'I've heard her singing,' Noah says.

'Who?'

'Your mum.'

'Oh, right,' I say, my fingernails digging into my thighs.

'She's good.'

I nod. Because Bonnie *is* good. It's easy to forget sometimes, to let my anger overshadow her talent.

'She should do it professionally,' Noah adds.

'She already does.'

'Really?' he says, his eyes full of wonder. 'That's so cool.'

'I guess.'

As long as I can remember, Bonnie has spent her weekends gigging. After Dad left, every Friday and Saturday night she dropped me off with a steady rotation of women she'd met on the gigging circuit – women called things like Mandy and Tanya and Shona, who parked me in front of the TV and fed me fizzy drinks and bags of violently potent salt and vinegar crisps. A few times, she couldn't find anyone and had to take me with her, smuggling me backstage where I'd sit in the wings, watching through the tatty velvet curtains as she belted out power ballads like her life depended on it. When I turned 11, Bonnie started leaving me home alone, ringing to check in between sets, but ultimately trusting me to put myself to bed.

'My mum's a tax accountant,' Noah says, wrinkling his nose.

'What about your dad?'

'He's . . . between jobs at the moment.'

Based on Mr Hornby's irregular comings and goings, this makes perfect sense.

There's another long pause.

Outside the hail has stopped and the rain has slowed, pattering gently against the felt roof now.

Noah pulls at a loose thread on his T-shirt.

Now what?

My eyes roam the shed for possible conversation topics. They fall on the crate. I stand up and walk over to it, peering in. It contains a plastic watering can, a couple of pairs of battered gardening gloves, a tin of white paint and, at the very bottom, a rectangular box.

'Do you know how to play chess?' I ask, pulling it out and peeking inside the box. It's just a cheap, flimsy thing – cardboard and plastic – but all the pieces appear to be there.

Noah shakes his head.

'I don't suppose you fancy learning?'

I kneel down and unfold the board. Noah shifts towards me on his bottom. His hair has dried oddly, sticking up in two tufts making it look like he's sprouted a pair of horns. It suits him.

'Who taught you to play?' Noah asks as I line up the pieces.

'My dad,' I say. 'I'm a bit rusty though.'

Noah is a complete natural, picking up the rules quickly. As we play, we gradually loosen up, our chat finally beginning to flow as we debate our favourite music, the places in the world we most want to see, the best flavour of Krispy Kreme doughnut, whether we'd prefer to fight one hundred duck-sized horses or one horse-sized duck.

And it's fun.

Actual real-life fun.

We're on our third game when we hear yelling. I scramble to my feet and open the door. It's stopped raining and the sun is peeping through the clouds.

'Noah!' Mr Hornby is shouting. 'Noah!'

I look down at Noah. His mouth is set in a grim straight line.

'My dad,' he says, his voice flat.

He stands up and just like that – *poof!* – the cosy spell is broken.

Deflated, I crouch down and begin to dismantle the game.

'Wait,' Noah says. He shifts his weight from one foot to the other. 'Couldn't we leave the board as it is? That way we can pick up from where we left off, next time.'

Next time.

He wants there to be a next time.

Tingles shoot down my arms and legs.

'OK, sure,' I say, fighting to keep my tone casual. 'When were you thinking?'

'The thing is, I'm going back to school tomorrow,' he says.

'On a Sunday?'

'I go to boarding school.'

'Oh.' The disappointment cuts through me like a knife.

'When will you be back?' I ask.

'Half term maybe?' Noah says.

Half term is at the end of October. Week and weeks away.

'Maybe we could swap numbers?' Noah suggests. 'So we can arrange it properly.'

'Sure,' I say, trying not to look too excited and handing him my battered old phone so he can tap in his number.

'Noah!' Mr Hornby's voice is full-on angry now.

'I'd better go,' Noah says, giving me my phone back and slipping his feet back into his soggy slippers.

We step out into the garden.

'Look,' Noah says, pointing up at the sky.

A faint outline of a rainbow is peeking out from behind the clouds. We watch in silence as it dissolves from sight.

We're standing on the patio now. Noah still hasn't mentioned the state of the house. I know it's impossible but it's almost as if he can't even see it.

'Thanks again for taking me in,' he says.

'No worries.'

'October, then?'

'October,' I echo.

'Noah!' Mr Hornby's furious voice sails over the fence, making us both flinch.

'My cue to leave,' Noah says.

And just like that, he's gone.

AUTUMN

10

The corridors are packed with students hugging and squealing like they're re-enacting footage from when the Berlin Wall was torn down.

'Oh my God, I missed you so much!' a Year Nine girl shrieks as I make my way to morning registration, lifting up her friend and swinging her round in a circle.

I manage to flatten myself against the wall just in time to avoid being whacked in the shins by her flailing legs.

My form tutor for Year Ten is Ms Cameron. She's there hunched over a stack of paperwork, her glasses perched on the very end of her nose. The rest of the classroom is empty so I have my pick of desks. If I'm lucky, there'll be an uneven number of students and I'll get one to myself again. I quickly scan the room and settle on a desk at the front by the window. I'm about to sit down when Ms Cameron glances up.

'No, no, not there,' she says in her trademark rasp.

'Sorry?' I say.

She lets out an impatient sigh. 'Did you not see the name cards?'

That's when I notice the pieces of card propped on each of the desks, like place cards at a wedding breakfast.

'They're in alphabetical order,' Ms Cameron adds impatiently. 'Starting with A at the front.'

I retrace my steps and try to think of any other students in my form with a surname beginning with S.

S, S, S.

Then it hits me.

Emerson Saxby.

My heart sinks.

I've known Emerson since primary school. He's loud and hyperactive, always bouncing up and down in his seat, telling stupid jokes and doing comedy farts. He means well, I suppose, but the prospect of sitting next to him for an entire academic year fills me with intense dread.

I locate my name card on a desk at the very back of the room.

Ro Snow, it says in Ms Cameron's old-fashioned swirly handwriting. I brace myself for Emerson's name on the card next to it but when I look closer I see it's an entirely different name altogether – *Tanvi Shah*.

I frown.

Tanvi Shah?

Confused, I lower myself into my seat as the rest of my classmates trickle into the room, every single one of them grumbling over the seating arrangements.

'Miss, are you joking!' Ryan Attah exclaims.

'I don't joke,' Ms Cameron replies in a bored tone of voice, not even bothering to look up.

By the time the bell rings, there's still no sign of Tanvi Shah. Maybe she's not coming. Maybe Ms Cameron got confused and wrote Tanvi's name on the card by mistake and I'll have a desk all to myself after all. I allow myself to relax a little, moving Tanvi's name card aside and spreading out my things.

Ms Cameron is halfway through the register when the door bursts open and a needle-thin girl with wispy black hair and a pair of lively chocolate brown eyes slightly too large for her face tumbles into the classroom, almost head-butting Ryan who is sitting in the front row.

'Sorry I'm late, miss!' the girl gasps. 'I got *so* lost!'

Ms Cameron's usually stern face visibly softens. 'Not to worry, Tanvi,' she says gently. 'Welcome back.'

Welcome back?

'Take a seat next to Ro,' she adds, pointing in my direction.

It's only as Tanvi careers down the aisle towards me, her too-large backpack bouncing against her back, I twig why I recognized her name earlier, and from the whispers and nudging elbows around me, everyone else has figured it out too.

Of course.

It's Tanvi Shah.

Back from the dead.

*

One frosty December morning two and a half years ago, the whole of Year Seven was summoned to the hall for an impromptu assembly. I remember what the weather was like that day because someone had drawn a massive willy and balls on one of the frosted-up windows and people were pointing and giggling. Then Mrs Hibbert, the head teacher, and Mr Liu, the head of Year Seven walked onto the stage looking sad and serious, and everyone quickly shut up. They exchanged grave looks before announcing they had some bad news, and that following a series of tests, Tanvi Shah of form 7D had been diagnosed with cancer.

Lots of people cried. I didn't though. Not that it wasn't sad, or that Tanvi didn't deserve our tears; it just weirded me out to watch all these kids who I was pretty sure didn't even hang around with Tanvi break down in mass hysterics like they were the best of friends.

For a few days, Tanvi's illness was the main topic of conversation in the playground and lunch queue. There was a suggestion of doing a fundraiser for her family, but it never quite got off the ground, and Tanvi quickly faded from everyone's minds. I thought of her sometimes, on cold frosty days usually, briefly wondering what had happened to her, whether she'd pulled through or not. All I knew was that there were no follow-up assemblies and Tanvi never returned to school.

She was in limbo.

That is, until now.

A very much alive Tanvi throws herself into the seat next to me. Everything about her is small and delicate-looking, from her sloping shoulders to her slender wrists, so tiny I reckon I could wrap my thumb and index finger around one with ease. Tanvi's blazer is stiff and new and far too big for her, only the very tips of her fingers poking out from the sleeves. Combined with her calf-length skirt and baggy blouse, she looks more like a Year Seven pupil than someone entering Year Ten.

'I got completely lost,' she whispers as Ms Cameron continues down the register. 'Nothing is where it used to be!'

Of course. Tanvi left before the school was fully renovated the summer between Year Eight and Year Nine.

I search her face for any signs of illness, but her eyes are bright and her cheeks lightly flushed. The only clue is her small size but I don't know whether that's down to the cancer or just plain old genetics.

Tanvi picks up my name card and studies it. 'I remember you though,' she says, putting the card back down and pulling out from her overstuffed backpack a red plastic pencil case with a Hello Kitty charm attached to the zip and plonking it on the desk next to my plain metal one.

I blink. She must be mistaken.

'No you don't,' I say.

'What do you mean?' Tanvi asks, tilting her head to one side, her mouth quivering into an amused smile.

'You must be mixing me up with someone else,' I say.

'Nope.'

I frown.

Tanvi throws back her head and laughs, gripping my arm

with a child-sized hand. 'There's no need to look so upset about it!' she says. 'I remember everyone pretty much.'

I carefully remove Tanvi's hand.

'I'll prove it to you,' she continues. 'Pick anyone in this classroom, anyone at all, and I'll tell you all the stuff I remember about them.'

'No, you're all right, thanks,' I say.

'Quiet, please!' Ms Cameron barks.

'Oh, go on,' Tanvi says, lowering her voice to a whisper. 'Please.'

'I said no,' I hiss back.

'Fine, I'll choose someone then,' Tanvi replies, her eyes roaming the classroom for a suitable candidate.

'OK, her,' she says, pointing at Sienna Blake. 'Sienna Blake. She's got a mouth the size of the Channel Tunnel, is allergic to peanuts and in Year Seven she dressed up as Kim Kardashian for *Children in Need*. She shoved a cushion down the back of her pants and paid Tre Morgan a fiver to come as Kanye.' She turns to me and beams triumphantly.

'So? Everyone knows who Sienna is,' I point out.

'Pick someone else then,' Tanvi says. 'Someone harder.'

'Look, I really don't care.'

'Oh, please,' Tanvi says.

'I mean it, I'm really not interested.'

'How about Justin Nowak,' Tanvi says, ignoring me. 'OK, let's see. He once had a nosebleed in assembly and fainted, he's really amazing at art and he always wears odd socks. Look.'

Sure enough, Justin is wearing a plain red sock on one foot, a Homer Simpson one on the other.

'I'll do you now,' Tanvi says. 'You're Ro Snow and—'

I cut her off. 'Please stop.'

'But why?'

'I told you, I'm not interested.'

But it's too late – Tanvi's already talking over me.

'You're Ro Snow,' she recites, undeterred. 'You like to wear your hair in a plait, there's always a Baby Bel in your packed lunch and in netball you play wing defence. Oh, and your mum is really pretty. So are you, by the way. Just in a different way to your mum.'

'How do you know my mum?' I ask sharply.

'Oh, I don't. Well, not really. I just remember her coming to parents' evening one time and thinking how fun and glamorous she looked.'

I shudder as I remember that night. Bonnie was en route to a 1960s themed gig and turned up in a purple mini dress, thigh-high boots, full stage make-up and her hair teased into a massive beehive. Another parent asked her if she was on her way to a fancy dress party and Bonnie laughed like a hyena and everyone stared. I hate that Tanvi remembers it too.

Tanvi drags her backpack onto her lap. 'Mint?' she asks, unzipping the front pocket.

I peer in. The pocket's full of loose mint imperials.

'No thanks,' I say.

Tanvi shrugs and pops two in her mouth at once.

The second Ms Cameron completes the register, Emerson – who is sitting directly in front of us – turns all the way round in his chair and rests his elbows on our desk.

'All right, Tansy?' he says.

'It's Tanvi actually,' Tanvi replies. 'T. A. N. V. I. Tanvi. And I'm fine, Emerson, thanks for asking. Mint?'

Emerson takes a greedy handful, shoving them in his mouth all at once so his cheeks look like they've been stuffed with marbles. 'I'm not gonna lie,' he says, chomping away. 'But I kind of assumed that you'd, you know.' He grimaces.

Abi Rix, the girl sitting next to Emerson, clasps her hand over her mouth to mask her shocked giggles. I roll my eyes at the ceiling on Tanvi's behalf. Emerson really is a tool sometimes.

'I don't think I follow you,' Tanvi says, fiddling with the Hello Kitty charm on her pencil case. It boasts a tiny pink light that flashes on and off when she touches it.

'Yeah, you do,' Emerson says, shifting in his seat. 'I mean, it's been ages, what were we supposed to think?'

'I don't know. Why don't you tell me?'

I sneak a sideways glance at Tanvi. Her face is entirely neutral. Emerson's, on the other hand, is rapidly crumpling at the realization Tanvi is going to make him spell it out.

'You know,' he says quietly, his eye line hovering about three inches above Tanvi's eyebrows.

She bites her lip and performs an exaggerated shrug.

Emerson's Adam's apple contracts as he takes a nervous swallow. 'We thought you'd died,' he whispers, his face practically purple.

'Oh!' Tanvi says, clapping her palm to her forehead. 'You thought I'd croaked it, was six feet under, dead and buried, kicked the bucket. You'd basically killed me off, yeah?'

There's an awkward silence. Kids at the surrounding desks have stopped what they're doing to listen in on the exchange, their eyes flicking between Emerson and Tanvi like they're spectators at a Wimbledon final.

There's a beat before Tanvi bursts out laughing. She leans across the desk and punches Emerson on his arm. He blinks rapidly.

'Duh! I'm pulling your leg!' she says.

'Oh, right. Ha ha ha . . .' Emerson's unconvincing laughter trails off. His mouth is still half-full of soggy mint imperials.

'God, your face,' Tanvi continues, slapping the desk with her hand. 'You looked like you were about to cry!'

'Everything all right over there?' Ms Cameron barks.

'Yes, miss,' Emerson squeaks.

Ms Cameron narrows her eyes and summons him to the front of the room.

I take out my pack of fluorescent highlighter pens and start to annotate the timetable Emerson drops on the desk in front of me a few minutes later.

'Oh, boo,' Tanvi says, prodding at it with her skinny index finger. 'We're in none of the same classes. Just PE.'

I glance at her timetable. She's in top set for everything.

'I'm *so* happy to be back,' Tanvi continues. 'I can't even tell you! I've been going mad at home. I got the all-clear seven whole months ago, you see, but my parents didn't think I was ready to come back to school full-time until now.'

She says all of this with remarkable cheer, like having cancer for three years was a mere inconvenience to her academic career.

'Hey, do you mind if I borrow these?' she asks, pointing at my highlighters.

'OK,' I say. 'Just make sure you put the lids back on.'

As Tanvi makes a proper meal out of selecting which pen to use first, I try to remember who she was friendly with before she got ill. I have a vague recollection of her hanging around with a blonde girl whose family emigrated to Australia midway through Year Eight but I'm not absolutely sure.

The bell rings for first period. I gather up my pens. As I feared, Tanvi has mixed up the lids, the pink on the yellow, the yellow on the green and so on. I sigh and shove them into my bag to sort out later.

'I don't suppose you know where room sixteen-one is?' Tanvi asks, thrusting her timetable under my nose as we stand up. 'I've got design and technology there.'

'It's in the art and design block. There are signs.'

'Well, where are you going?' Tanvi asks, plucking the timetable from my hands before I have the chance to stop her. 'Hey, you've got art in sixteen-two,' she says. 'Perfect! I'll just follow you.'

Great. Just great.

The corridors seem even busier than usual. The teachers, with their holiday suntans and slightly too short haircuts, bark at everyone to keep moving, their eyes on fresh alert for untucked shirts and non-regulation footwear. Tanvi scampers along at my side, her eyes barely level with my shoulder. She chats the whole time, mostly about how hungry she is despite the fact she had 'four Weetabix, a banana, and a strawberry Nesquik' for breakfast.

‘Mr Bagshot,’ Tanvi says, peering at her timetable. ‘What’s the verdict? Still as scary as he was three years ago?’

After Ms Cameron, Mr Bagshot is the longest-serving member of staff in the school and, like her, possesses a distinctly old-fashioned approach to discipline. His shouts can be heard several classrooms away and he makes no secret of his sadness that corporal punishment is no longer an accepted practice.

‘I don’t know, I’ve never had him for anything,’ I say.

‘Lucky,’ Tanvi says. ‘He once told me off for talking in one of his lessons and I swear I did a bit of a wee, I was that terrified.’

Wow, this girl really has no *filter.*

‘Tell me to shut up if I’m getting on your nerves,’ Tanvi adds merrily, as we head down a flight of stairs and through a set of double doors. ‘I’m just a bit over-excited to be making conversation with someone who isn’t either my tutor, a member of my family, or a medical professional.’

I stop abruptly outside room 16.1 and point to the sign above the door.

‘Oh my God, thank you *so* much,’ Tanvi says. ‘I’d have never found my own way here.’

‘I’m sure you would have figured it out eventually,’ I say, turning on my heel and walking away before Tanvi can ask me anything else.

I’m sitting on a bench at lunch trying to decide whether it’s too soon to text Noah or not when I hear someone calling my name.

I look up. Tanvi is weaving her way towards me, a huge grin on her face.

'There you are!' she says. 'I've been looking for you everywhere!'

'Why?' I ask, not even bothering to hide my confusion.

She just giggles and shoves a paper plate with a slab of flapjack on it into my hand.

'But I didn't ask you for anything,' I say, trying to give it back.

'I know that, silly. Consider it a thank you, for being my tour guide earlier.'

'But I don't want it. Seriously, take it back.'

'Oh, relax,' Tanvi says, batting me away. 'It's a piece of flapjack, not a trip to Disneyland.' She bites into her own slice and lets out a gasp, clutching my arm with her spare hand. 'Oh my God, Ro,' she cries. 'I've been dreaming of this stuff. Literally! Like full-on sex dreams!'

Admittedly, the flapjack at Ostborough Academy *is* legendary – gooey and floppy and at least fifty per cent golden syrup. My slice has already soaked through the paper plate, leaving a sticky residue on my fingers.

'Napkins in there,' Tanvi says, nodding down at the breast pocket of her blazer. 'Now, budge up.'

With little choice in the matter, I scoot along the bench and give in to the flapjacky goodness.

'This place is blowing my mind,' Tanvi says with her mouth full. 'I knew they'd modernized it, but I didn't know how much. *Nothing* is where it used to be. Hey, want to hear something a bit weird?'

'Do I have a choice?' I venture.

'You're funny,' Tanvi says, punching me gently on the arm.

'It wasn't a joke.'

She doesn't seem to hear, angling her body towards me, her knees brushing my thigh. I try to shift away but I'm already perched on the very edge of the bench.

'OK, so here's the thing,' Tanvi says. 'I always assumed I'd come back to school at some point, like even when I was really, really ill and my mum and dad were crying all the time and clearly thought I was a goner, at the back of my mind I just had a feeling it wasn't over, you know?'

But of course I don't. How can I?

'But every time I imagined being back here,' Tanvi continues, jabbing the bench with her non-flapjack-holding index finger, 'it was the old school I pictured, not this one. So now I'm actually here, it's kind of thrown me a bit, like I'm living in an alternate reality or something. Does that make me sound like a loon?'

'Uh-huh.'

'Cheeky!' Tanvi says, elbowing me in the ribs.

We're interrupted by Marissa Rossdale, appearing out of what seems like nowhere and flinging herself at Tanvi, almost catapulting the plate of flapjack out of her hand and into the bushes behind us.

'Oh my God, it's true!' she cries, pulling Tanvi to her feet and clutching her skinny body to her wobbling chest. 'You're alive!'

'Yep,' Tanvi says, patting Marissa on the back and

mouthing 'Help!' over her shoulder. 'How have you been, Marissa?'

'Never mind *me*,' Marissa gasps, releasing Tanvi from the embrace but continuing to grip her by both shoulders, shaking her for extra emphasis. 'How are *you*?'

I spy an opportunity to escape.

'I think I'm gonna leave you guys to catch up,' I say, rising to my feet.

Tanvi widens her eyes, as if to say 'please don't leave me!'

I pretend not to notice. If it's a friend Tanvi Shah is after, Marissa Rossdale is surely a much better fit than me.

11

After school, Tanvi intercepts me at the school gates and tries to offer me a lift. Even though she eventually accepts my refusal, I still feel uneasy as I walk home, glancing over my shoulder every few steps.

I'm turning into Arcadia Avenue, when my phone buzzes. My heart does a little lift when I see Noah's name on the screen. It's only a short message – hello and how was school – but I don't care, quickly tapping out a reply. We message back and forth for the next few minutes. Our conversation is nothing special – notes on our respective days – but it feels significant somehow, like the beginning of something real.

I'm in the kitchen adding dried pasta to a saucepan of boiling water when Bonnie staggers through the back door wearing a tie-dyed kaftan and a pair of jewel encrusted flip-flops, a floppy straw hat on her head. Her face is flushed and her eyes are shining. Combined with the bulging carrier bags looped over her wrists, this means just one thing – she's been shopping. And just like that, my good mood evaporates.

'Oh, hello,' she says, dumping the bags on the already heaped kitchen table.

I wait for her to ask me how my first day back went, but despite the fact I'm wearing my school uniform, she's clearly forgotten.

'What's in the bags, Bonnie?' I ask instead, trying my hardest to keep my voice steady.

'Oh, just a few groceries,' Bonnie says vaguely, running her fingers through her hair. 'Lidl have some brilliant offers on at the moment.'

I peer in one of the bags. 'But we already have peas,' I say, noting the half dozen tins. 'And rice. And since when do we use that much soy sauce? There are like ten bottles here.'

'I like to dip my prawn crackers from the Chinese in it,' Bonnie says, pouting.

'So buy one bottle.'

'It was buy one get one half price.'

'So buy two bottles.'

'And then run out and have to go back and buy them at full price?' Bonnie tuts and wags her finger. 'I thought you were supposed to be clever, Ro Snow.'

According to whom exactly? I always give Bonnie my school reports to read, but I doubt she gives them much attention. If she did, she'd know I'm totally average in every single subject – middle set across the board.

I spot a packet of cigarettes nestled on top of at least six tins of fruit cocktail. 'I thought you were giving up,' I say, holding them up.

'I'm cutting down,' Bonnie replies, plucking them from my hands and clutching them to her chest. 'This pack will probably last me all month.'

Yeah, right. I've emptied her ashtray at least five times in the past week alone.

I move on to the next bag. It's full of greetings cards. Annoyance stirs deep inside me. I take out a handful and leaf through them – 'Congratulations On Passing Your Driving Test!' and 'I'm Sorry For Your Loss' and 'Happy Hanukkah!'

'Who are these for this time, Bonnie?' I ask. It's getting harder and harder to keep calm.

'Just people,' Bonnie says vaguely, picking up a bottle of soy sauce and studying the label.

'What people?'

Bonnie and I don't *know* people. Bonnie isn't in touch with any of her family, and apart from her singer friends – women who enter and exit her life like they're riding a carousel – she has no other significant relationships I'm aware of.

'I don't know yet,' Bonnie says.

'So why did you buy them?'

'Because you never know when they might come in handy.'

I turn one of the cards over. 'This one cost three pounds seventy-five!'

'Oh, did it?' Bonnie says. 'It must be all the embellishment. Isn't it pretty?'

I wouldn't mind so much if Bonnie sent the cards, or even just put them away carefully. But she doesn't. She just dumps them wherever she feels like it, just like she randomly dumps everything she brings into this house, regardless of its value.

I look at the rest of the price tags, adding up as I go. 'You've spent over forty pounds on cards, Bonnie.'

'I told you, they're an investment,' she says, snatching them from my hands and stuffing them back in the bag.

'Did you pay for all of this with cash or card?'

'Card. Why?'

'The water bill comes out of the account on Friday. This lot is going to send us over our overdraft limit.'

God, I hate the way I sound right now. Like a middle-aged nag. Everything is the wrong way round. I'm 14. I should be the one being told off for wasting money; it should be Bonnie worrying about all this stuff, not me. My chest burns with familiar resentment.

'Well, there's no point it getting in a tizz over it, is there?' Bonnie says cheerfully. 'It's done now. Besides, I've got three gigs at the weekend – Friday, Saturday *and* Sunday. Pip who, eh? Come this time next week, we'll be back on track, you'll see. Now, are we done here, because I'm dying for a wee.'

She doesn't wait for an answer, dropping the bag of cards on the floor and humming as she disappears into the hallway.

My fists tighten. I want to scream, to take every one of those soy sauce bottles and smash them against the concrete paving slabs outside.

But I know I won't. I can't. Because I'd be the one who'd have to clean it up, so what would be the point in that?

The boiling water hisses as it foams over the side of the saucepan. I swear under my breath and reduce the heat.

I can hear Bonnie singing 'Son of a Preacher Man' at the top of her voice – not a care in the world. I shut the door to the hallway to block it out and reach into the back pocket of my jeans for my mobile.

After listening to three separate automated menus and successfully passing through security, I finally make it through to a human being.

'Hello,' I say in my very best grown-up voice. 'My name is Bonnie Snow. I'd like to extend my overdraft please.'

12

'Over here! Over here!' Tanvi cries.

She's been scampering about the netball court like an overexcited puppy for the past forty minutes now, her hands permanently in the air even when the ball is nowhere near her. As someone whose chief aim is to *avoid* contact with the ball wherever possible, it's both exhausting and confusing to watch.

The second Ms Bello blows her whistle I rip off my bib and break into a run towards the changing rooms, ignoring Tanvi's cry of 'Ro! Hey, Ro, wait for me!'

Seriously, when is she going to get the message and leave me alone? Despite offering to give me a lift home every afternoon this week and getting a firm brushoff every single time, she's showing no signs of backing off. If anything, she's acting keener than ever.

Today is no exception, Tanvi cornering me as I tie up my shoelaces.

'Hi!' she says.

I look up. She's half-dressed, her jumper hanging round her neck, and one leg in her tights, the other bare and goose-pimpled.

'Can I help you?' I ask, my flat delivery hopefully making it clear it's not an invitation.

It doesn't work.

'You can actually,' Tanvi says, sitting down next to me on the bench, her skinny thigh pushed up against my less skinny one, her grasp of 'personal space' *severely* lacking. 'Can you help me find room twenty-one-four?'

'Not really. I've got stuff to do this lunch time.'

As I say this I feel mean, but 'distant yet polite' doesn't seem to be doing the trick. If I'm going to get Tanvi to back off, I'm going to have to be a little more direct.

'Oh please!' Tanvi says, clasping her hands together in prayer position. 'I'll probably be wandering around lost for ages if you don't.'

'Can't someone else help you?' I ask, gesturing desperately at the changing room full of people. 'What about Marissa?'

Tanvi leans in, her flapjack breath warm and sweet on my cheek. 'Between you and me, Marissa is a bit too full-on.'

I raise an eyebrow. *Marissa* is too full-on for *Tanvi*?

'I promise this is the last time I'll ask!' Tanvi says, swiping her hand across her heart. 'I'm just *so* hopeless with directions. Please, Ro. Pretty please with a cherry and whipped cream on top!'

Room 21.4 is in the music department. If we walk quickly, it will take me five minutes at most to escort Tanvi there. Hopefully, after that, she'll stick to her promise and seek out a new tour guide.

'OK, fine,' I say. 'But this is absolutely the last time, got it?'

'Cross my heart and hope to die!' Tanvi cries.

As we walk against the tide of students making their way to the canteen, Tanvi fires questions at me like she's a red carpet reporter. What's your favourite film? Do you like cats? Do you think Emerson Saxby is cute? (My answers: I don't know, I'm allergic, and NO.)

'Who *do* you like then?' Tanvi asks, as we enter the music department.

'What?'

'You know! As in, who do you fancy?'

'No one,' I reply, trying and failing not to picture Noah's face.

Since hearing from him on Monday, we've exchanged dozens more texts, mostly about schoolwork and television shows we like.

'What?' Tanvi says. 'But there must be someone.'

'Well, there isn't.'

'I'll tell you who I like, if you tell me you like.'

'That really won't be necessary.'

'I know, I'll guess! Um, Kai Clarke? Tre Morgan? Theo Gold?' Tanvi asks, reeling off the names of the best-looking boys in our year. 'Ryan Attah? Jacob Shapiro? Jamie Cannon?'

She lets out a gasp of delight.

'See, I knew there'd be someone!' she cries, looking incredibly pleased with herself.

'I don't know what you're talking about,' I stammer.

'Oh really? Then why else did your face go all red when I said Jamie's name?'

'It didn't.'

'Oh yes, it did,' Tanvi says gleefully. 'It was like I'd turned on the switch to your blood vessels! Oh, don't worry, I won't tell anyone. I'm an excellent secrets keeper.'

'Look, I don't fancy anyone, OK?' I snap.

'OK,' Tanvi agrees, biting her lip to stop myself from smiling.

'I don't!' I cry.

'No, no, I totally believe you . . . Not!' she says, cackling in delight.

God, she's irritating.

'Aha, new blood!'

Tanvi and I whirl round in unison.

Mr Milford, one of the music teachers has emerged from room 21.4 and is rubbing his hands together like the child catcher.

'Come in, come in,' he says, beckoning us across the threshold.

That's when I notice the poster on the door behind him.

CHOIR
EVERY FRIDAY LUNCH TIME
NEW MEMBERS WELCOME!

I take a very large and very deliberate step backwards. 'I'm not staying,' I say.

'Ah, a dagger to my heart,' Mr Milford cries, clutching his chest with both hands and staggering about on the spot.

'Oh, please stay, Ro,' Tanvi says, waggling my arm. 'It'll be fun.'

I stare at her in horror. 'But I already do an extra-curricular activity,' I say.

'So? You can do more than one.'

'Tell you what, why don't you just give it a try,' Mr Milford says. 'And if you're not keen, I promise I won't be offended if you don't come back next week. Well, not *too* offended.'

'But I don't sing,' I say.

'All the more reason to come to choir,' Mr Milford says.

'Exactly!' Tanvi chimes in, pulling me into the room, her grip surprisingly strong.

I attempt to shake her off but Tanvi clings on for dear life.

'Get off,' I hiss. 'I'm not staying.'

'Just try it,' Tanvi says serenely, the tranquil expression on her face at odds with her pincer-like fingers.

'But I don't want to.'

People are starting to look.

'OK, so from left to right, we've got sopranos, mezzos, altos, tenors and bass,' Mr Milford says, ignoring the kerfuffle and pointing at the rows of chairs arranged in a semicircle around an upright piano. 'Put very simply, high voices to low voices. Don't worry if you're not sure which you are, nothing is set in stone.' He pauses, his hands on his hips. 'So, ladies, are we staying or leaving?'

Tanvi and I are still standing in the centre of the room,

Tanvi's fingers wrapped around my forearm, digging in, even through the double layer of my blouse and blazer.

'Staying,' Tanvi says. 'Right, Ro?' She fixes me with a dazzling smile.

The room is suddenly silent. Practically the entire choir is looking at us now.

'Right, Ro?' Tanvi repeats, somehow immune to the daggers I'm shooting from my eyeballs.

'Right,' I mutter.

Tanvi finally lets go of my arm.

'Great stuff!' Mr Milford says. 'Now, if you're not sure, I'd suggest starting out with the sopranos – they tend to get to sing the tune most of the time – and seeing how you go from there.' He directs us to two empty chairs.

I sit down in semi-shock. How exactly has this happened? Next to me, Tanvi is oblivious to my annoyance, humming happily as she removes her blazer and drapes it over the back of her chair.

Mr Milford rolls up his shirtsleeves and sits down at the piano. 'Welcome, everyone,' he says. 'It's great to see so many new faces. Now, how about we start with a warm-up.'

The warm-up consists of scales and tongue twisters and breathing exercises, similar to the ones Bonnie does around the house before her gigs. I join in half-heartedly, my eyes trained on the clock above Mr Milford's head. Next to me, Tanvi is singing at the top of her voice, hitting maybe 50 per cent of the notes at most. I steal a sideways glance at her. Despite the awful din she's making, she looks ecstatic. It's very, very weird.

After the warm-up, Mr Milford hands out sheet music. It's a pop song from the 1970s called 'Lean on Me'.

'There are a few solo lines towards the end,' he says. 'Any takers?'

Tanvi actually has the nerve to give me a nudge. I respond with a fierce shake of my head and the dirtiest look in my arsenal.

'Why not?' Tanvi whispers.

'Because I'd rather have my toenails pulled out?'

She giggles, clearly under the misapprehension that I'm joking.

In the end, a sixth former called Bailey raises her hand.

'Great! Thank you, Bailey,' Mr Milford says. 'Right, let's take it from the top.'

Mr Milford breaks down the lines individually, hammering them out on the piano one by one until he's satisfied all the groups have got the hang of their harmonies. I continue to sing quietly, happy to be drowned out by the other singers.

'OK, let's be brave and have a go at putting it all together!' Mr Milford says.

I'm surprised by how good our first attempt sounds. It's not perfect by any stretch, but even I have to admit that some of the harmonies sound really quite nice. Even more surprising is just how satisfying it feels, like slotting together the final pieces of an especially tricky jigsaw.

'What a way to start to the term!' Mr Milford says, playing a closing flourish on the piano. 'Sadly, though, I think that's all we have time for today.'

'Aw,' at least half of the choir chorus.

I glance up at the clock, startled to discover time is up.

'To be continued,' Mr Milford says. 'In the meantime, if you could help me get the classroom back in order, that would be great.'

'What should we do with our music, sir?' Tanvi asks, waving her copy in the air.

'Ah. Well, that all depends. Have I done enough to entice you back?'

Tanvi nods her head enthusiastically.

'In that case, feel free to hang onto it until next week's session. I'm sorry, I don't know your name.'

'Tanvi Shah,' Tanvi replies happily.

'Brilliant. Very happy to have you on board, Tanvi Shah. And how about you?' he says, turning to me. 'I'm sorry, I don't know your name either.'

'Ro Snow,' I admit.

'And how did you find it, Ro Snow?'

'OK,' I say, shrugging.

'See you next Friday, "OK"?' Mr Milford asks, wiggling his eyebrows up and down.

'I don't think so, sir,' I say, picking up my bag and leaving the room without looking back.

'Wait!' Tanvi calls after me.

I increase my speed but Tanvi catches up with me within seconds.

'Did you really not like it?' she asks, scampering alongside me.

'Why do you sound so surprised? I told you I didn't want to do it.'

'But you're a really good singer.'

'Don't be mental.'

'I mean it,' Tanvi insists. 'You literally *have* to come back to choir next week. It would be, like, criminal if you didn't.'

'I don't *have* to do anything.'

'Oh, please, Ro! Pleeeeeease!'

'Ugh, I'll think about it,' I say, more to get her off my back than anything.

'Hey, what are you doing after school today?' Tanvi asks. 'Do you want to come round to mine?'

'What for?' I ask, my voice laced with suspicion.

'To hang out? Watch some telly maybe? My mum went shopping yesterday so we've got loads of yummy stuff in. I think we might even have some cookies and cream Häagen-Dazs.'

I blink in confusion. No one has asked me over to their house since I was at primary school.

'I can't,' I say.

'Tomorrow then?'

'Sorry?'

'Fancy coming round to mine tomorrow instead? It's going to be proper hot apparently. We could get the paddling pool out.'

'I work on Saturdays,' I say.

'You've got a job?'

'Yeah.'

'Where?'

'I deliver leaflets.'

'Cool! Whereabouts?'

'Near the park.'

'Sunday, then?' Tanvi asks. 'We could do our homework together then watch a film or something. I have my brother's Now TV password so we've got loads to pick from.'

'Sorry, family stuff.'

'Have you got a big family too?' Tanvi asks, her eyes lighting up.

'Not exactly.'

I can tell Tanvi wants me to elaborate. I don't, of course.

'Canteen?' Tanvi asks as we reach the bottom of the stairs.

We've got ten minutes to grab food before the bell rings for registration.

'I've already got a sandwich,' I say.

The canteen is for canteen-bought food only. Plus, I'm still annoyed at the way she tricked me into going to choir.

'Oh, OK,' Tanvi says, hiding her disappointment behind a smile. 'See you in registration then.'

'Yeah, see you there,' I mutter.

I walk away, Tanvi's eyes burning a hole in my blazer.

13

I have an earworm. 'Lean on Me' has embedded itself in my head and shows no signs of going away. I literally. Cannot. Stop. Singing. It.

I blame Tanvi Shah entirely.

It's Saturday and I've been leafletting for the past two hours. As Tanvi promised, it's officially hot and my T-shirt clings to my back as I drag my trolley behind me.

Long, wide and lined with cherry trees on either side, Hopewood Gardens is probably the prettiest street on my route. In the spring, the trees sprout petals that fall to the ground like wedding confetti, cloaking the pavements with a blanket of baby pink.

Despite my earworm, I'm feeling the most relaxed I have in days. Avoiding Tanvi all week proved surprisingly exhausting in the end and I'm grateful for the break. I may have a full trolley of leaflets to deliver, but at least I don't have to worry about her pouncing on me.

I'm about halfway down the street when I hear a familiar voice yelling my name.

No.

No, no, no, no.

Slowly, I turn round.

The front door of the house I just leafletted is wide open and Tanvi is heading down the driveway towards me wearing a cow-print onesie and unicorn slippers.

My heart sinks.

Is this actually happening to me?

'When you said you delivered leaflets near the park, I had a feeling you might do my road,' she says, a wide grin on her face.

Wait, she hasn't been waiting for me all morning, has she?

'It's so funny I've never seen you before,' Tanvi continues. 'Don't you think?'

'Hilarious,' I murmur.

'How long did you say you've been doing this job for?'

'I didn't.'

'How many more houses have you got to do?' she asks, trying to peer into my trolley.

'Quite a lot,' I say, pulling it behind me. 'In fact, I really need to get on.'

'Do you want some help?'

'You're not dressed.'

'It would only take me a second.'

Considering how long she takes to get changed before and after PE, I doubt this.

'Seriously, please don't,' I say.

'Why not? It'll be fun doing it together. Not to mention waaaaaay quicker.'

'Thanks, but no thanks.'

'Well, why don't you come back here when you've finished?' Tanvi suggests, scampering next to me, the silver unicorn horns on her slippers flopping from side to side with every step. 'My mum always makes pancakes on Saturday mornings. French style ones with bananas and Nutella. They're insanely good!'

My stomach chooses that exact moment to let out an angry rumble. I cough to disguise it, not wanting to give Tanvi any ammunition. It's becoming increasingly obvious that this girl doesn't understand 'no' in the usual sense of the word.

'No thank you,' I say.

'Next week then?'

'I don't think so, Tanvi.'

'Well, you know where I am if you change your mind.'

I keep walking, Tanvi's hopeful voice ringing in my ears.

After my shift, I head home for lunch and a rest before my weekly pilgrimage to the launderette. For the past three years, ever since the washing machine stopped working and Bonnie refused to get it fixed, I've spent my Saturday afternoons at Luna's Launderette.

Luna's is a 1970s time warp. A pink neon sign hangs in the window, but I've never seen more than two of its letters illuminated at once. All the washing machines are a lurid mint green and take for ever, rumbling violently on their final cycle. The flooring is made up of peeling black-and-white checked lino, the white bits scuffed and closer to grey than the gleaming white they must have been once upon a time.

I'm the only person in here. This is not unusual. Occasionally, the bell above the door lets out a mournful tinkle and someone shuffles in to drop off a service wash, but most of the time, apart from a few stalwart regulars, I more or less have the place to myself.

I empty the two huge laundry bags I dragged from home. As usual, Bonnie left her dirty things in a heap on the bathroom floor for me to pick up. And, as usual, I left them there until the very last minute, seriously flirting with the idea of ignoring them and letting Bonnie run out of clean things. Ultimately, though, I knew I'd pick them up. Because if I didn't, Bonnie certainly wouldn't bother. And although a big part of me thought that was exactly what she deserved, another, bigger part of me couldn't be doing with the inevitable fallout.

I wait until the machine has started to whir before climbing up on top of it, leaning my back against the woodchip wall and taking out my phone.

I get comfy and scroll through my latest conversation with Noah. Until now, we haven't really talked about personal stuff but the other day he started to moan about his dad and, before I knew it, I was joining in and moaning about mine (albeit with some heavy editing). The weirdest bit was, I felt better afterwards – like something small but significant had shifted.

I'm reading our messages for the third time while munching on a cereal bar when I notice a familiar face squished up against the glass.

Tanvi.

Twice in one day? OK, this is getting ridiculous now. And *not* in a good way. What on earth is she doing here? We're nowhere near Hopewood Gardens.

She straightens up and waves through the glass, grinning and oblivious. Behind her, two men and a woman – who I guess must be Tanvi's family – are sitting in an olive green car.

Don't come in, Tanvi. Please don't come in.

She comes in.

'Hi!' she says. 'I'm not stalking you, I promise! We were just passing by and I saw you through the window and I was like "Stop the car!"'

I'm still sitting on top of the washing machine, cereal bar crumbs clinging to my lips. I wipe them away with the back of my hand before climbing down.

'What are you doing here?' Tanvi asks, trailing a finger across the row of dryers.

'Well, we're in a launderette so why don't you take a wild guess,' I say.

Tanvi giggles. 'How come you're stuck doing it, though?' she asks.

It's a fair question. I doubt many 14-year-olds are solely responsible for their household's laundry, and Tanvi's reminder stings a little.

'My mum's not very well,' I lie.

Tanvi's face sags with concern. 'Oh no! What's wrong with her? Is it serious?'

'Oh, just a cold. She's fine,' I say. 'Just not up to doing to the washing this week.'

'Oh, OK. Well, that makes sense,' Tanvi says. 'For the record, I'm not usually this dressed up.'

She's wearing a faded denim jacket over the top of a cerise pink sari.

'I mean, in case you were about to ask. We're just on our way to my grandparents' house. They're having a party for their wedding anniversary. Fifty years! Can you believe that?'

I'm not sure how long my grandparents have been together. Dad's parents live in Spain these days and I've never met Bonnie's. From what I can gather, they haven't been in contact since way before I was born.

'Look, shouldn't you get back to your family?' I ask, glancing at them through the window. They're chatting happily.

'Oh, they don't mind,' Tanvi says, waving at them.

They smile and wave back.

'See!' she says brightly.

My stomach tenses. Other people's parents make me nervous.

Tanvi opens the door of one of the unoccupied washing machines and peers in. 'Do you reckon I could fit in one of these?' she asks.

'I wouldn't know,' I say, one eye still on Tanvi's family.

'I reckon I could. If I try, do you promise not to lock me in?'

'Seriously, your family is waiting, Tanvi.'

'Oh, they're fine,' she says, with a dismissive wave of the hand. 'We're early anyway. So, do you promise?'

'Promise what?'

'That you won't lock me in?'

'I'm not a monster.'

'Just checking!' Tanvi says, removing her jacket and bundling it into my arms.

She squeezes inside the washing machine, giggling the entire time.

'Oh my God, it's really warm in here!' she cries. 'Hey, can you take a picture? My phone's in my jacket pocket.'

I sigh and retrieve Tanvi's phone.

'The passcode is two-four-one-two-one-seven,' Tanvi says.

As I'm typing it in, Tanvi pulls the door to, pressing her face up against it, her breath steaming up the glass.

I can't help it, I start to laugh. In response, Tanvi hams it up, pretending she's stuck.

'Save me!' she cries. 'Heeeeeeeelp!'

Her muffled shouts are interrupted by the sharp tinkle of the bell above the door.

I spin around. Linda, one of the regulars, is waddling towards me, a plastic basket of dirty laundry tucked under her arm.

'All right, Ro,' she says, dumping the basket on the skinny bench running down the centre of the launderette and opening one of the empty machines. 'God, time flies. Has it really been a week already?'

Shut up, Linda. Please just shut up.

She clocks Tanvi, still in the washing machine.

'Brought a little friend with you this week, have you?'

Tanvi wriggles out. 'Hi, I'm Tanvi,' she says, extending her hand for Linda to shake.

'Linda,' Linda replies, looking amused.

'She's just going actually,' I say, pressing her phone and jacket into her arms. 'Aren't you, Tanvi?'

Tanvi shoots me a confused glance but, miraculously, seems to take the hint.

'I'll see you at school then,' she says, glancing from me to Linda then back to me.

'Yeah, see you at school,' I say, turning away and pretending to squint at the dial on the dryer, even though I know every setting by heart. I don't look up until the bell above the door has rung to indicate Tanvi's departure.

14

Avoiding Tanvi Shah is proving a full-time occupation. She's clearly memorized my timetable, and as a result, I've had to resort to sprinting out of my lessons the second the bell rings in a bid to escape her ambushes. If Tanvi's at all bothered by my behaviour, she shows no sign of it, playfully scolding me for my elusiveness when I see her in registration but otherwise remaining her cheerful self. I just wish I knew what it was about me she finds so appealing, because, from where I'm standing, her interest in me makes absolutely no sense.

'Choir?' Tanvi asks, catching up with me as I walk back to the changing rooms after Friday's PE lesson.

OK, time to be firm.

'I've had a think, like I said I would, and I'm not coming,' I say.

'But you're so good!' she cries.

I smile tightly, not wishing to point out that I don't exactly trust Tanvi's musical ear.

'What will you do instead?' she asks.

'What I usually do. Eat my lunch outside.'

'But it's going to tip it down.'

As if on cue, the sky darkens and the heavens open, forcing us to break into a run to avoid getting drenched.

In the changing rooms, I dress quickly, slipping out of the door while Tanvi's back is turned and heading straight for the seldom used disabled toilet at the far end of the maths corridor – my favoured wet-weather lunch spot. When I try the handle though, it's locked. Frowning, I press my ear against the door. I can hear tinny music and giggling coming from inside, suggesting its occupants are not planning to vacate any time soon.

Great.

I back away and peer out of the window. The glass is streaked with fat raindrops. Maybe I can just hang out here. I perch on the windowsill and take out my sandwich. I'm unwrapping the foil when a loud 'Oi!' echoes down the corridor. It's one of the sixth form lunch monitors, easily identifiable by their blue sashes and overzealous enforcement methods.

'You know the rules,' the boy barks, his power trip at full throttle. 'If you want to eat your packed lunch you either go outside or to the designated social area for your year group.'

'But it's raining.'

'Did you not hear what I just said? That's what your social area is for.'

I get the feeling it's not worth arguing with him and slope away, leaving him to hammer on the door of the disabled toilet, bellowing: 'I know you're in there!'

I head up to the social area and peer through the glass panel in the door. All the popular kids are lounging on the beanbags as usual, forcing everyone else onto the hard seating around the edge of the room. Jamie is amongst the crew in the middle. He's sprawled on the biggest beanbag of them all, his legs spread, Sienna nestled between his knees. He glances up and for a few seconds our eyes meet. I pull away, my heart beating, and walk away as fast as I can.

The warm-up has already started by the time I slip into choir practice. Mr Milford gives me a thumbs up from behind the piano as I slide into the spare chair next to Tanvi.

'Yay! You came!' she whispers.

'Only because of the rain,' I say. 'This is strictly a one-off.'

I'm not sure she believes me though, her smile a bit too knowing for my liking.

After the warm-up, Mr Milford announces we're going to be working on a song from a brand-new Broadway musical.

'You all did so well with "Lean On Me" last week, I thought we might step things up and try something a bit more advanced today. I saw this show in previews when I was in New York at the end of August and the second I heard this number, I just knew I wanted you guys to give it a go.'

He plays us a recording of the song. He's right. It's beautiful, and when it's over I'm surprised to discover I'm itching to sing it.

Mr Milford breaks it down, starting in the middle, with the chorus, working through it bar by bar, before returning to the opening verse – a solo.

'Anyone fancy having a try?' he asks.

No one responds.

'Oh, come on, don't be shy!'

Tanvi sticks her hand in the air.

I raise an eyebrow. Say what you like, but there's no denying this girl has serious guts.

'Fantastic,' Mr Milford says, clapping his hands together. 'Thank you, Tanvi. Now, how about we take it from the top, nice and slow.' He begins to make his way back to the piano.

'Oh no, sir,' Tanvi calls after him. 'Sorry, I wasn't suggesting *I* sing the solo.'

Mr Milford stops in his tracks and turns to frown at her. 'You weren't?'

'Uh-uh,' she says. 'I was thinking Ro should do it.'

What??? I turn to look at her in horror. Tanvi beams back, all big brown eyes and oblivion.

'That OK with you, Ro?' Mr Milford asks, continuing to stride towards the piano as if it's a done deal.

'No!' I yelp.

He stops walking. 'No?' he repeats.

'No, thank you,' I repeat in a quieter voice, my heart pounding.

'Are you sure you don't want to just give it a go?' Mr Milford asks. 'No pressure or anything.'

No pressure? Who is he kidding? The entire choir is gawping at me.

I nod firmly, my face hot with embarrassment and annoyance and a big dollop of anger reserved for the pint-sized interferer sitting next to me.

'Oh, go on, Ro,' Tanvi says, nudging me with her elbow. 'You'll slay it. Honestly, sir, Ro has *such* a nice voice.'

Oh my God, I want to kill her. Strangle her skinny little neck with my bare hands.

'Ro?' Mr Milford says, cocking his head to one side. 'Anything I can do to persuade you?'

Giggles break out across the room and my face flames even hotter.

'Quiet please,' Mr Milford says, irritation flashing across his face. 'Ro?'

I raise my eyes to meet his and shake my head. 'No, sir,' I say.

He holds my gaze for a few seconds. 'Fair enough,' he says eventually. 'Bailey? You up for giving it a go?'

'Are you mad with me?' Tanvi whispers as Mr Milford goes over the tune with Bailey.

'Yes,' I hiss back.

'Oh, please don't be,' Tanvi begs. 'I was only trying to help.'

Help? By making me look like an idiot in front of the entire choir?

'Please, Ro,' she adds. 'I wouldn't be able to stand it if you were mad with me.'

'Too late,' I say, burying my head in my sheet music and keeping it in there until the rehearsal is over.

The second Mr Milford dismisses us, I leap to my feet,

gathering up my things as quickly as I possibly can and doing my best to ignore Tanvi's continued pleas for forgiveness.

I'm heading for the door when Mr Milford calls my name.

'Can I grab you for a quick word before you go?' he asks.

Panic sloshes in my belly. *What an earth can he want?*

'Do you want me to wait for you?' Tanvi asks.

Is she crazy? I'm so cross I can barely look at her. 'No,' I snap.

'OK,' she says in a small voice, sloping out of the room with her head down.

As the room slowly empties out, I hover awkwardly at the back of the room, trying to work out what on earth Mr Milford could want. When the last person has left, Mr Milford sits down at the piano and beckons for me to sit next to him. I do as I'm told. Without saying a word, he begins to play the introduction to the song we've just been working on.

'Do you read music, Ro?' he asks.

I nod. The house is full of sheet music. When I was little, I'd follow with my finger as Bonnie practised songs for her gigs, matching the notes and lyrics to her voice, and reminding her of the words if she forgot.

'What do you say? Fancy giving it a go?' he asks. 'Just you and me.'

I look over his shoulder. The room is empty. 'But why?' I ask.

'Just to see how it feels,' Mr Milford says.

I hesitate.

'No pressure,' he adds softly. 'I promise.'

He starts to play the introduction. It really is a beautiful song.

I don't know if I'm going to sing or not until the very last moment, the first few notes that leave my mouth taking me almost entirely by surprise.

When I reach the end of the verse, I expect Mr Milford to stop playing, but instead he urges me to 'keep going!' and before I know it, I've sung the entire song.

When we're finished, we sit side by side in silence. My palms are sweaty. I rub them on my school skirt but the scratchy polyester isn't exactly absorbent and just seems to move the sweat about.

'Have you sung that piece before, Ro?' Mr Milford asks.

'No, sir.'

'Were you familiar with it at all? Before today's rehearsal, I mean.'

'No, sir.'

He pauses and looks thoughtful. 'I'm going to try something if that's OK, Ro. Do you think you can sing an A for me?'

I steal another glance over my shoulder. There's definitely no one else in the room. It's just me, Mr Milford and the piano. I take a deep breath and sing an A.

Mr Milford lets it carry for a few seconds before playing it on the piano. The notes match.

'And a D,' he says.

I sing a D. Again, Mr Milford plays the note on the piano. Again, they match.

Next, he tries a G, an A flat and a B sharp.

'Ro,' he says, resting his clasped palms on his lap. 'Have you ever heard of something called perfect pitch?'

'Don't you mean *Pitch Perfect*? As in the film?' I saw it at the cinema with Dad years ago. He fell asleep halfway through.

Mr Milford laughs. 'No, not the film.'

'Oh. Then no. I don't think so.'

He turns to face me, tucking his right leg under his left. 'Ro, perfect pitch is a rare auditory phenomenon, characterized by the ability of a person to identify or recreate a given musical note without the benefit of a reference tone. In plain English it means the majority of people cannot do what you did just then.'

The word 'phenomenon' makes my brain fizz. It just doesn't fit. He must have got it wrong. I'm ordinary, average, unremarkable, as far from 'phenomenal' as you can get.

'Are you joking, sir?' I ask.

He smiles. 'No, Ro. I'm pretty certain you have perfect pitch. Not to mention a very beautiful singing voice.'

I stare hard at the piano keys, my vision blurring so the black and white melt into each other.

'You seem surprised,' Mr Milford observes.

I shrug it off.

'Is anyone else in your family musical?'

'My mum,' I answer reluctantly. 'She's . . . she's kind of a singer.'

Mr Milford's eyes light up. 'Really?'

'Just weddings and social clubs and things.'

'Do you ever sing together?'

Once upon a time we did. Back before the house got really bad and I began to spend more and more time holed up in my room.

'Not really,' I say. 'She's pretty busy . . .'

'I see.'

The bell rings for afternoon registration. I stand up.

'It was a privilege to hear you sing today, Ro,' Mr Milford says. 'Truly.'

'Thank you, sir,' I murmur.

'See you next week?'

I nod, scoop up my bag and hurry out of the classroom, the words 'perfect pitch' and 'phenomenon' ricocheting around my brain like the ball bearings in a pinball machine. And although I know my dominant emotion should be anger towards Tanvi and her meddling, it's completely obliterated by the unfamiliar yet really rather pleasant sensation of pure unadulterated excitement.

15

I take a deep breath and half run, half walk up Tanvi's drive-way with my head down. The leaflets are halfway through her letter box when the door springs open and out she jumps, like a human jack-in-the-box.

'Hi!' she says.

She's fully dressed today, wearing skinny grey jeans and a T-shirt with the Cookie Monster on the front, her wispy hair pulled into two slightly wonky Princess Leia-style buns.

Even though her appearance isn't exactly a surprise, it still makes me jump, the leaflets slipping from my fingers and fluttering to the ground.

'Sorry,' Tanvi says as I bend down to pick them up. 'I didn't mean to scare you. It's just that I've been sitting here for the past hour waiting for you.' She claps her hand to her mouth. 'Oh my God, did that sound super stalkery? I promise I'm not obsessed with you! Well not *that* much, ha ha ha! It's just that I've been feeling sooooooo bad about what happened in choir yesterday.'

'It's fine,' I growl, heading back down the driveway.

This is a lie, of course. I'm still absolutely furious with her.

'No,' Tanvi calls after me. 'I was totally out of order and I want to make it up to you. Which is why I got you this.'

Curiosity gets the better of me and I turn round. Tanvi is holding out a big wicker picnic hamper, the sort posh people fill with champagne and fancy cheese at Christmas time.

'A peace offering,' she says. 'Well, don't you want to know what's in it?' she asks when I don't respond.

'Not especially.'

I know I'm being rude but I refuse to feel guilty about it. Not after yesterday.

'I promise it's nice,' she says.

'I don't care what it is.'

'Oh, just have a look, will you!'

She flips open the lid of the hamper to reveal an Aladdin's cave of goodies – mini freshly baked baguettes, three different flavours of kettle chips, little tubs of olives and sun-dried tomatoes, hummus, chocolate chip cookies, Percy Pig sweets and bottles of pink lemonade. And that's just the stuff I can see. My stomach lets out a quiet grumble. Breakfast was half a custard cream from the very bottom of the biscuit tin at work.

'I thought we could eat it in the park once you've finished,' Tanvi says, setting it down on the doorstep. 'Have you got much more to do?'

Before I can answer, she's already got her nose in the trolley.

'You've hardly got any left!' she exclaims. 'Amazing!'

I open my mouth to protest but she's already bounded back into the house, leaving the door wide open. She re-appears less than a minute later, wearing a lilac hoodie over the top of her T-shirt and carrying a rolled-up tartan picnic blanket under her arm.

'I really don't have the time for this,' I say.

'But I really want the chance to make things up to you. I felt so bad last night I could barely sleep.'

'Seriously?'

'Uh-huh,' she says solemnly. 'Check out my eye bags.'

I frown. Tanvi's under-eye area looks perfectly smooth to me.

'Please,' she says. 'It would really mean a lot if you let me do this for you.'

She looks so hopeful, her hands in prayer position, her stupidly big eyes blinking expectantly. With every bat of her eyelashes, I can feel myself softening.

Damn it.

'OK,' I say. 'But I haven't got long.'

'Yay!' Tanvi cries, tying the blanket around her shoulders like a cape and picking up the hamper.

She insists on helping me with my last few leaflets.

'This is so much fun!' she exclaims, scampering back down the final driveway, her eyes shining.

'You're very easily entertained,' I say.

'I know,' she replies, grinning. 'It's one of my very best qualities.'

I glance up the street. A middle-aged man is hovering

about five metres behind us. The second he realizes I've clocked him, he widens his eyes in panic and leaps behind a bush.

'OK,' I say. 'This is going to sound weird but I think we're being followed.'

'Huh?' Tanvi says.

'There,' I say, pointing at the pair of legs with an overgrown gorse bush for a body.

Tanvi lets out a deep groan. 'Seriously, Dad?' she says, her hands on her hips. 'It's a good job you're a pharmacist and not a private detective, because you'd be utterly rubbish at it.'

Dad?

The man steps out from behind the bush and walks towards us with his hands up in surrender. He is short with a rounded belly and bushy moustache.

He smiles sheepishly.

'Ro, this is my dad. Dad, this is Ro – the girl I've been telling you about. He's a *tad* overprotective,' she says, turning to me. 'And by a tad, I mean a colossally mortifying amount.'

'But this is your first time going to the park by yourself,' he says.

Tanvi covers her face with her hands. 'Dad!' she wails.

'But it is, *bachcha*.'

'Well, it isn't really. Since I'm not actually by myself, am I? You're here.' She jabs him in the chest with her index finger before whirling round to face me. 'How long have you been going to the park without your parents, Ro?'

'Er, I don't know,' I say, trying to think what an appropriate age might be. 'Um, since I was ten or eleven maybe.'

'See!' Tanvi says, spinning back to face her dad. 'You and Mum are being totally over the top!'

'I prefer to think of it as being careful.'

'Well, whatever it is, it's annoying and totally unnecessary. I'm fourteen! Juliet was married at fourteen!'

'Considering what happened next, that's probably not the best example,' her dad points out.

'Well, maybe if she'd been allowed to go to the park by herself instead of being cooped up at home with her parents all the time, she wouldn't have bothered with running off with Romeo in the first place? Ever thought of that? We're just going to sit on the grass and eat our picnic. And if something does happen, *which it won't*, I've got my phone.' She pats the pouch of her hoodie.

'We won't be long,' I add. 'I've got to be home in a bit anyway.'

Tanvi's dad looks from me to Tanvi. 'OK then,' he says. 'Just . . . be careful.'

'It's my default state, Dad,' Tanvi says. 'Now go. Preferably somewhere out of sight.'

'Nice to meet you, Ro,' he says.

'Er, yeah, you too.'

'Love you, *bachcha*.'

'Love you too,' Tanvi says with a dismissive wave of her hand.

'What does "bachcha" mean?' I ask as we watch Tanvi's dad slope back up the street.

'It's Hindi for "baby",' Tanvi says, rolling her eyes hard.

*

Ostborough Park is pretty busy. After much one-sided debate on Tanvi's part, we settle for a spot of grass near the tennis courts, one of which is occupied by two elderly women wearing immaculate tennis whites.

'Help me with this, will you?' Tanvi says.

Together, we spread out the blanket on the grass, weighing it down in each corner with our shoes, and begin to unload the contents of the hamper.

'I didn't know what you liked,' Tanvi says. 'So I got a bit of everything.'

'No kidding,' I murmur, surveying the spread. There's enough food to feed an entire family.

'Sorry about before,' Tanvi adds, prising the lid off a tub of hummus.

'Before?'

'With my dad. Like I said, he and my mum are a bit overprotective.'

'Is this *really* your first time in the park by yourself?' I ask.

That sort of concern is kind of hard to imagine when I've been left to my own devices for so long.

'Yes,' Tanvi admits, her cheeks glowing. 'I bet you think I'm super lame, right?'

'No. It's nice they care so much.'

When it comes to parents, I'm hardly in a position to judge. I could probably tell Bonnie I'm off to join ISIS, or sell my body in Soho, and she wouldn't even blink. And Dad is only capable of parenting when I'm right under his nose. Tanvi's situation is so far removed from mine it's not even worth comparing.

'They've always been pretty protective,' Tanvi says, pausing to dunk a kettle chip into the hummus. 'But I definitely think my cancer sent things up a gear. Like, when I was in Year Seven, they let me walk to school on my own, but now they insist on dropping me off and picking me up.'

'How come? I mean, what exactly do they think is going to happen to you?'

Tanvi grins, obviously pleased by my question. 'OK, so I have a few theories. So, the kind of cancer I had, it's called rhabdomyosarcoma, and it's pretty aggressive. It's also really rare, like fewer than sixty kids are diagnosed with it every year and most of them are boys under the age of ten. And I was a twelve-year-old girl. Based on the tumour location and stage, I was given a forty per cent chance of survival. Put all that together, and the odds were stacked against me the entire way. And yet here I am. Which is obviously amazing, but has also made my parents super crazy and convinced there must be a catch or something.' She pauses and dunks another kettle chip. 'Ever watched the film, *Final Destination*?' she asks.

'Isn't that a horror film?'

'Uh-huh. They're my absolute obsession by the way. Well, one of them. I kind of have a few.'

'You're into horror films? Really?'

With all her peppiness and overflowing optimism, Tanvi strikes me as more of a Disney fiend. The idea of her getting off on blood and gore is more than a little unexpected.

'Yep,' Tanvi says, grinning. 'I love 'em.'

'But why?' I ask. 'I don't get it.'

'I dunno. I just really like being scared, I suppose,' Tanvi says. 'I like the adrenaline rush I get. My mum and dad would go bonkers if they knew.'

'Wait – they don't know you're into them?'

'No way. You met my dad just then. As if he's going to be cool with me watching *The Texas Chainsaw Massacre*.'

'He'd be upset?'

'Big time. He thinks *The Great British Bake Off* is too tense half the time. Anyway, back to *Final Destination*. So, in it, a load of high school students narrowly avoid being in this massive plane crash when one of them has a premonition about it and tells them all not to get on the plane, but after that they all start dying in really bizarre accidents.'

'Right,' I say, not quite sure where Tanvi is taking this.

'See, the thing is,' she says, shuffling in closer, 'it turns out they were *supposed* to die in the crash, which is why they're all getting killed now, because Death is ultimately in charge and they're on borrowed time.'

'Wait, are you saying you think you were supposed to die? That you cheated death or something? That's kind of messed up, Tanvi.'

'Well, it is when you put it that way! It's more like I get the feeling my parents think we were *so* lucky, that they don't quite trust that we're out the other side yet. It's not quite like in the film, obviously. It's not like they actually think I'm going to be impaled on a kitchen knife or decapitated by flying shrapnel any second now. They just worry *a lot*, and want to know I'm safe at all times, hence my dad's stalkery behaviour before.'

I take a deep breath and ask the question that's been playing on my mind since Tanvi started talking.

'*Could* you get ill again? I mean, *could* the cancer come back?'

'The doctors don't think so. There's a possibility I might develop side effects in later life: a possible reduction in bone growth, infertility, a change in the way the heart and kidneys work, a slight increase in the risk of developing another cancer' – she ticks them off on her fingers, the way you might items on a shopping list – 'and my immunity is still a bit weak, but there's no point in fixating on any of that stuff. It's all ifs and maybes. Try telling that to my *mental* parents though.' She rolls her eyes and drowns a veggie Percy Pig in hummus.

Another deep breath. 'How close *were* you to dying?' I ask.

Tanvi's face changes slightly and for a second I'm worried I've gone too far.

'I was pretty poorly for a while,' she says slowly. 'I never thought I'd actually die though, even when things were really touch and go and my parents had puffy eyes from crying all the time, even though they always pretended it was hay fever. Like I said the other week at school, I kind of always knew I was going to get better.'

'Wow,' I say softly.

'Anyway, enough about me. What about *your* mum and dad?' she asks, licking her fingers. 'Are they ever overprotective?'

'Not exactly.'

'Lucky.'

'Maybe.'

'Do you have brother and sisters?

'Not really.'

The second the words leave my mouth, I regret them. Why didn't I just say 'no'?

Tanvi tilts her head to one side '"Not really?" What does that mean?'

I should have known she wouldn't let that one slide in a million years.

'It's no big deal,' I say, picking at a piece of bread. 'It's just that my dad's wife has a daughter.'

'So you have a half-sister? Cool!'

'We're not related by blood,' I say stiffly. 'She was four when my dad got together with her mum.'

'So he's not her dad?'

'Not biologically, no.'

'Wow, that must be hard for you,' Tanvi says, reaching over and giving my knee a gentle squeeze.

Her sympathy makes me feel uncomfortable. Time to deflect.

'Not really,' I say swiftly. 'So how about you? Brothers? Sisters?'

'Two brothers.' Tanvi says. 'Anish and Devin. Both older than me. Anish has got a family of his own and Dev's doing his masters at the moment. He's living back at home to save money and driving me up the wall. His girlfriend just dumped him, so he's being a total misery. And when he's not moping around, he's winding me up. They both do that actually, at the same time as being ultra-protective. It's a very annoying combination.'

I used to fantasize about having a big brother – Jake, I called him. Jake was kind and wise and knew exactly how to handle Bonnie, and together we were a united front – strong and capable and in control. With Jake on the scene, there were no worries about Social Services. With Jake on the scene, we were untouchable.

I'm relieved when the conversation moves on to safer topics – school, *Brooklyn Nine-Nine*, how to make the ultimate toasted cheese sandwich, the future colonization of Mars, whether Tanvi should get a fringe cut in.

And it's actually sort of fun.

'Try one of those seedy cracker things with a dollop of hummus, a couple of olives and a Percy Pig,' Tanvi instructs. 'I promise you, it's heaven in your mouth.'

'You sure about that? It sounds horrible.'

'I know! That's what's so amazing about it. Go on, try it.'

I grimace but for some reason find myself doing as I'm told. As I suspected, it's beyond disgusting and I have to spit it out into a tissue.

'You've got messed up taste buds, Shah,' I say, swigging down some pink lemonade to get rid of the taste.

'I prefer to think of them as sophisticated,' Tanvi replies in a posh voice. She loads up another cracker, this time adding a sun-dried tomato and a wedge of Brie into the mix, cackling with delight when I pull a face.

'I meant what I said before,' Tanvi says, breaking a chocolate chip cookie in half, crumbs going everywhere.

'About what?'

'Yesterday. In choir. I really am sorry.'

Weirdly, Tanvi mentioning it doesn't reignite my anger the way it did earlier.

'It's . . . fine,' I say. 'Well, it's not *fine*. I don't know, just don't do anything like that again, OK?'

'I absolutely promise,' Tanvi says, swiping her finger across her heart. 'I just didn't want that Bailey girl taking another solo. Especially when you're *so* much better than her.'

I make a face.

'But you are!' Tanvi insists. 'She can hit the notes and make a pretty sound and all that, but then so can loads of people. When you sing I get all goose-pimply.'

'Whatever.'

'It's true! Sing something and I'll prove it.' Tanvi yanks up the sleeve of her hoodie and thrusts her bare arm in front of my face.

'Don't be a dick,' I say, batting it away.

'I'm not! I'm telling you, your voice makes me all tingly.'

'Shush, no it doesn't.'

'It does! If I had a voice like yours I'd never shut up. I'd sing entire conversations, the way they do in *Les Mis*.' She plucks a broken cookie from the packet. 'This cookie is delicious,' she trills, holding it aloft. 'Don't you agree?' She pauses, gesturing for me to reply in song.

I roll my eyes at her. *As if.*

'But don't you want to show off?' Tanvi asks.

'Nope.'

'What?' she asks, incredulous. 'Not even a teeny bit?'

'Not even a teeny bit.'

'Interesting,' Tanvi says, reaching for another cookie. 'You know what you are, Ro?'

'What?'

'An onion.'

'An onion? Wow, thanks.'

Tanvi punches me on the arm. 'I mean it in a good way! Because onions have loads of layers that need peeling away and that's exactly what you're like.'

'No, I'm not,' I say. 'I'm more like a . . .'

My brain frantically gropes for the most straightforward of vegetables.

'. . . a turnip!'

'A turnip?' Tanvi repeats, sitting up straight and putting her hands on her hips.

'Yes!'

She shakes her head. 'I must say, I'm not sure I've ever witnessed someone align themselves with a root vegetable quite so enthusiastically.'

'What can I say? Typical turnip behaviour.'

'You're crazy,' Tanvi says, chucking a Percy Pig at me.

It bounces off my shoulder and lands in the hummus. I fish it out and throw it back at her. She attempts to catch it in her mouth and misses and it ends up in the grass. She lunges for it, popping it in her mouth without even looking at it.

'Five-second rule,' she declares before chucking a ball of mozzarella at me, somehow managing to get it down the front of my V-neck T-shirt.

'Tanvi!' I shriek, jumping up and un-tucking my T-shirt, freeing the offending (and surprisingly cold) mozzarella ball while Tanvi rolls about on the blanket, howling with delighted laughter.

Using a kettle chip as a scoop, I catapult a dollop of dip in Tanvi's direction. My aim is perfect, the hummus hitting Tanvi square on the nose with a satisfying splat.

Tanvi blinks in shock, and for a moment I'm worried I've taken things too far.

There's a beat. Slowly, Tanvi sticks her tongue out of her mouth and licks the tip of her nose, her eyes glinting.

'OK, Snow,' she says, reaching for the breadsticks, brandishing one in each hand like they're Samurai swords. 'This means war.'

Five minutes later, the picnic is pretty much demolished. I'm soaked and sticky from a dousing of pink lemonade and Tanvi has crumbs in her hair from where I crushed two massive handfuls of kettle chips directly over her head. Giddy and exhausted, we lie on the blanket, our heads just centimetres apart, chests heaving up and down as we catch our breath.

'Is that your phone?' Tanvi asks, propping herself up on her elbows.

I sit up and listen. My phone rings so rarely I'm not entirely familiar with its nondescript tone.

'Hello,' I say.

'Ro, it's Eric. Everything OK?'

'Fine. Why?'

'It's just that it's nearly two and you're usually back by now.'

'It's nearly two?' I say, jumping up. 'I'm so sorry, I'm on my way now.'

I hang up and begin stuffing our rubbish into the empty hamper. How did I manage to lose track of time quite so spectacularly? If you'd asked me what time it was, I'd have said midday at the latest.

'Do you have to go?' Tanvi asks, her eyes clouding over with disappointment.

I blink at her. I feel a bit like I've just woken up from a weird dream. 'I really do,' I say.

'But we haven't opened the eclairs yet.' She digs a packet of chocolate eclairs out from the bottom of the hamper. 'Ta-da!' she says, stroking the packaging. 'They've got salted caramel cream inside them.'

'Sorry, but I'm already really late,' I say, pulling on my shoes, the blanket they were holding down flapping in the breeze.

'Time flies when you're having fun and all that,' Tanvi says, reluctantly returning the eclairs to the hamper. 'Give me a few minutes to pack up and I'll come with you.'

'Sorry, but I need to go now. Er, thanks for the food and stuff. I'll see you at school.'

I stride towards the gate without looking back. I may have had fun just now, but the very last thing I need is a new friend, especially one as nosy as Tanvi Shah.

16

I feel a little shy as I walk into registration on Monday morning. Even though I've gone over our conversation over and over in my mind and concluded I didn't reveal anything *too* personal to Tanvi on Saturday, I'm still gripped with nerves as I approach our desk. Tanvi doesn't seem to notice my discomfort, smiling broadly and launching straight into an energetic monologue about the rest of her weekend as I slide into my seat.

She's recounting an argument she had with Devin when Ms Cameron calls me to the front of the class and hands me an envelope with my name printed on it in unfamiliar writing.

'What is it?' Tanvi asks as I return to my seat.

'I don't know,' I say, angling my body away from her and slicing open the envelope with my fingernail.

I reach inside and pull out a leaflet with an orange post-it note stuck on the front. The Post-it note says the following:

I think this could be right up your street! Application deadline midnight on Friday.

Mr Milford's signature is at the bottom.

I remove the Post-it and take a closer look at the leaflet. On the front there's a photograph of dozens of singers wearing smart white shirts and navy blue waistcoats. They must be singing about something happy because their eyes are bright and shiny, their open mouths upturned at the corners.

'The National Youth Choir of Great Britain,' Tanvi reads aloud over my shoulder.

Quickly, I turn the leaflet over, placing it face down on the desk.

'Aren't you going to read the rest?' Tanvi asks.

I shrug.

'Can I, then?'

'If you want to.'

She turns over the leaflet and spreads it open on the desk. '*The National Youth Choir of Great Britain is one of the most prestigious youth choirs in the world*,' she recites in an overly loud and theatrical voice. 'Fancy schmancy! Ooh, listen to this, they get to perform all over the world!' She skims the rest of the leaflet, reading aloud the highlights – the residential rehearsals, the travel, the concerts. 'Oh my God, it sounds *amazing*,' she squeaks. 'You have to apply, Ro, you have to!'

'I don't think so.'

'But why not?'

Because girls like me don't do things like join fancy choirs.

And even if they did, who would take care of Bonnie and the house while I was off jetting around the world? With Bonnie left in charge, Social Services would be on our case within days.

'I told you the other day,' I say. 'I'm not interested in getting up on stage.'

'But this is a choir,' she says, flapping the leaflet in front of my face. 'You'd be singing as part of a group.'

'Still not interested.'

Emerson chooses this moment to turn round. 'All right, ladies?' he says.

'Hello, Emerson,' Tanvi replies primly. 'Can we help you?'

'You talking about the National Youth Choir?'

'We are. Why?'

'My sister applied for that once.'

'Oh, really?' Tanvi says, giving me a nudge.

'Yeah,' Emerson continues. 'Didn't get in.'

'See!' I say triumphantly. 'It'd be a waste of time even applying.'

'I dunno about that,' Emerson says. 'I heard my sister practising and it was like listening to a cat getting strangled.'

Tanvi giggles.

'Mr Saxby, face the front of the classroom please!' Ms Cameron barks.

Emerson rolls his eyes and turns back round.

'You should at least try,' Tanvi whispers.

'I won't get in,' I whisper back.

'Mr Milford thinks you might.'

'He's probably just saying that.'

'And why would he do that?'

'I don't know. Maybe so I'll go back to choir on Friday?'

'No offence, but I don't think he needs to make up the numbers that badly. He clearly thinks you've got a shot.'

'At least read the leaflet,' she adds, pushing it towards me.

'There's no point,' I say, pushing it back.

'Oh my God, you're stubborn.'

'Or realistic.'

'No, *definitely* stubborn.'

The bell for first period rings. I stand up, heaving my backpack onto my shoulders.

'Hey, you forgot this,' Tanvi says, waving the leaflet in her hand.

'I know,' I say over my shoulder, before heading out of the classroom.

I forget about the leaflet until later that day. I'm at home, emptying my backpack, when it falls from between the pages of my Spanish folder and flutters to the ground.

Tanvi must have put it into my bag during afternoon registration, the sneaky thing.

I let out an exasperated sigh, screw it up into a ball and throw it at the wastepaper bin, only my aim is off and it bounces off the rim. Sighing again, I peel myself off the bed and retrieve it from under my desk. It's unfurled a little, a cluster of slightly wrinkled choir members beaming right back at me.

I intend to throw it straight in the bin but end up veering off course and heading back to the bed. Feeling self-conscious,

I sit down and smooth out the creases. I look over my shoulder and immediately feel ridiculous. I blame Tanvi Shah. Thanks to her track record, the idea of her bursting out of the wardrobe or wriggling out from under the bed, crowing 'I knew you'd read it!' doesn't exactly seem far-fetched right now.

I curl up on the bed, my back to the rest of the room, and begin to read.

I stare at the glossy photographs and try and fail to imagine myself slotting in at the back. Although the choir's members come in lots of different shapes and sizes, they all share a certain neatness – from their perfectly ironed shirts to their immaculate hairstyles – that I just know is out of my reach. I'm just not like the Melanies of this world – pristine and perfect and spotlessly turned out at all times. No matter how hard I try, something – a loose thread, a scuffed shoe, an oily forehead – always seems to let me down, as if the universe can't bear to pass up the opportunity to remind me where I come from.

For a second, I imagine filling in the online application form and attending the audition, but the pictures fail to form in my head properly. The choir simply isn't for people like me. It's for kids who have the sort of mums and dads who take them to ballet and piano lessons, and check their homework, and ask them questions about their day.

Kids like Izzy.

Not to mention the fact the rehearsals are residential. The last time I was away, it took Bonnie just five days to almost entirely block the route from the kitchen to the living room. I dread to think what kind of state she might get into without me around for longer.

No, the choir is definitely not for me.

And yet, here I am, reaching for my laptop and typing 'The National Youth Choir of Great Britain' into the YouTube search bar. I don't know why. I mean, what exactly am I hoping to achieve here? In fact, I should probably just stop now, put my laptop away and stop being so stupid.

Only then the choir on the screen starts to sing.

And all I can do is stop and stare.

Because they're amazing.

More than amazing.

Mind-blowing.

I turn up the volume, my eyes and ears glued to the screen.

The choir, dressed in their signature navy blue waistcoats, is assembled on the stage of what looks like a huge concert hall. The harmonies they're singing are precise and difficult, yet playful and almost unexpected, the resulting sound almost painfully beautiful.

When they finish, the audience breaks into thunderous applause, and as the camera zooms in on the glowing faces of the choir, I feel an ache deep in my belly – a brand-new kind I'm not sure I've experienced before.

I watch the next video. And the next. And the next.

You can't do this, I keep telling myself. You can't leave her on her own, you know you can't.

At the same time, I can't stop watching.

The ache doesn't go away.

If anything, it gets stronger.

17

Three nights later, the itching begins.

I scratch and scratch but the itching is only getting worse. Unable to sleep, I turn on my lamp, the pale yellow glow revealing raised red spots on both wrists. There must be a mosquito in here. I listen for its buzz, but I can't hear anything over the sound of the falling rain outside. It's the satisfying sort of rain I like – big fat heavy drops that splatter rhythmically against the window pane and make me feel safe and cosy in a way few other things can. Only tonight, I'm too uncomfortable to enjoy it.

I grope for my phone, on charge by the side of the bed, and check the time: 2.28 a.m. Frowning, I turn off the light and lie flat on my back, arms outside the duvet, and desperately try to resist the temptation to scratch my insanely itchy wrists. Over the next few hours, I experiment with every possible sleeping position, but no matter which one I go for, my wrists feel like they're on fire. I finally drop off around dawn, sleeping for what seems like about two seconds before my alarm goes off and it's time to get up.

In the bright light of day, the spots look even angrier and redder than they did in the night. Even though they're still itching like crazy, at least I can hide them under the cuffs of my school shirt.

By the time I reach school though, the itching has spread to my neck. I duck into the toilets before registration to assess the damage. The back of my neck is covered with raised red bumps identical to the ones on my wrists. Reluctantly, I release my hair from its usual sensible plait and arrange it down my back.

I should have known my change in hairstyle wouldn't escape Tanvi's attention.

'Your hair!' she gasps as I sit down. 'It looks so pretty! Emerson, Abi, doesn't Ro's hair look pretty?'

Emerson and Abi turn round.

'Sure,' Abi says, shrugging.

'Er, yeah, really nice,' Emerson says, barely looking at me.

Who is Tanvi kidding? Since leaving the toilets and sprinting across the courtyard in the drizzle, my hair has practically doubled in size, wiry hairs sticking out in all directions like I've been freshly electrocuted.

'It's just so thick and wavy,' Tanvi continues to gush. 'Mine is *so* wispy. When my hair grew back last year, I ended up with all this weird baby hair. See!' – she points to her hairline – '*Super* annoying.'

I hadn't considered the fact that Tanvi probably lost her

hair during her cancer treatment. I picture her sitting in a stark white hospital bed with a bald head covered with downy tufts of hair, big startled eyes dominating her delicate face even more than they already do.

'What made you wear it down today?' Tanvi asks.

My stomach turns over. 'No special reason,' I say, sitting on both hands to stop them from reaching to scratch my flaming neck. 'Just fancied a change.'

By third period, PE, it's still raining.

The rain makes me think of Noah and our afternoon cooped up in my shed. This weekend, it'll be three whole weeks since our game of chess. It feels like longer. We've been texting loads still, but it's still not the same as speaking in person.

'Dodgeball in the sports hall,' Ms Bello announces to widespread groans.

I join in. Dodgeball is the *worst*.

I change quickly, my back to the rest of the changing room, pulling my bottle green hoodie on over the top of my white Aertex top so no one will see my wrists.

'Aren't you going to be boiling?' Tanvi asks.

The windowless sports hall is well known for being the stuffiest, sweatiest, smelliest room in the entire school.

'I'm quite cold actually,' I say, feigning a shiver.

Tanvi's face sags with concern. 'Maybe you're coming down with something.'

'Yeah, maybe,' I echo.

'Come on, ladies!' Ms Bello says, clapping her hands

together. 'I haven't got all day. Jewellery off, hair up please. Tanvi, what exactly are you doing?'

Tanvi has so far removed only her blazer, jumper and one shoe.

'Folding my clothes, miss.'

'Admirable, Tanvi, you clearly have a future in high-end retail. But for now, I need you to prioritize speed over aesthetics. In other words, can you get a move on please?'

'Sorry, miss,' Tanvi says, vaguely speeding up her movements.

Ms Bello turns to me. 'Hair up, please,' she says. 'You know the rules.'

'I don't have a bobble, miss.'

'I have a spare!' Tanvi says, peeling a hairband off her wrist and waving it round her head like she's won it in a raffle.

Of course you do.

'Thanks,' I say, smiling tightly and tying my hair into the loosest ponytail I can get away with.

Five minutes later, I'm standing with my back against the wall of the sports hall, waiting for the rest of my classmates, including Tanvi, to finish getting changed and join me. The painted brickwork feels nice and cool against my itchy legs.

Wait a second, since when were my legs itchy?

I peer down at the backs of my legs as discreetly as I can. The backs of both knees are red and blotchy, just like my wrists.

My heartbeat begins to quicken. This is the work of no mosquito.

Tanvi bounds into the sports hall, her laces undone, her too-large PE skirt sitting low on her hips. 'You OK?' she asks, coming to an abrupt stop in front of me. 'You look worried.'

'I'm fine,' I say, not quite meeting her eye.

Ms Bello strides into the centre of the room, the whistle she wears on a rainbow-coloured cord round her neck dangling from her lips. She blows it once and motions for everyone to gather around.

Tanvi can't help herself, skipping to the front. I peel myself away from the wall but remain at the back of the group. Ms Bello is midway through a lecture on 'aggressive throwing' when I hear whispering behind me. I glance over my shoulder. Sienna Blake, Cassie Harris and Paige Wilkinson are looking at the back of my legs. A thick bead of sweat makes its way down my back, pooling at the waistband of my skirt.

'What's wrong with your legs?' Sienna asks. 'You got leprosy or something?'

'It'd better not be contagious,' Paige chimes in with a theatrical shudder.

'Guys,' Cassie says. 'Don't be such bitches.'

Ms Bello blows her whistle, making me jump. 'Do we have a problem here, girls?' she asks. 'Because I could really do without the chat right now.'

'Yes,' I blurt. 'I'm not feeling very well.'

Ms Bello rolls her eyes. 'Another one bites the dust, eh? Fine. Go take a seat on the bench. I'll with be with you in a minute.'

Ignoring Sienna and Paige's continued whispers, I make my way round the edge of the sports hall and slide onto the wooden PE bench by the fire exit door along with the usual skivers – Lena Lomas who is *always* on her period and hasn't been sighted in PE kit since Year Seven, and Becca DeSilva, who is currently snivelling into a grotty length of toilet roll.

Across the sports hall, Tanvi, still waiting to be chosen for a team, jumps up and down, waving to attract my attention.

'You OK?' she mouths.

I mime another shiver and feel like the hammiest actress that ever lived. Tanvi pouts in sympathy. A few seconds later, Georgia Purnell picks her for her team.

'OK, so what's the deal here?' Ms Bello asks once the game is underway. 'You seemed fine back in the changing room.'

I stand up, my back to Lena and Becca, and peel back my right sleeve.

'It's on the backs of my legs and my neck too,' I say in a low voice.

'I think maybe you need to take a trip to see the nurse,' Ms Bello says, taking a small but unmistakeable step backwards. 'Go grab your stuff and head straight there.'

'Now?' I ask.

'Now.'

Lunch time is over and afternoon lessons have started by the time Bonnie arrives to pick me up.

'Where have you parked?' I ask as we walk through the

quiet corridors towards the exit. The rain has stopped but the sky is still grey and ominous.

'A couple of streets away,' Bonnie says. 'The car park was chock-a-block.'

Thank you, universe.

Bonnie is wearing an uncharacteristically modest outfit – jeans, boots, a tight black polo neck and a belted trench coat. The only real giveaway is the bulging handbag hanging over her left arm, the clasp and stitching visibly straining under the weight of its contents.

'I thought you were about to drop dead from the way that school nurse of yours summoned me to come get you,' she says, laughing.

My eyes bulge. Trust Bonnie to find this funny.

Away from its usual spot on the driveway, parked alongside all the nice, normal cars with their empty seats and clear views out of their back windscreens, Bonnie's car looks even worse than usual.

'Where am I supposed to sit?' I ask, annoyance bubbling in my belly.

The car is stuffed, newspapers and empty fast food cartons and plastic bottles and random bits of stage costumes, feathers and fans and odd shoes piled so high I can barely see in.

'Oh,' Bonnie says, as if registering the mess for the very first time. 'Hang on a second.'

She opens the passenger door. Stuff comes pouring out onto the pavement. Bonnie tuts cheerfully, humming as she battles to stuff it back in. A man walking his dog passes by, his eyes widening at the sight. He catches my eye and frowns.

This isn't my fault, I want to yell after him. *She's the one who wants to live like this, not me!*

It's pointless though. As long as I live with Bonnie, we'll continue to be lumped together as joint offenders.

'OK, give this a try,' Bonnie says, straightening up.

She's moved just about enough stuff about so I can sit in the passenger seat, albeit elevated on top of a stack of ancient magazines, the top of my head brushing the roof, and my knees drawn up under my chin. I feel like a circus clown. I yank the seat belt across my body but the buckle is completely buried. In the end I have to settle for holding it in place so it at least looks like it's done up.

'There!' Bonnie says, starting the engine. 'Sorted.'

She actually has the nerve to look triumphant.

18

'Look,' Bonnie hisses as we sit on plastic chairs in the doctor's waiting room. She's peering over the top of an out-of-date copy of *House Beautiful*.

House bloody *Beautiful*. I'm tempted to rip it from her hands and hurl it across the room.

'What?' I ask.

'Over there,' Bonnie says, pointing at the staff list on the wall. 'Dr Ali is a locum.'

'So? Locums are still doctors.'

'Hmmmmmm,' Bonnie says, folding her arms across her chest.

'I'm sure Dr Ali will be fine.'

Bonnie flips the page. 'We'll see.'

Dr Ali turns out to be a young woman with a shiny black bob and a kind smile. I like her straightaway.

'So, what seems to be the problem?' she asks as we sit down.

I show Dr Ali my wrists. Within about three seconds she makes a diagnosis.

'Scabies,' she says.

'Scabies?' I repeat. I've never heard of it.

'It's a contagious skin disease,' Dr Ali explains. 'Caused by tiny mites that burrow under the skin. They're called *Sarcoptes scabiei.* They feed using their mouths and front legs to penetrate the epidermis to lay their eggs.'

'How can you tell?' Bonnie asks.

Dr Ali rubs some ink on my left wrist, then wipes it off. 'See that?' she says, her finger tracing the line of ink that remains. 'That's a mite tunnel or a burrow. A sure sign of scabies basically.'

A shiver ripples down my spine.

'Not to worry though,' Dr Ali continues. 'Scabies may be unpleasant but it's very easily treated. A special cream called permethrin usually does the trick.' She turns round in her swivel chair and begins to tap away at her computer keyboard.

'How did I get it?' I ask.

'It's hard to pinpoint for sure,' Dr Ali says, continuing to type. 'But most commonly it's passed from human to human, via some sort of skin-to-skin contact, usually a family member or romantic partner. The contact has to be prolonged, though – we're talking fifteen to twenty minutes skin-to-skin.'

I glance at Bonnie, who is rifling determinedly through her handbag. As usual, it's overflowing with pointless things – broken pens, a long defunct phone charger, endless used tissues, a Chapstick with the lid missing, an empty Smints box, a crumpled Happy Easter card with a grinning bunny rabbit on the front.

'Have you been itchy?' I ask.

Bonnie's head snaps up. 'Sorry, were you talking to me?'

'I was just wondering who I could have got this from.'

'Does it matter?' Bonnie says. 'You heard what the doctor said; the cream will sort it out.'

I try to think of the last time I had any sort of prolonged skin-to-skin contact with anyone. Even with Bonnie.

Then I remember.

That night in front of *The Sound of Music.*

But that was over a month ago.

'The incubation period can last up to eight weeks,' Dr Ali continues as if reading my mind. 'So, it's possible you were infected quite some time ago.'

Bingo.

'Show me your wrists,' I say, turning to Bonnie.

'What?'

'Roll up your sleeves and show me your wrists.'

'What for?'

'I just want to see.'

'Don't be daft,' Bonnie says, panic flickering in her eyes. 'Look, we're wasting the nice doctor's time.'

'Not at all,' Dr Ali says. 'Perhaps it *is* worth me having a look. I was actually about to say, we recommend that anyone the infected person may have come into close contact with has the treatment too, even if they're not displaying any symptoms, just as a precaution.' She wheels her chair over to Bonnie. 'If you wouldn't mind letting me take a look, Mrs Snow,' she says, gesturing at Bonnie's wrists. 'Just to confirm either way.'

Bonnie opens her mouth, then closes it again before reluctantly shrugging out of her coat and rolling up the left sleeve of her jumper.

The spots on Bonnie's wrists are fainter than mine but they're undoubtedly the same thing.

'Mystery solved,' Dr Ali says. 'How long have you had these, Mrs Snow?'

'Oh God, I don't know,' Bonnie says irritably, yanking her sleeve back down. 'Not long. I've barely noticed them.'

As if, I think.

As. If.

'What?' Bonnie says, clocking the fury on my face. 'I just assumed it was eczema!'

'There doesn't appear to be anything about eczema in your notes,' Dr Ali says, squinting at her computer screen.

'Well, there should be,' Bonnie says indignantly.

More lies. Miraculously, Bonnie's health has always been oddly robust.

'Without treatment, the mites can survive on the body for up to two months,' Dr Ali explains.

'But how did Bonnie – I mean, my mum – get them in the first place?' I ask.

I can't leave it here. I *need* to get to the bottom of this.

'It's hard to say for sure,' Dr Ali says.

'Like, could a dirty house be to blame?' I ask, my face reddening to match my wrists.

That gets Bonnie's attention. I can feel her eyes on me, sharp and alert, like a rabbit emerging from its burrow.

'A dirty house?' Dr Ali repeats, her brow furrowing a little.

'I mean, just for example,' I add quickly.

'Well, it's entirely possible,' Dr Ali says slowly, her eyes flicking from me to Bonnie. 'It's certainly a lot easier for mites to breed in a less hygienic environment.'

There's a pause.

'Is there any particular reason you ask, Rosie?' she asks gently. Her brown eyes are feather-soft, gentle and full of concern. With a glimmer of something else. Suspicion.

I catch it just in time.

'No, nothing like that, just a bit curious,' I say quickly, desperate to throw her off the scent.

It doesn't work. Dr Ali's frown is deepening.

'So, what happens now?' I continue stammering a little. 'You were talking about a cream?'

'I'll give you a prescription,' Dr Ali says, the frown not leaving her face. 'You should also wash all your bed linen, nightwear and towels on at least fifty degrees. If you're unable to wash certain items, place them in a plastic bag for at least seventy-two hours. That ought to kill off the scabies mites. I would advise giving your entire house a good vacuum too. Just in case.'

But how do you vacuum floors you can't even see? My eyes brim with tears of frustration.

'Are you all right, Rosie?' Dr Ali asks.

I blink the tears back. I need to pull myself together. And fast. The last thing I need is Dr Ali making a well-meaning report to Social Services because I got emotional and slipped up.

'It's just a bit, um, overwhelming,' I improvise. 'All the instructions . . .'

'Would you like me to write them down?' Dr Ali asks gently, glancing at Bonnie who has stopped paying attention and is fiddling with her phone.

'No, no, it's fine. Vacuum, wash everything on fifty, put everything else in a plastic bag for seventy-two hours.'

'Perfect,' Dr Ali says.

'Er, what about school?' I ask. Dr Ali's form is now blurry through the watery film covering my eyes. *Don't cry, don't cry, don't cry.*

'Are sure you're OK, Rosie?' she asks, her head tilting to one side.

Bonnie's fingernails stop tapping at her phone.

'I'm fine,' I say. 'Just a bit upset about the scabies, you know . . .'

Dr Ali smiles sympathetically. 'Not to worry. I know it's not nice, but we've got you covered, and providing you start the treatment tonight, you'll be all good to go back to school on Monday. I have to warn you though; the itching may last for up to two weeks.'

She prints off two prescriptions and hands them to Bonnie.

'Is that it?' Bonnie asks, stuffing them in her coat pocket.

'That's everything,' Dr Ali says. 'Unless there's anything else you'd like to talk about?' She's looking at me as she says this.

'No, thank you,' Bonnie replies, stalking out the room. 'Come on, Ro.'

I stand up.

'Rosie?' Dr Ali asks softly. 'What about you? Is there anything else we haven't covered?'

I swallow.

'Anything at all?' she adds.

For a moment, I imagine telling Dr Ali absolutely everything – letting all the hurt and frustration and anger pour out of me along with the tears I'm currently fighting to keep from falling. As I stand there, my mouth full of cotton wool, I feel a bit like I'm teetering on the top of a tall building, the wind in my hair, as I look down at the roaring traffic below.

To jump or not to jump.

'Rosie?' Dr Ali prompts.

Her interruption snaps me back to reality. What on earth was I *thinking*?

'No, that's everything, thank you,' I say. I pick up my backpack and walk slowly after Bonnie.

I don't say anything until we're in the car.

'How long?' I demand.

Bonnie doesn't answer, turning on the engine and flicking on the radio, flooding the car with 'Waterloo' by ABBA. I turn it off again.

'How long, Bonnie?' I repeat.

'How long what?' Bonnie asks, lighting a cigarette, filling the car with smoke.

'How long have you had it?' I ask, wafting the air.

'Not long.'

'*How* long?'

'I don't know.'

'Bonnie!'

'You heard what the doctor said – it's easy enough to get rid of.'

'But I shouldn't have got it in the first place!'

'Stop getting at me! I'm not a child.'

'And I'm not an adult! I shouldn't have to be dealing with this . . . rubbish.'

Because that's what most of my life is. In every sense of the word.

'People saw, Bonnie,' I say, my voice trembling.

'What people? When?'

'Girls in my PE lesson.' My skin prickles with shame as I picture the disgust on Sienna and Paige's faces, and the pity on Cassie's. I can't decide which felt worse.

Bonnie sighs and shakes her head. 'You know what your problem is, Ro?' she says. 'You worry about what people think far too much.'

'Well, one of us has to give a toss about something other than themselves!' I snap.

'I didn't know it was contagious! You're acting like I gave it to you on purpose!'

'That's not the point and you know it.'

Bonnie lets out an impatient sigh. 'I'm sorry, Ro. OK?'

But sorry isn't good enough. Not when I know Bonnie has no intention of backing up her apology with a change in behaviour. Coming out of Bonnie's mouth, 'sorry' is a nothing word – flimsy and meaningless. She may as well be saying 'teapot' or 'dragonfly' or 'vanilla custard'.

Bonnie starts the engine and reverses out of the space, almost clipping the car parked next to us. It's started to rain again, the miserable grey sky suiting my mood perfectly. I rest my head against the window and watch the raindrops roll down the glass, tracing their watery tracks as I try my hardest not to cry.

By the time I've changed my bedding, been to the launderette and cleaned as much of the house as logistically possible, it's way past my usual bedtime. Noah messages to ask how my day's been, but I'm too ashamed to even reply.

I put my phone away and perch on the edge of the overflowing bathtub and read the permethrin instruction leaflet. As directed, I remove all of my clothes and smother every centimetre of my body with the thick sticky cream, my body trembling with cold and resentment.

This is all Bonnie's fault, and she didn't even have the decency to help me clean up the place. After I refused her apology, she spent the rest of the car journey in a sulk and the moment we got home from the pharmacy she retreated to the living room, shutting the door and turning on both the TV and radio at full blast like a moody teenager.

I hate you, I think as I apply the cream between my toes.

'I hate you,' I say out loud as I rub it under my armpits and in the creases of my elbows.

I begin to cry – my scalding hot tears making my entire body shake.

‘I hate you,’ I sob as I use a cotton bud to apply the cream under my finger and toenails.

My sobs become louder, wetter, angrier. It feels good to let some of the fury and frustration and pain out. It isn’t enough though. I need more. More of a release.

‘I hate you,’ I yell as I pull on my pyjamas, the cotton clinging to my slightly sticky body. I hold my breath, before realizing there’s no way my voice can be heard over the blizzard of noise coming from the living room below.

‘I hate you!’ I yell again, louder this time. ‘I hate you! I hate you! *I hate you!*’

By the time I collapse into bed, I’m weak with exhaustion. The anger is still raw, but I feel a little calmer, my breathing slow and even.

I’m about to turn out my light when I catch sight of the creased National Youth Choir of Great Britain leaflet on my desk. I’ve been meaning to get rid of it all week, but for some reason I haven’t got round to it. I slip out of bed and retrieve it, climbing back under the duvet and staring at the otherworldly faces of the smiling singers.

What would Bonnie do in this situation? I don’t have to ponder. I *know* what she’d do. Because in Bonnie’s world, Bonnie always puts herself first. My entire life revolves around protecting her and this stupid house. Why shouldn’t I do something for myself for once?

I check the time: 11.52. I pull out my laptop from under my bed, open it up, and before I can talk myself out of it, type the choir’s website address into the search bar.

19

The week starts quietly, mainly because Tanvi is on a geography field trip on Monday and Tuesday.

'Did you miss me?' she asks when we're reunited in registration on Wednesday morning.

'Terribly,' I deadpan.

'Knew you would,' she replies, grinning.

'What happened to you on Friday by the way?' she asks.

'Friday?'

'Yeah. In PE.'

'Oh, period pain,' I say quickly. 'Came on really suddenly.'

'Oh, poor you.'

Even though the spots have faded a bit, my skin continues to itch like mad.

I brace myself for Tanvi to comment on not seeing me on Saturday (unable to cope with an ambush, I'd missed out Hopewood Gardens on my round) and feel relieved when she doesn't mention it, bombarding me with gossip from the field trip instead.

*

It's Friday morning and I'm drying my hair before school when there's a knock at my bedroom door. I switch off my hairdryer and set it down on the bed.

'Come in,' I say.

The door eases open and Bonnie steps inside. In her leopard-print silk dressing gown and pink fluffy slippers, she looks totally out of place in my sparse white room.

I haven't seen her much all week. I've been avoiding her, carefully timing my visits to the kitchen and bathroom, and I get the feeling she's been doing the same, hiding out in the living room with the door firmly shut.

Her eyes roam around the room, taking in the empty surfaces, the bare walls, the light streaming in through the unobscured windows.

'What's up, Bonnie?' I ask, my voice flat.

'Oh. This came for you,' Bonnie says, looking uncharacteristically awkward. 'It looked important so I thought I'd better bring it up.'

She hands over a white envelope. I take it from her and place it face down on the duvet next to me. As Bonnie continues to hover, it dawns on me that this might be her idea of a peace offering.

Too little, far too late.

I pick up the hairdryer and continue drying my hair. The roar in my ears triggers a memory. On cold nights when I was little, Bonnie used to peel back my duvet and blast the sheets with a hairdryer to warm them up. The rattling wheeze of the hairdryer – an ancient old thing with a frayed cord – used to scare me, so Bonnie came up with a special dance for us to do as a distraction – the 'hairdryer boogie'.

I glance up at Bonnie and just like that the memory dissolves. The woman in front of me may look like the woman who used to make me giggle until my stomach hurt, but right now I refuse to connect the two.

Bonnie seems to get the message, taking one last look around before backing out of the room, gently closing the door behind her.

I wait until she's returned downstairs before turning over the envelope, blinking in surprise at the sight of the National Youth Choir of Great Britain logo stamped next to the postmark.

My heartbeat quickening, I open the envelope and skim-read the letter inside.

I have an audition a week on Saturday.

After PE, I head to choir with Tanvi with no arguments. When Mr Milford asks for a volunteer to sing solo on the new song we're working on, she mimes zipping her lips before sitting on her hands.

After the rehearsal is over, I tell her to go ahead without me. I expect her to press me on it but she doesn't, agreeing to see me in registration.

I hover at the back of the classroom while the classroom empties.

'Good to have you back, Ro,' Mr Milford says, catching sight of me. 'I was worried I'd scared you off when I didn't see you last week.'

'Oh, I was ill,' I say, instinctively pulling the sleeves of my jumper down over my fingers.

'I'm sorry to hear that. All better now?'

'Yeah, I think so.'

'So, what can I do for you?'

I hand him the audition notification letter. As he reads it, a broad smile spreads across on his face.

'You applied,' he says.

'Yeah . . .'

'I'm so pleased.'

'I'm not sure I'm going to go,' I blurt.

Mr Milford frowns. 'Why's that?'

'I just don't think it's for me.'

'Then why did you apply?'

Because I was angry.

Because I was upset.

Because I wanted to do something for myself for once.

Only now a week has passed and the anger I felt has been replaced with guilt and doubt and fear.

'I don't know,' I say.

'I wouldn't have encouraged you to apply if I didn't think you had a chance, you do know that, don't you?'

I shrug.

'What makes you think it's not for you?'

'Well, it's for posh kids, isn't it?'

'Am I posh?'

'I don't know,' I stammer.

Mr Milford laughs. 'Ro, I grew up on one of the toughest estates in Sunderland. Believe me when I say there was nothing remotely posh about my upbringing. Didn't stop me joining the choir, though.'

'You were a member?' I ask.

'Yep. For seven years. Had the time of my life.'

'Really?'

'Too right. It's where I met some of my very best mates.'

'But weren't all the *other* kids posh?'

'A few were. Loads weren't though. And none of that matters anyway. There's something about it being totally separate from home and school that puts everyone on level pegging. There's no hierarchy – you're all just in it together.'

I hadn't thought of it like that. If I were in the choir, there'd be no risk of anyone finding out about Bonnie the way there is at school. I could start all over again, be anyone I wanted to be. The thought gives me a jolt of excitement.

'But isn't it really expensive?' I ask.

'Not as much as you'd think. And there are bursaries for families struggling to cover all the costs. That's how I managed to do it. We can cross that bridge though, if and when we come to it. Our priority right now is the audition and picking you a killer audition song. Any ideas?'

'God, I don't know,' I say.

'We've only got a week so it's probably best to go for something you're already comfortable with. Anything spring to mind?'

I shake my head, my mind completely blank.

'It doesn't have to be complicated. At this stage, they just want to get an idea of pitch and tone and so on. What sort of music do you like?'

'All sorts,' I say.

Mr Milford nods encouragingly.

'Er, The Carpenters, Tori Amos, Kate Bush, Fleetwood Mac . . .' I say, listing the artists I grew up listening to via Bonnie – the soundtrack to my childhood.

'Nice! I approve! Do you have a favourite song?'

'I don't know . . . Um, I guess I quite like "Rainy Days and Mondays" by The Carpenters.'

For a while, Bonnie performed as a Karen Carpenter tribute act. She'd spend hours singing along to The Carpenters' most famous songs, trying to make her voice blend with Karen's. 'Rainy Days and Mondays' was the track I'd always listen out for. I'm not sure why that one stuck out so much, only that there was something about the mournful saxophone solo and the sadness in Karen's voice that made my heart twist and yearn for something I couldn't quite put my finger on.

Mr Milford sits down at the piano and begins to play the introduction from memory. 'Do you know the lyrics by heart?' he asks.

'I'm not sure.'

'Let's give it a go. I can prompt you if you get stuck. I'm a BIG Carpenters fan so I've got you covered.'

I'm surprised when I get the first lyric correct. And the next one, and the next, the words flowing without hesitation. They must have been tucked at the very back of my brain this entire time.

When I finish singing, I notice Mr Milford is frowning slightly.

'Did I do something wrong?' I ask, fiddling with my shirt cuffs.

'No, no. I mean, technically it's great. I just feel like you're not quite connecting to the lyrics yet.' He pauses to recite the first verse. 'Pretty powerful stuff, right?' he says.

'I suppose.'

'So how do these words make you feel?'

'I don't know,' I say, shifting from one foot to the other.

'You sure about that?' Mr Milford asks, cocking his head to one side.

I bite my lip. I understand the lyrics perfectly well. Maybe too well. Perhaps it was a mistake to pick this song. Perhaps it's *too* reminiscent of Bonnie, *too* close to home. I should have suggested something pretty and light and superficial. Something I can smile my way through.

'Look, I get what they're saying,' I say hurriedly. 'But I can't force feelings.'

'I'm not asking you to force anything, Ro. But here's the thing, the panel will be looking for good voices and musicianship, of course, but they're going to want to see that you can put across the meaning of a song too. It's all about connecting with your audience. No matter how powerful, the lyrics can only take you so far. It's up to the performer to communicate the emotional heart of the song.'

'Even as part of a choir?' I ask.

'Especially as part of a choir. That's part of their magic.'

I know he's right. I've watched enough YouTube videos of the National Youth Choir of Great Britain now to realize their success is about so much more than just hitting the right notes.

'How about we take it from the top,' Mr Milford suggests. 'And I want you to really think about the lyrics this time.'

'OK.'

'Forget I'm even here,' Mr Milford says as he plays the introduction. 'Turn your back on me if you need to, go stand in the corner, look out the window, close your eyes. Whatever works.'

I take this advice, angling my body in the opposite direction and shutting my eyes. As the introduction plays, the same bittersweet cocktail of emotions I used to experience when Bonnie sang along with The Carpenters begins to stir. Instead of trying to ignore them and squash them down, I let them swirl and build. And for maybe the first time ever, I *really* listen to the lyrics. I've always found them sad, but I've never thought to apply to them to my own life before. It startles me to discover just how apt some of the references are.

And how sad they make me feel.

I'm used to anger and irritation and annoyance and resentment, but it's rare I let sadness float to the surface. I had no idea I had so much of it inside me – I'm full up with it.

Then Mr Milford is applauding. And I'm blinking hard. I've finished the end of the song without even realizing it. I lift my fingers to my cheeks. They're wet. Quickly, I wipe them dry with the sleeve of my jumper before turning back to face Mr Milford.

'Now that's what I'm talking about!' he says, his eyes shining.

And I can't help it – my lips curl up into a massive grin.

'Oh my God, Ro, you sounded amazing just then!' Tanvi squeaks, scrambling to her feet as I close the door to Mr Milford's classroom behind me.

'What are you still doing here?' I ask.

'Duh! Waiting for you,' Tanvi says happily.

'But I told you to go ahead without me.'

'I know. What was that song you were singing just then?'

'Nothing special. Just something Mr Milford's helping me with.'

'What for? Ooh, is it to do with that fancy choir?'

My hesitation gives me away.

'It is, isn't it?' Tanvi cries, skipping sideways along the corridor. 'So you *did* apply! That's so great! When's the audition?'

'Next weekend,' I admit.

'Is that the song you're singing for it?'

'I don't know. Maybe.'

'Oh my God, you're *so* going to get in!' Tanvi says, gripping onto my arm with that watertight grip of hers. 'I can feel it in my skinny little bones!'

'I'm really not,' I say.

'We'll see, Ro Snow,' Tanvi calls over her shoulder as she pirouettes down the corridor. 'We shall see.'

20

As usual, Melanie looks momentarily surprised to discover me on the doorstep after school.

'Has it really been a month since your last visit?' she asks, wiping her hands on her frilly pink apron and stepping aside to let me in.

'So it would seem,' I say, squeezing past her into the immaculate hallway, automatically taking off my shoes.

'Izzy! Ro's here!' Melanie trills up the stairs.

No answer.

Dad and Melanie love to keep up the charade that Izzy 'worships' me when the truth is that Izzy appeared entirely indifferent to my visits right from the beginning, regarding me with weary eyes even as a four-year-old.

'I'll just go dump my things and make a start on my homework,' I say.

'Good idea,' Melanie replies, absent-mindedly patting me on the shoulder before drifting back into the kitchen.

I trudge up the stairs, past the numerous photographs of Dad, Melanie and Izzy. They go to a professional photographer every summer, posing against a white background wearing coordinating primary colours, hugging and giggling and looking every inch the textbook happy family.

On my way to the spare room, I glance in on Izzy. Her room is headache-inducing pink. The star attraction is her bed, with its heart-shaped headboard and ruffled canopy, dozens of tiny fairy lights sewn into the gauzy material. Izzy is currently lying on it, her head propped up on a pile of fluffy cushions as she taps away on her iPad. If she senses my presence, she doesn't feel the need to register it.

Dinner is beef tacos. As we eat, Dad grills Izzy about her day at school in forensic detail, expressing delight and fascination at every single mundane revelation.

'How about you, Ro?' he asks once he's accounted for what feels like every second of Izzy's day. 'Good few weeks?'

'Not really,' I say.

Ordinarily, I give Dad the bland answers he wants but today I'm not in the mood to play along.

'Why's that, Rosebud?' he says, reaching for a handful of cheese to sprinkle on top of his fourth taco.

'Oh, where shall I start?' I say. 'The scabies? The fact I just had to extend our overdraft *again*? The twenty-four bottles of soy sauce under the kitchen table?'

He and Melanie exchange panicked looks. Izzy sits up straight, for once actually interested in something I have to say.

'What are scabies?' she asks.

'Mites that bury under your skin,' I reply.

'Ew!' she squeals.

'Rosie, that's enough,' Dad says.

'Oh, don't worry, they're only contagious if we hug for like twenty minutes or something and I'm pretty sure there's no chance of that.'

'Rosie! I said that's enough. We're eating here.'

'Don't ask me questions if you don't want to hear the answers.'

'We can talk about it later,' Dad says. 'You and me.'

Yeah, right. He has a new life now – clean and ordered and photogenic – and he'd rather chuck himself in a moving river than willingly confront the mess he left behind.

'More guacamole, anyone?' Melanie says, her voice artificially bright.

'Yes please, darling,' Dad booms back. He spoons a dollop on the side of his plate before turning back to Izzy. 'Now, sweet pea,' he says. 'Tell me more about your maths test. How many people did you beat again?'

'The whole class,' Izzy says as I crumble a shard of taco shell between my fingers. 'So, twenty-seven.'

'My clever daughter!' Dad says, beaming.

He's always referred to Izzy as his daughter – he did right from the beginning, trading in his frizzy-haired real-life daughter for an adorable blonde version. I like to tell myself it doesn't hurt, and I'm so used to it now, most of the time it doesn't. But then there are moments that catch me off guard, like this one, and it takes my breath away.

21

The following morning, Dad drops me off in Ostborough before driving Izzy to her weekly tap-dancing lesson. I keep waiting for him to bring up last night's conversation but, as I kind of predicted, he doesn't, keeping up a steady stream of chatter with Izzy the entire journey.

I'm later than usual, and by the time I make it upstairs, Jodie and Moses are preparing to leave.

'Nice outfit,' I tell Jodie with a grin.

She's wearing a plastic Alton Towers poncho over the top of her Aztec-print leggings and purple hi-tops.

'Sexy, huh?' she says, striking a pose. 'I made you a cuppa by the way. *And* I saved you the last Jammie Dodger.' She presses her hands into prayer position and flutters her eyelashes. 'I know, I'm a saint.'

It's not until half an hour later, when the heavens open and tip their contents on my head, that I twig why Jodie was wearing the poncho. I drag my trolley under the nearest tree and zip up my hoodie, pulling the drawstring tight so just my eyes and nose poke over the top. It does little to protect me from the driving rain though, the thick jersey material quickly growing heavy with moisture.

Within minutes, I'm soaked to the skin. This must be how Noah felt that time I found him shivering outside his front door. Only then it was August and now it's October and the rain is icy cold, stinging my cheeks and hands.

It's no good just standing here though. These leaflets aren't going to deliver themselves, and from the look of the determinedly gloomy sky, the rain seems unlikely to let up anytime soon. With grim resignation, I reach for my trolley and continue on my round.

It's raining just as hard when I enter a deserted Hopewood Gardens almost an hour later. I'm drenched, water sloshing in my didn't-stand-a-chance Converse. I'm trudging up Tanvi's driveway, my head down, when I hear knocking. I look up to see Tanvi's face pressed up against the living-room window, palms splayed, her breath steaming up the glass.

It's such a predictable sight I almost burst out laughing.

'Wait there!' she yells, reappearing a few seconds later at the door.

'Oh my God, look at you!' she cries in dismay.

'I'm fine,' I say, handing Tanvi a wodge of soggy leaflets.

'Oh no you're not,' Tanvi says. She sounds like an audience member at a pantomime.

'I honestly am,' I say.

'Oh no, you're not,' Tanvi repeats, touching my sopping

sleeve. 'You're wet through. Quick, come in.' She leans past me and drags my trolley into the hallway.

'But I'm not finished,' I say.

'Don't be crazy! If you keep going like that you're going to get pneumonia or something.'

She grabs me by the arm and pulls me into the hallway, slamming the front door shut behind us. Her house is warm and smells of coffee and toast and washing powder. 'Mum!' Tanvi yells. 'Can I use the tumble dryer?'

'Yes,' a voice calls back.

'Take your shoes off and follow me,' Tanvi instructs.

'Tanvi, I mean it, I'm fine,' I say, reaching for my trolley.

'Bloody hell, you're stubborn!' Tanvi says, whisking it out of reach.

'It's just rain.'

'Oh, stop being such a martyr.'

She shoves me in front of the mirror hanging over the radiator. I look like a drowned rat – strands of hair plastered to my forehead like seaweed, raindrops clinging to the tip of my nose and my eyelashes, my hoodie so wet it's at least five shades darker than it was when I set out.

'OK, OK, I surrender,' I say, sinking down on the bottom step and unlacing my trainers with freezing fingers, before following Tanvi upstairs.

On the landing, Tanvi pauses in front of a door with a poster of Garfield the Cat tucking into a dish of lasagne, its corners peeling away.

'*Chez* Tanvi,' she says with a flourish, opening the door and directing me inside.

Tanvi's room is an assault on the senses. Every inch of the wall is covered in posters and postcards and drawings and clippings from magazines – like one gigantic collage. There are fairy lights everywhere – chilli-shaped ones threaded through the spokes of her brass bed, star-shaped ones framing her window, Chinese style lanterns looping from one corner of the ceiling to the other. Her unmade bed is covered with well-loved cuddly toys, almost all of them falling apart – their stuffing hanging out, limbs hanging on by a few threads – and every available surface is littered with knick-knacks – china ornaments and action figures and novelty candles and jars filled with beads and buttons. It isn't messy exactly (there's remarkably little dust considering the sheer number of things and there *appears* to be some sort of system in place) – it's just a lot to take in, like an eccentric and slightly chaotic museum. Even though it's a million miles away from the scene at Arcadia Avenue, I can't help but feel uneasy as I move into the centre of the room.

'My brother Devin reckons I'm a hoarder,' Tanvi says.

I stiffen at the word.

'But I prefer "collector",' Tanvi continues. 'Much nicer.' She reaches for a dressing gown from the mound hanging on the back of her door. 'This should just about fit you,' she says, flinging it to me. 'Get your kit off then,' she adds, before bursting into a filthy laugh. 'Joking!' she says, when I don't join in. 'Obviously. I'll be just outside.'

She slips onto the landing, leaving the door slightly ajar and humming Christmas songs.

I peel off my wet things, hesitating when it comes to my

underwear. My pants are soaked but I feel peculiar just handing them over to Tanvi to take care of. On the other hand, keeping them on feels a bit grim, not to mention very uncomfortable. In the end, I slip them off and stick them in the pouch of my hoodie.

I'm pulling on the dressing gown when my eyes fall on a selection of photographs framing Tanvi's dressing-table mirror. I glance at the door. I can't see Tanvi, but I can hear her, belting out an extended version of 'Rudolph the Red-nosed Reindeer'.

I pad over to the mirror. My eyes zone in on a picture of Tanvi sitting up in her hospital bed. She's wearing a red paper hat, the sort you get out of a Christmas cracker. Her face looks puffier than it does now, her skin ashen, but the smile is exactly the same – broad and infectious. My eyes drift to another picture – Tanvi with her arms around a girl with short light-brown hair and a silver nose stud. They're wearing matching T-shirts and laughing. I inspect the other photos. The same girl features in another, on her own this time, wearing a pink wig and doing the peace sign at the camera, and another back with Tanvi, the two of them sticking their tongues out at the camera. I move over to the bedside table. There she is again, with Tanvi on her lap, in a frame with 'Friends Forever' etched into the metal. I feel a twinge of something.

Jealousy?

No, that would make absolutely no sense. Like I care who Tanvi is friends with.

'You OK in there?' Tanvi calls, making me flinch.

'Yeah,' I call back, belting the dressing gown and stepping out onto the landing.

Tanvi holds out a plastic washing basket for me to tip my wet things into.

'Is the rest of your family here?' I ask, peering left and right.

Although the dressing gown is full length and made of thick fluffy towelling material, I can't help but feel incredibly self-conscious.

Tanvi shakes her head. 'Nope, just me and Mum. Dad's working today and Devin's playing five-a-side.'

Downstairs in the kitchen, Tanvi shoves my clothes into the tumble dryer.

'Can shoes just go in with everything else?' she asks a petite woman with big round eyes who I'm guessing must be her mum.

'Probably best to stick them in a pillowcase, just in case,' Tanvi's mum says.

'OK, thanks,' Tanvi says, bounding out of the room again.

Tanvi's mum turns to me, and smiles. 'You must be Ro,' she says.

'Yes. Hi. Sorry about this . . .' I motion at the tumble dryer.

'Don't be silly. And please, call me Seema. Now, how about a nice hot chocolate to warm you up while I get started on the pancakes?'

'I'm fine, honestly,' I say.

'Don't believe you,' she says with a wink, flicking on the

kettle and reaching for a jar of hot chocolate granules from the open cupboard.

'Please don't go to any trouble,' I say.

'No trouble at all. Sit yourself down.'

I do as I'm told.

Just like Tanvi's room, the kitchen is packed full of stuff – pans in every possible size, pots filled with spatulas and wooden spoons and whisks and tongs, blenders and mixers, a huge rice cooker and the biggest knife rack I've ever seen. Photos and postcards and kids' paintings and novelty magnets adorn the fridge. It's cluttered, but there's an order to the clutter, a system, that makes it a million miles away from the interior of 48 Arcadia Avenue. In fact, teamed with the sunny yellow walls, red-and-white checked curtains hanging at the steamed-up windows and the Motown music on the radio, it's just about the cosiest, most cheerful room I've ever set foot in.

As my gaze drifts around the room, Tanvi's mum bustles around me, chatting away about the rain.

Tanvi reappears waving a pillowcase over her head. She pops my trainers in it and tosses them in the tumble dryer.

'Keep an eye on it,' Tanvi's mum says. 'You don't want to shrink poor Ro's jeans.'

'Will do.' Tanvi turns to me, 'I'm running you a bath by the way.'

'What?' I say. 'You don't need to do that.'

'Too late,' she sings. 'Everyone knows a bath is the only proper way to really warm up.'

Tanvi's mum sets a steaming mug of hot chocolate down

in front of me, mini marshmallows bobbing on the surface.

'Wow, thank you,' I say, blowing on the hot liquid and making the marshmallows quiver.

'Bring it up,' Tanvi says. 'You can't beat drinking hot chocolate in the bath.'

The bathroom is full of steam.

'Whoops, I forgot to turn the extractor fan on,' Tanvi says, wafting her arms as she makes her way through the haze. 'Want a bath bomb?' she asks once the gloom has cleared a little.

'I'm fine without,' I say.

'Don't be mental! A bath isn't worth having if it's not fizzy and full of glitter.'

She presents me with a choice of three.

'Um, that one,' I say, choosing the blue one at random.

'Excellent choice,' Tanvi says, dropping it in the running water. 'Now watch the magic happen.'

I peer over the edge of the bathtub as the bath bomb whizzes and fizzes through the water like it's got a mind of its own, Tanvi waving her hands in the air as if conducting its every twist and turn.

'Cool, huh?' she says. 'Now for the final touch. And don't you even think about arguing with me.'

She produces a box of matches from the cupboard under the sink and lights the tea lights on the windowsill.

'*Voila!* Help yourself to anything you want. Oh, and take as long as you like. I'll be downstairs.'

I lock the door behind her and take a sip of my hot

chocolate before setting it down on the toilet lid. I roll up the right sleeve of the dressing gown and dunk my hand in the bath. The temperature is perfect – hot but not too hot. I double-check the lock before removing the dressing gown and stepping into the still fizzing bright blue water.

I feel strange at first, overly naked and far too aware of the fact I'm taking a bath in a stranger's house. Plus, although I'm no longer infectious, I'm painfully aware of the faded remains of my scabies rash. Slowly, though, I start to relax, gradually letting my body sink under the water until just my face is poking above the surface.

As I lie there, my hair – free from its plait – floating around my face like a mermaid's, I try to remember the last time I took a bath. There's a bathtub at Dad's house, but I've hardly ever used it. Melanie always makes a big fuss about whether there'll be enough hot water left for Izzy, so it's never an especially relaxing experience.

I sit up and take another sip of hot chocolate. Tanvi is right – it *is* a pretty good combination. My eyes fall on a tub of body scrub on the edge of the bath. I remove the lid and sniff. It smells delicious – of lime and coconuts and summer holidays I've never been on. I hesitate before taking a modest handful, slowly scrubbing my arms and legs and the bits of my back I can reach. Then I take another handful and do my feet. The sharp granules feel the good sort of tickly between my toes and on my tired heels. Once I'm finished, I pick up another tub. This one contains a clay face-mask. I read the instructions before dipping in my hand. The thick grey goo heats up on application and makes my face tingle. I like it.

As it hardens, I top up the hot water and add a little bath foam. Within seconds, the tub is filled with snowy white bubbles. I scoop them up and press them between my palms before sinking back under the water.

The Shahs' bathroom, with its old-fashioned peach bathroom suite and spider plant on the windowsill, isn't exactly glamorous, but lying at the bottom of the bathtub, my cold bones tingling back to life, it feels like a little slice of heaven.

The water is getting cold. I'm tempted to top it up again but I'm aware I've been in here a while now. Reluctantly, I wash the clay off my face and remove the plug. I can't quite bring myself to get out though, remaining cross-legged at the bottom of the tub until the very last of the suds has disappeared down the drain. It takes all the strength I have to heave my warm, floppy body over the side. I wrap myself in a mint-green bath sheet and dry myself carefully, paying special attention to all the things I usually miss because I'm in such a rush to get out of the chaotic bathroom at home – between my toes, the backs of my knees, behind my ears. I find a bottle of body lotion and smooth it on all over. My parched skin drinks it up. By the time I pull on the dressing gown, wrapping the towel around my head turban-style, I feel smoother and softer and cleaner than I have done in years.

Downstairs, Tanvi's mum is transferring pancakes from a frying pan onto warmed plates.

'Perfect timing!' Tanvi says. 'A Tanvi special coming right up!'

'I'd better not,' I say. I'm going to Pizza Express later for lunch. Dad, Melanie and Izzy's weekly tradition.

'I could just do you a little one?' Tanvi offers.

'I'm good, thanks.'

I sit down and watch as Tanvi slathers almost half a jar of Nutella onto a pancake, before adding discs of sliced bananas and a sprinkling of chopped nuts. She folds it up and begins sawing at it with her knife and fork.

'Try some!' she says.

She doesn't wait for my answer, shovelling a massive chunk into my mouth.

It tastes like heaven.

'Tanvi was telling me you were auditioning for some sort of big choir,' Tanvi's mum says, sitting down to join us with a pancake of her own.

'Er, yes,' I say, wiping Nutella from the corners of my mouth. 'Next week.'

'How exciting! What do you have to do at it?'

As I explain the format of the first audition – a sight-reading test followed by the performance of a song of my choice – Tanvi's mum seems genuinely interested, her eyes shiny and alert. Talking to her about it doesn't feel scary though, just sort of nice and safe.

My phone buzzes.

'Excuse me,' I say, taking it out of my pocket.

It's a text from Bonnie asking if I've seen her red sparkly shoes.

Check the car, I reply.

As I'm putting my phone away, I register the time. Almost midday. Once again, time has flown.

'I should go,' I say. 'I need to be at my dad's by one.' I

retrieve my almost dry clothes from the tumble dryer and go back up to Tanvi's room to change.

'Are you sure you can't stay a bit longer?' Tanvi asks as I sit on the bottom step and pull on my significantly less damp shoes. 'It's still raining.'

For a moment I let myself imagine what an afternoon at Tanvi's might look like – warm and cosy with an endless supply of snacks.

I can't though. As much as I want to, I know I can't.

'I need to get back for lunch,' I say regretfully. Dad will be a proper pain if I'm late.

'OK,' Tanvi says in a small voice.

'I don't know, another time maybe?' I suggest.

She breaks into a huge grin. 'That would be great!' she says.

She walks me to the door and insists I take an umbrella.

I accept, selecting a black and white polka dot one from the stand by the door.

'Well, thanks,' I say. 'For the food and the bath and clothes and stuff.'

'What else are friends for?' Tanvi asks.

Friends. She says it so easily. Like it isn't loaded with all manner of complications.

'Right,' I murmur, smiling tightly before heading down the driveway.

When I get back to Dad's his car is missing from the driveway.

'Hello?' I call, taking off my shoes in the hallway.

No answer.

I touch the closest radiator.

Stone-cold.

In the kitchen, there's a note on the counter – *Ro, Izzy was starving after tap so we went straight to the restaurant. Soup in the fridge if you're hungry. Dad x*

I burst into tears. I don't know why.

I don't even like Pizza Express that much.

22

'How are you feeling about your audition tomorrow?' Tanvi asks as we leave choir on Friday afternoon.

'I don't know,' I admit. 'I've never been to an audition before. I've been practising loads though.'

'What about your leaflets?'

'I'll do them before I go.'

'But won't that mean getting up at crazy early?'

I shrug. Before my last shift I asked Eric if I could pick up my leaflets a bit earlier than usual and he'd agreed.

'But you'll be knackered!' Tanvi exclaims.

'I'll be all right.'

Tanvi's eyes light up. 'Hey, why don't I do them for you?'

'Don't be silly.'

'Why not? I know the area. And, no offence or anything, but it's hardly rocket science. Oh, go on. You'll be doing me a favour too.'

'How so?'

'You never know, if I can prove myself capable of delivering leaflets in my own neighbourhood without coming to harm, my parents might do something really radical like let me get the bus to school. And I'll do a good job, I promise. Not one leaflet will perish on my watch!' She salutes. 'Please,' she says, her expression suddenly serious. 'You'd really be helping me out.'

I take a deep breath. 'OK,' I say. 'Thank you.'

Tanvi squeaks with delight. 'Awesome! I will *not* let you down, Ro Snow! Hey, why don't you come round for dinner afterwards? Or for lunch on Sunday? Or I could come to yours if that's easier.'

'No,' I say sharply.

'No?' she repeats.

I swallow hard. I need to cover my tracks. And fast.

'You can't. Come to mine, I mean. The thing is, my mum isn't very well.'

'Still? Wow, that's some cold.'

'Cold?'

'Yeah, when I came by the launderette that time you said she had a cold.'

'Oh! No. Um, the thing is, I sort of lied about that.'

'OK . . .' Tanvi says.

'The thing is, my mum is ill, but it's kind of more serious than a cold.'

'What's wrong with her?'

'It's, um, not that easy to explain.'

'That's OK,' Tanvi says encouragingly.

I can feel my body getting hot. I can only hope the heat doesn't reach my face and give me away.

'The thing is,' I begin, faltering a little, 'there's not really a name for it. She just has to rest a lot. And have total peace and quiet. That's, um, why I do the washing at the launderette. And why I can't really have people over . . .'

It's not a complete lie, but somehow it feels almost worse to tell Tanvi a half-truth rather than telling her an out-and-out fib.

'Shit, I'm so sorry,' she says. 'Do you want to talk about it? I'm an excellent listener.'

'No, no,' I say. 'It's fine. It's always been like this so I'm kind of used to it now. I just wanted you to know why I can't have people over.'

'Totally understood. I won't ask again.'

'Thanks, Tanvi.'

My gratitude is genuine at least.

It's still pretty dark when I drop off the leaflets at Tanvi's house the following morning. I'm heading back down the driveway having left my trolley tucked behind the wheelie bins when I hear someone hissing my name. I turn round. Tanvi is creeping towards me wearing dolphin-print pyjamas, her wispy hair sticking up in all directions.

'What are you doing up?' I ask. It's barely 7.30 a.m.

'I wanted to wish you good luck,' Tanvi says in a loud stage whisper. 'How're you feeling?'

'OK, I think.'

I know my song inside out and I've had three separate sight-reading tests with Mr Milford this week, all of which went well. My train tickets (purchased in advance with leftover birthday money) and a map detailing the route from the train station to the audition venue are nestled in the inside pocket of my bag along with a bottle of water, my sheet music and a hairbrush. Despite at least three careful inventories, I can't shift the feeling that I've forgotten something vital.

'That's not the only reason I'm up so early though,' Tanvi says. 'I also wanted to give you this.' She thrusts a small square package wrapped in glittery red paper into my hands.

I stare at it.

'Open it then,' Tanvi says.

'What? Now?'

'No, two weeks on Tuesday,' Tanvi says, rolling her eyes. 'Yes, now, you wally.'

I turn the package over and slide my index finger under the paper, easing it away to reveal a small grey box. I open it. Nestled inside is a delicate silver chain with a charm in the shape of a treble clef hanging from it.

'It's a good-luck present,' Tanvi explains. 'In case that wasn't obvious.' She laughs.

I continue to stare at the necklace. It's without doubt one of the loveliest things I've ever seen. 'You shouldn't have,' I murmur, stroking it with my fingertip.

'Don't be a loon,' Tanvi says. 'It's not like it's an engagement ring or anything, and it wasn't super expensive if that's what you're worried about. Not that it's tat either! It's proper sterling silver so it's not going to turn your neck green or anything.'

'It's beautiful.'

'You're sure it's OK? I wasn't sure if you really wore

jewellery, but the second I saw it, I knew I had to buy it for you.'

'No, it's lovely,' I say. 'Really.'

'Here, let me help you put it on.'

Tanvi removes the necklace from the box. I lift my plait out of the way and stoop down so Tanvi can reach to do up the clasp.

'There,' she says, lowering down from her tiptoes. 'It looks great on you!'

The silver feels cold and strange against my collarbone. I'm not used to wearing jewellery.

I don't know what else to say. No one has done anything like this for me before. 'I should get going,' I say eventually. 'You sure you're OK doing the leaflets?'

'All under control,' Tanvi says. 'Now go and blow their socks off!'

I've never been to Birmingham before. As I make my way through the bustling train station, map in hand, it dawns on me just how few places I've actually been to, just how small my life in Ostborough with Bonnie truly is. The audition venue, an arts centre, is sleek and modern, all glass and sharp angles. Boys and girls my age and a little older mill about on the steps. My competition. The sight of them makes my tummy flutter. Until now, I've been focusing purely on getting through my performance.

Most of the other auditionees appear to be accompanied by their parents, even the older ones. My heart puckers. Quickly I scold myself for being so silly. *You operate best when you're on your own, remember?*

In the foyer I'm directed to the registration table. A smiling woman wearing a red National Youth Choir of Great Britain T-shirt who introduces herself as Carla, ticks my name off on a list and gives me a number to pin to my shirt.

'Now, where's your parent or guardian?' Carla asks, looking expectantly over my shoulder.

'I'm sorry?' I say.

'All auditionees under the age of sixteen need to be accompanied by an adult.'

My heart begins to beat faster. How did I not know this? I've read the audition letter at least twenty times. Was there some small print I'd somehow missed?

'I-I didn't know that,' I stammer.

'It's just that it's an official requirement. For insurance,' Carla says. 'We need a signature.' She taps the list with her pen and gives me an apologetic smile.

'Does it mean I can't audition?' I ask. Disappointment surges through my body; all those hours of practice flashing before my eyes.

'I could keep an eye on her,' a voice with a thick Birmingham accent says.

I turn round.

'I'm here with these two anyway,' a tall woman with long jet black hair and an expertly contoured face continues, nodding at the twin boys at her side. 'It'll be no bother.'

'I'm not sure if that's really acceptable,' Carla says.

'Oh go on, the poor kid's come all the way here.'

'You're sure you're happy signing for her?'

'I think I'll manage.' The woman winks at me and scribbles her signature.

'Thank you,' I say once she's registered her two sons.

'Don't mention it,' she replies with a wave of her hand. 'It's a daft rule anyway. How old are you?'

'Fourteen.'

'Exactly, you're not a little kid. And it's a choir audition, not an illegal rave.'

I smile gratefully.

'Well, good luck,' the woman adds. 'C'mon, lads.'

She struts off, the boys trotting after her. I watch them go, resisting the urge to follow.

For the next little while, I mill about, trying not to feel intimidated by the unmistakeable confidence of the other auditionees warming up around me. With their straight backs and self-assured faces, they remind me of the singers on the front of the leaflet. As I quietly siren up and down the scale, I hope beyond hope that someone might think the same of me.

While I'm waiting, I get a message form Noah asking what I'm up to today. I lie and tell him I'm hanging out with friends, scared I'll jinx things if I mention the audition. I'll tell him if I get through, I decide.

After about half an hour, my name is called along with nine others.

I hover by the door while they say goodbye to their parents, averting my eyes as they're showered with kisses and enveloped in 'good luck' hugs. En masse, we follow a woman with a clipboard out of the room, down a maze of corridors and up a set of stairs. As we walk, the other auditionees chat away, the girls in front of me exchanging audition anecdotes like veterans. I hang back, the nerves that have been steadily building all morning coursing their way down my legs, making them tremble like jelly.

Outside the audition room there are ten chairs. The woman tells us what order to sit in. I'm fourth in line, sandwiched between a confident-looking redhead and a boy wearing a tuxedo. Although most people are dressed casually like me, in my jeans and flannel shirt, some are much more formal, wearing suits and dresses, like they're about to perform a solo concert at the Royal Albert Hall.

The girl to my right takes out her phone and plugs in a pair of headphones.

'You don't want to get psyched out by the competition,' she says knowingly.

'Right,' I say, swallowing hard.

A skinny Asian boy wearing little round glasses is called in. About a minute passes before his voice, clear and self-assured, leaks through the walls. Everyone pretends not to react, suddenly engrossed in their sheet music or fingernails or shoes, but it's impossible not to be unnerved, not to sit up that little bit straighter at his obvious talent. The redhead, her eyes closed and volume turned up to maximum, is blissfully unaware. Maybe she's on to something.

A girl with curly blonde hair is up next. When her voice cracks on a high note, the boy wearing the tuxedo screws up his face like he's just been force-fed something disgusting.

'Far too ambitious,' he says to no one in particular. 'That's the golden rule of auditioning. Never *ever* pick a song that exposes your weaknesses.' He turns towards me. 'What are you singing?' he asks.

I show him my sheet music.

'A pop song,' he says. 'Interesting.'

It doesn't sound like a compliment.

The girl emerges from the audition room, her face as red as a tomato. I take a small mirror out of my bag and check my reflection. My cheeks are pink and my forehead is covered with a fine sheen of sweat. I don't have any powder so I have to make do with a tissue, blotting my forehead and nose. I'm thrown by the sight of the necklace from Tanvi hanging round my usually bare neck, the silver treble clef glinting at my throat. I stroke the cool metal with my finger and feel a bit calmer.

The boy in the tuxedo is up next. From what I can hear through the wall, his audition is technically perfect – clean and crisp.

When he comes out, he looks pretty pleased with himself.

'Best of luck, everyone,' he says. 'Hopefully I'll see some of you in London.' He does a little bow and struts down the corridor with the confidence of someone used to getting what they want.

'Number one-two-five-four,' the lady with the clipboard says. 'Ro Snow.'

I stand up. My bottom has left behind a sweaty imprint on the plastic chair I just vacated and I'm glad the girl next to me still has her eyes closed.

I catch my foot on the doorframe and stumble into the audition room, regaining my balance just in time to present myself in front of the panel. There's four of them in total (two men and two women), crowded around a table covered with mugs and paperwork. They all look very posh.

'If you'd like to give your music to Sean,' the skinnier of the two men says. 'He'll be your accompanist today.'

My wobbly legs somehow carry me across the room to Sean. Although they look nothing alike, with his twinkly eyes and encouraging smile he reminds me a little of Mr Milford.

I hand over my sheet music and make my way back to the centre of the room.

'And who do we have here?' one of the women asks in a deep husky voice.

'Ro Snow,' I say, my voice wafer thin.

'And where do you go to school, Ro?' the second man asks.

'Ostborough Academy.'

They nod as if they've heard of it.

'Very good,' the man continues. 'And how old are you?'

'Fourteen.'

'Super,' the second woman says. 'OK then, we're going to start with some scales, just to get a sense of your range. Then we'll go into the sight-reading section, followed by your chosen piece.'

I nod. Can the panel see how badly my legs are trembling? They must. The quaking feels almost cartoon-like.

For the scales, I sing at a spot on the wall far above the panel's heads. When it's time to sight-read, I hide behind my sheet music.

'We'd really love to see your face, Ro,' the husky-voiced woman says gently.

'Sorry,' I stammer, lowering the piece of paper and wishing I possessed even an eighth of the self-confidence the tuxedo boy exuded.

'Not to worry, Ro,' the woman says, smiling. 'Let's take it from the top.'

I take a deep breath and make it through the rest of the piece with my head up.

'Perfect pitch?' the skinny man asks.

'Er, yes.'

'Thought so. It's a very useful thing for a singer to have.'

'Yes, sir.'

'And what piece have you brought with you, Ro?' the second woman asks.

'"Rainy Days and Mondays" by The Carpenters.'

'Lovely,' the woman says, giving absolutely nothing away with her bland smile. 'Whenever you're ready.'

Sean gives me an encouraging smile and begins to play the introduction. I choose a new spot on the wall, half a metre or so above the panel's heads and open my mouth to sing.

It takes a few bars to register that the voice coming out of my mouth and filling every cubic centimetre of the room actually belongs to me. The proficient voice that sang scales and carefully sight-read a few minutes ago has been replaced by something big and gutsy, full of longing and passion and soul. Just like that time in Mr Milford's classroom, I lose myself in the lyrics, singing every word like it's coming straight from the heart.

The song comes to an end. I realize my legs aren't shaking any more.

I drop my gaze and look at the panel. They're smiling, only these are different kinds of smiles to the fixed sort they've been wearing up to this point. They aren't big toothy grins or anything like that, rather small private smiles that tug that tiniest bit at the sides of their mouths.

'How old did you say you were again, Ro?' the husky-voiced woman asks.

'Fourteen, miss. Fifteen in February.'

She nods and makes a note on her pad of paper.

'Thank you, Ro,' the skinny man says. 'I think I'm probably speaking for the rest of the panel when I say I enjoyed your audition very much.'

The rest of the panel nod in agreement.

'Thank you,' I croak.

I scurry to collect my music from Sean. As he hands it over he grins and winks, making my heart balloon.

'Bye,' I say.

'Bye,' the plumper of the two women says. 'And see you soon, Ro.'

See you soon.

I fall out in the corridor in a daze. The waiting auditionees turn to look and it dawns on me that they would have heard my audition, just like I heard the others. To my surprise, I realize I didn't mind. More than that, I feel proud that they heard me.

As I push open the double doors, I catch sight of my reflection in the glass panels.

And for once, my eyes don't look sad at all.

23

I feel different. Lighter somehow. Like one of the knotty balls of anxiety that seems to sit permanently in my belly has been shrunk to almost nothing overnight.

When I arrive at school on Monday morning, Tanvi is waiting at the gates, her hands clasped together in anticipation.

'So? How was it?' she asks, hopping from foot to foot.

'It was . . . good, I think.'

'That's amazing!' Tanvi shrieks, grabbing my hands and bouncing up and down. 'I knew you'd smash it, I just knew it.'

'I'm not sure I smashed it,' I say, gently wriggling free from Tanvi's grasp.

'Hush now! Actually, don't! Tell me everything. "Good" is waaaaaaaay too vague. I need details! Description! Dialogue! In fact, you might as well just start at the very beginning,' Tanvi says, feeding her arm through mine as we walk. 'That way you won't leave anything out.'

Apart from the bit about almost not being able to audition, I tell Tanvi pretty much everything – from my exchange with the boy in the tuxedo, to the wink the pianist gave me as I left.

I've been replaying the day in my head on loop pretty much all weekend but there's something extra thrilling about reporting it out loud to a captive audience.

'Oh my God, it sounds like they loved you!' Tanvi gasps, when I admit the panel's final words to me were 'see you soon'.

'I don't know,' I say. 'They might say that to everyone.'

'Don't be mad! Hey, we should celebrate!' Tanvi says. 'Shake It Off after school? My treat.'

'You don't have to do that.'

'I know that, silly! Did it not cross your mind that I might want to?'

That's the thing though – I'm still struggling to understand what Tanvi sees in me.

'What are you doing a week on Thursday by the way?' she continues, as per usual hurtling from one subject to the next.

'Um, I don't know. Why?'

'Would you like to come to a party?'

'A party?' I repeat. I haven't been invited to a party since I was at primary school.

'Yeah. My family always throw a massive do for Diwali and this year it's my mum and dad's turn to host. Anyway, I was talking to them about it yesterday and I asked them if I could invite a friend along and they said yes, and well, spoiler alert, that friend is you.'

'But isn't it a family thing?' I ask.

'Nah! We always have loads of random extras. Not that you're a random extra, but you know what I mean; there are always tons of neighbours and friends and people like that kicking around. It's really fun, I promise. There's fireworks, and music, and dancing, and more food than you'll ever see in your life.'

There's a pause.

'So?' Tanvi says, sitting on her hands and looking hopeful. 'Fancy it?'

And the weird thing is, I actually think I do.

'Go on then,' I say.

Tanvi blinks. 'Seriously?' she repeats.

'Yeah, why not.'

'Oh my God, really?' Tanvi squeaks, her face lighting up with delight.

'I just said so, didn't I? What do you want me to do? Give you a vial of my blood?'

'Yay!' Tanvi cries, chucking her arms round my neck. 'Oh my God, Ro, we are going to have so much fun.'

I'm sitting outside the staffroom eating my sandwich when I hear knocking on the glass above my head. I look up. Mr Milford is cranking open the window, a huge grin on his face.

'So, how'd it go?' he asks, perching on the windowsill. 'I've been dying to know.'

I stand up to face him. 'I think it went well,' I admit, before delivering an edited version of the account I gave Tanvi.

'That sounds fantastic,' Mr Milford says, grinning. 'No matter what happens from here, you should be really proud of yourself, Ro.'

As I nod, I realize I am.

'On a slightly different subject, I wanted to run something by you,' Mr Milford continues. 'The Christmas concert. I usually mix things up a bit with a couple of big solos, and I was wondering if you fancied having a stab at "O Holy Night"?'

'But I don't sing solo,' I say automatically.

Mr Milford tilts his head to one side. 'What about at the audition?'

'That was different,' I say.

That was a means to an end.

'Look, I'll level with you here,' Mr Milford says, leaning in as if about to impart a juicy secret. 'This song is *hard*. Really hard. I would only ask you to do it if I was confident you'll ace it.'

'I don't know, sir,' I say.

Just the thought of stepping out onto the centre of the stage in front of so many people creates a full-on butterfly farm in my belly. I'm safe as part of a choir. On stage, all alone, I'm exposed and vulnerable.

'Tell you what, why don't we try it out after choir sometime. Just to see how it feels. No pressure, I promise.'

I know I should just say no, shut it down immediately, but the chance to try out a new song with the piano is just too appealing to turn down. At least not straightaway.

'OK,' I say.

Mr Milford beams. 'Great stuff! I'll see you in choir on Friday. And well done, again. I'm proud of you, Ro.'

He shuts the window and I plop back down on the grass. As I lift my sandwich to my lips, I realize I'm smiling. And not just a small smile either – a massive grin, the sort that makes your cheeks hurt if you hold it for too long.

People believe in me. Really believe in me.

I never guessed it would feel quite so nice.

The letter arrives three days later. I get home from school to find it lying on the doormat, the National Youth Choir of Great Britain's distinctive logo beaming up at me.

My heartbeat starts to quicken. I've spent the last few days trying to convince myself that the result doesn't matter, that the positive experience of auditioning is enough, and if it's bad news I'll just forget it and move on, but as I take the envelope in my hands, I know I'm kidding myself.

I want this.

I want it badly.

I open the letter slowly, taking care not to rip the envelope. My vision blurs as I skim the first page, words like 'pleased', 'successful', 'recall' and 'London' leaping out at me.

Happiness surges through my body.

I passed the audition.

I didn't imagine the panel's reaction.

I, Ro Snow, might just be good enough for a place with the National Youth Choir of Great Britain.

I'm reading the letter for the third time when Bonnie

struggles through the back door, two bulging plastic bags in each hand.

'What have you got there?' she asked, dumping her bags at her feet and flexing her fingers.

'Nothing,' I say, hiding it behind my back.

In that second, I decide against telling Bonnie about the audition. The novelty of having a nice secret for once, one that makes me feel warm and fuzzy inside instead of sick and nervous, makes it far too precious to risk sharing with her.

I've been getting on pretty well with the audition process up to now. Why ruin it all by getting her involved? I'll tell her if I get in. Until then, there's no need to say anything. In the meantime, I need to identify an adult willing to come to London with me.

'Jodie, can I ask you a humungous favour?' I ask on Saturday morning.

'Course you can, babe,' Jodie replies.

'What are you doing on Thursday the thirtieth of October?'

'Hmmmm, I don't usually have any lectures on a Thursday so lying in bed eating biscuits probably. Why?'

'Do you fancy a trip to London? All expenses paid.'

I've done the calculations and I've got just enough money left in my bank account to pay for two return train tickets to London, plus tube fares and a bite to eat somewhere.

'Colour me intrigued. What for?' Jodie asks.

I tell her about the audition and the small print on the

letter – *all under-sixteens must be accompanied to the audition by an adult.* I thought about chancing it and relying on another kindly parent to fill in on the day, but it seems like a risky approach considering what's at stake.

'I didn't know you were a singer,' Jodie says, a grin spreading across her face.

'I'm not really,' I say. 'I don't sing solos or anything – it's just being part of a choir I'm interested in.'

'But you must be good to get called back.'

'I don't know. Maybe . . .'

'You sure you don't want to take your mum or someone instead? Someone a bit more, you know, responsible?'

'My mum's got something on that day.'

There's a pause.

'So, do you think you can come?' I ask, biting down hard on my lip.

Jodie puts her hand on her heart. 'Ro, it would be my absolute honour.'

24

Tanvi's house is glowing.

Dozens of candles in tiny clay pots line the driveway and windowsills. A cluster of candles on the front doorstep illuminates stencilled patterns chalked onto the concrete in vibrant shades of pink and blue and red. A foil banner with the words 'Happy Diwali' is stuck to the door. The party sounds like it's already in full swing, belly laughter and traditional Bollywood music leaking through the open living-room window.

A wave of anxiety ripples through my body. I agreed to come so easily, but now I'm here I'm not so sure. Ever since I told Tanvi about Bonnie's unnamed illness, she's been remarkably restrained on the subject, occasionally asking how she is but not pushing me for any further details. What if her extended family is a little more probing? That's not the thing that's worrying me most though. Tanvi's dad has insisted on driving me home after the party, and every time

I think about us pulling up outside number 56, my stomach turns somersaults.

I check my phone: 6.35 p.m. No one has seen me yet. I could leave now, send Tanvi an apologetic text message complaining of period pains or a migraine. Before I can change my mind, I turn on my heel and head back down the driveway. I've almost reached the pavement when the volume from the house increases and a voice calls out my name.

Tanvi.

She's standing in the open doorway wearing a shimmering turquoise sari.

'Where do you think you're going?' she calls in a teasing voice.

'I, er, dropped something,' I improvise. I bend down and pick up a pebble, slipping it into my pocket before Tanvi can see what it is.

'You coming in or what?' she asks.

'Course,' I say, hurrying up the driveway.

'Happy Diwali!' she says, ushering me through the front door.

It's only once I'm inside I'm able to take a proper look at her. In her glittering sari, gleaming black hair styled in glossy ringlets and eyes ringed with black kohl, making them look even bigger than usual, she looks like a glamorous stranger.

'You look totally different,' I say, slipping off my shoes.

'I know!' Tanvi says, fingering one of her curls. 'My sister-in-law, Prisha, helped me get ready. She's *so* ace. I can't wait for you to meet her, for you to meet everyone actually! Come in, come in.

'Mum! Ro's here!' she yells.

Tanvi's mum emerges from the kitchen wearing an apron with 'World's Best Mum' on it, over the top of a pink and gold sari. Her cheeks are flushed and she's smiling broadly.

'So good to see you again, Ro,' she says, taking my hands in hers.

'You too,' I say. 'Er, Happy Diwali.'

She beams. 'Thank you, Ro. Now, let me take your coat.'

'Yeah, before you boil to death,' Tanvi adds. 'Just to warn you, my grandparents are *always* cold, so when they come round we have to whack the heating up to sub-tropical temperatures to stop them from moaning. Honestly, prepare to sweat.'

'Tanvi,' her mum scolds. She's smiling though.

I feel seriously underdressed in comparison to Tanvi and her mum in their beautiful saris and dramatic make-up – like a pigeon sandwiched between a pair of exotic birds. I kick myself for not asking about the dress code.

'I'm sorry I'm not wearing something nicer,' I whisper as Tanvi's mum hangs my jacket on a peg in the downstairs toilet. I'm wearing my nicest pair of jeans and a black jumper. 'I didn't realize it was going to be so fancy.'

'Don't be dumb,' Tanvi says. 'I don't care what you wear. I'm just happy you're here. Unless . . .' A mischievous grin spreads across her face.

'Unless what?' I ask.

Tanvi doesn't answer, grabbing my hand and pulling me up the stairs, the gold bangles on her wrists jangling.

'Unless what, Tanvi?' I yelp.

'Prisha? Prisha, you still up here?' Tanvi calls, pushing open her bedroom door.

A woman with the shiniest hair I have ever seen in real life is kneeling in front of Tanvi's full-length mirror, applying mascara to her already ridiculously long lashes.

'Well, hello,' she says, lowering the mascara wand and sitting back on her heels. 'You must be the famous Ro. I'm Prisha, Tanvi's unofficial big sister.' She twists round and extends an elegant hand for me to shake.

'Hi,' I say, trying not to feel intimidated.

Prisha turns her attention to Tanvi. 'So, what's up, monkey?'

'I just wanted to ask you a teensy weensy favour,' Tanvi says.

'Here we go,' Prisha says, laughing. 'Come on then, what are you after?'

'I was wondering if you had the time to do Ro's hair and make-up too?'

My eyes widen with panic. 'Don't be mental,' I say quickly. 'I'm fine like this, really.'

'Oh, I don't mind,' Prisha says, reaching for a bulging make-up bag. 'I'm pretty sure I've got some colours that would work on you. Plus it means another half an hour without the kids in my face.'

'Prisha's studying to be a make-up artist,' Tanvi says, flopping on the bed. 'Her make-up collection is epic.'

'Special effects make-up is what I'm really interested in though,' Prisha says, removing the lid from a tube of lipstick and peering at it, then at me, one eye closed, then back at the lipstick again. 'The gory stuff especially. Wounds and burns and lacerated flesh and all that. I might have gone a bit overboard in the realism stakes with the kids at Halloween last year though. No one would go near them, poor sods.' She stands up. 'Right, let's get started.' She twizzles a make-up brush between her fingers.

I hesitate. Apart from concealer on my spots and a bit of lip balm, I don't wear make-up. The one time Melanie made me wear some, I looked like a clown.

'I promise I don't bite,' Prisha says. 'Grab me that headband, would you, Tanvi?'

Tanvi tosses Prisha a black elastic headband. Prisha slips it over my head to hold the hair off my face, by which time it feels too late to protest.

Prisha works quickly, calling out brisk instructions like 'eyes closed' and 'look up' as she applies various creams and powders and liquids to my face.

It all feels very strange, from the unexpectedly tickly texture of the make-up brushes against my skin, to the alien sensation of my eyebrows being tamed with some sort of gel.

'They're great, by the way,' Prisha says.

'Sorry?'

'Your eyebrows. They're fab. Cara Delevingne, eat your heart out.'

'Um, thank you,' I say. Until this moment I'm not sure I've ever given my eyebrows a second thought.

'Just promise me you won't pluck them,' Prisha adds. 'I plucked mine to obscurity when I was a teenager and I still regret it to this day. You OK with eyelash curlers?'

I have no idea but say yes anyway, hiding my alarm as best I can as Prisha clamps my lashes with what looks like a miniature medieval torture device.

From my position on the bed, I can't see my reflection in the mirror so I have no idea what Prisha is actually doing, only that my face feels strange and almost heavy, like I'm wearing some sort of mask.

The whole time, Tanvi bounces about the room delivering enthusiastic updates on how I'm looking. All I can do is smile weakly.

'I'm thinking we work with the natural wave in your hair,' Prisha says, removing my hair from its plait and plugging in a pair of hair straighteners.

She sections up my hair, winding pieces around the barrel of the hair straighteners in turn. The waves feel warm against my neck. Once she's done my entire head, Prisha sprays them for ages. The smell of hairspray reminds me of Bonnie. Quickly, I push the thought from my mind. I don't want to think about home. Not tonight.

I hear Prisha set the can back down on Tanvi's desk and open my eyes.

'Can I look now?' I ask, eyeing the mirror.

Prisha and Tanvi stand side by side in front of me, their arms folded, heads cocked to the left. Prisha glances at Tanvi.

'Are you thinking what I'm thinking?' she asks.

A grin spreads across Tanvi's face. 'Yes!' she says.

Prisha dashes out of the room.

'What? Where has she gone?' I ask Tanvi, but she just grins and tells me to 'wait and see'.

Prisha returns about thirty seconds later with a heap of purple material embroidered with gold thread draped over her forearms.

'Eeeeeeeeee!' Tanvi cries, clasping her hands together in excitement. 'It's perfect! Ro, take your jeans off.'

'What?'

'Take your jeans off,' she repeats. 'Unless you're planning to wear this over the top of them, which kind of might ruin the effect.'

The penny finally drops. 'No way. I'll look completely silly,' I say, backing up against Tanvi's wardrobe.

'You'll look amazing,' Tanvi assures me.

'But won't people mind?' I stammer. 'What about your grandparents and stuff? I don't want to offend them? I mean, I'm not a Hindu.'

Tanvi wrinkles her nose. 'They won't give a monkey's. And if Kate Middleton can wear a sari, so can you.'

'You've had your hair and make-up done,' Prisha adds. 'You may as well go the whole hog and dress the part too.' She holds out the sari.

'Do it, do it!' Tanvi chants.

Prisha joins in and even though I'm terrified, I can't help but laugh at their animated faces.

'OK, OK!' I say before I can change my mind.

Tanvi lets out a whoop, hands me the underskirt and matching blouse for the sari and ushers me to the bathroom to change, remembering just in time to duck in there ahead of me to cover the mirror with a towel.

'No peeking!' she says with a stern wag of the finger before leaving the room.

I shiver as I step out of my jeans and top and change into the underskirt and blouse. What am I doing? I'm supposed to be keeping my head down tonight, not playing dress-up. And yet, there's something oddly thrilling about the swish of unfamiliar material against my legs and the weight of mascara on my lashes. I swallow my doubt and head back to the bedroom.

I'm surprised by just how long the sari itself takes to put on. Prisha's brow is furrowed with deep concentration as she makes her way around my body, tucking and pleating and pinning, the expanse of material gradually getting shorter and shorter. My attempts at checking my reflection in the mirror are thwarted by Tanvi's insistence that we do a 'grand reveal' at the very last moment.

'Tanvi!' a voice yells up the stairs.

'I'll be right back,' she says, bolting out of the room and thundering down the stairs.

Prisha shakes her head and laughs. 'That girl has enough energy to power an entire village, I swear.'

I nod in agreement. I swear I wouldn't be surprised to discover Tanvi is half-human, half-Duracell bunny.

'She talks about you loads, you know,' Prisha says, as she continues to work on the sari.

'She does?' I ask doubtfully. I'm still baffled by why Tanvi seems to like me so much. We're like chalk and cheese in almost every possible way.

'Oh yeah,' Prisha says. 'It's all Ro this and Ro that.'

'Wow, sorry. That must be so boring for you.'

'Not at all! It's nice she's found someone she gets on with so well. Especially after the few years she's had. She's still quite fragile under that cheerful facade of hers.'

My eyes fall on the picture of Tanvi in hospital looking frail but happy. They drift to the numerous photos of her and the girl with the nose piercing. I notice details I hadn't registered the first time round – the dimple in the girl's left cheek, the fact she has blue eyes, the mole next to her right eyebrow. The whole time, I'm asking myself the same question, over and over. Why isn't she here tonight instead of me?

I glance down at Prisha. She must know who the girl in the photos is. I want to ask her about her, but I feel too shy and by the time I've plucked up the courage, Tanvi returns.

Five minutes later, I'm standing in the centre of the room with my eyes closed.

In unison, Tanvi and Prisha count down from three. I peel my eyes open one by one and look in the mirror.

I blink, my cheeks growing hot as I study my reflection.

Instead of its usual frizzy plait, my hair falls in smooth, glossy waves, and my complexion appears clear and even under the expertly applied layers of make-up. It's the sari that makes the biggest difference though. My wardrobe consists almost entirely of black, grey and navy, clothes carefully selected to help me fade as far into the background as possible. The rich purple sari does the exact opposite and I have no idea how I feel about it.

'Say something then!' Tanvi says, shaking my arm. 'Do you love it?'

'I don't know,' I say truthfully, still trying to get my head around the idea that the girl in the mirror is actually me. 'I don't usually wear make-up and stuff. And are you sure I don't just look like a massive bar of Dairy Milk?'

'No!' Prisha and Tanvi cry, laughing.

'You look fab-u-lous,' Prisha says. 'And I'm not just being biased.'

'You look awesome,' Tanvi adds. 'And should basically wear nothing but purple from this day forward.'

In all the excitement, I realize I haven't thanked Prisha.

'Thank you,' I say. 'That was a lot of work.'

'You're very welcome,' Prisha replies, patting me on the shoulder. 'And no work at all. I have to say, you're a much easier subject than this one' – she jerks her head in Tanvi's direction – 'who's a right fidgeter.'

'Oi!' Tanvi says.

Prisha blows her a kiss.

The doorbell downstairs rings and Tanvi lets out an excited squeal. 'C'mon, I want to introduce you to everyone,' she says, taking my hand. 'Coming, Prisha?'

'In a minute. I'm milking this downtime all I can get right now. Just don't tell your brother.' She winks and lies down on Tanvi's bed, crossing her legs at the ankle, resting her hands on her stomach and closing her eyes.

'Ready?' Tanvi asks, tugging on my arm.

I'm not entirely sure, but I nod and follow anyway.

25

I pause at the top of the stairs, gripped by nerves, the swell of voices coming from downstairs making my belly swoop. Prisha has lent me a pair of glittery sandals to wear. The heel is only small but I still feel wobbly and uncertain in them.

I feel Tanvi's breath on my neck. 'You look great,' she whispers, prodding me gently in the ribs.

A part of me knows she's right. Another part wants to hide in the bedroom until the party is over. I know I can't though. Prisha has gone to far too much trouble for me to back out now.

My hands trembling, I gather the folds of the sari in my left hand, grasping the bannister with my right. For a sliver of a moment, I'm so overwhelmed by it all, I'm scared I might cry.

Stop being so silly, I scold myself, my fingernails digging into the wooden rail. *It's just a bit of make-up and a fancy outfit.*

Only it's not, I know it's not. I've never been the centre of attention like this and I have no idea how I'm supposed to act.

I take a deep breath and follow Tanvi. I put one foot in front of the other. And again. And again. Until I'm almost at the bottom of the stairs.

Just below me, four members of Tanvi's extended family are giving Tanvi's dad their coats.

'Is that Ro?' he asks, squinting up at me. 'I didn't recognize you there.'

The group's heads twist towards us and my cheeks grow even hotter under my powdered cheeks.

'Everyone,' Tanvi says, reaching across and taking my sweaty hand. 'This is my best friend, Ro.'

Best friend. She says it so easily, so proudly, entirely without hesitation or self-consciousness. 'Ro, this is my auntie Preti, my uncle Raj, and my cousins, Kamla and Krish.'

'Hi,' I say, pulling myself together just in time.

'Nice sari,' Kamla, a girl of around nineteen, says.

'It's not mine,' I blurt, instantly feeling stupid.

'It's Prisha's,' Tanvi supplies. 'Doesn't Ro look awesome in it?'

Although Kamla says 'totally' and nods enthusiastically, I still feel awkward, folding my arms to cover up my exposed strip of bare stomach.

Tanvi leads me through into the living room, now packed full of people – aunts and uncles and cousins and grandparents and family friends and neighbours, every sofa cushion and arm taken, kids on laps or perched on cushions on the floor like frogs on lily pads.

Tanvi parades me around the room, again introducing me as her 'best friend' with the same ease and confidence as before. I keep waiting for someone to laugh or make a face at my appearance, but everyone is friendly and welcoming, even Tanvi's brother Devin, who Tanvi promised me was a 'miserable poo bum'. Just like Prisha, they all seem to know exactly who I am, asking unprompted questions about school and the choir and even my upcoming audition. My voice still shaking a little, I answer them politely, taking care to keep my answers brief and to the point. By the time we've made a complete circuit of the living room, I've managed to relax a little.

Formal introductions over, Tanvi and I stick our heads in the kitchen, observing the various dishes bubbling away on the stove and marvelling at the dozens of boxes of sweets the family have been given as Diwali gifts. After that, we visit the home temple on the landing, where I hover at Tanvi's side as she bows her head and prays.

The dinner table (made up of various different tables pushed together, all covered with a giant paper tablecloth) is so long it extends from the dining room right through into the adjoining living room, the seating a mismatched assortment of traditional dining-room chairs, patio furniture and several office chairs on wheels.

I watch, mesmerized, as the table fills up with steaming hot dishes of food – rice and curries and dahls and chutneys. Tanvi loads up my plate until it's so heavy I can barely lift it.

The eating portion of the evening goes on for what seem like hours, every single dish delicious and packed full of flavour. The conversation is loud and chaotic, jokes and conversations shooting across the table in a mixture of English and Hindi, Tanvi translating where necessary. As I eat, I keep catching sight of my reflection in the patio doors, and every time it takes a split second to twig the girl with the gleaming hair and kohl-rimmed eyes is actually me.

After dinner, the guests pile into the living room, collapsing onto the furniture or floor and lamenting over their full bellies.

Tanvi suggests playing *Just Dance* on the PlayStation.

'Are you crazy?' Prisha cries, flopping on the sofa, her kids immediately climbing on her, making her groan in pain as their hands and feet knead her stomach. 'I can barely breathe, never mind dance.'

'I'm with Prisha,' one of Tanvi's aunts agrees, rubbing her stomach. 'This food baby needs some serious R&R.'

'*Sing Star*?' Tanvi says hopefully.

'Can we do that sitting down?' Prisha asks.

'Yes.'

'*Sing Star* it is, then.'

I help Tanvi set up the PlayStation.

'Oh God, you're going to absolutely trounce us all,' Tanvi says as we kneel on the carpet, untangling wires.

'Huh?'

'Have you not played this before?'

I shake my head.

'Well, it's a bloody singing game, isn't it?' Tanvi says.

'You're going to take the entire Shah family to the cleaners!'

'Speak for yourself!' Anish pipes up. He has collapsed on the sofa next to Prisha, his head resting on her shoulder. 'My voice has been compared to Sir Michael Bublé himself.'

'Oh please,' Tanvi says. 'You make Devin sound good.'

Devin throws a scatter cushion at Tanvi's head. 'Oi!' he cries. 'I heard that!'

'I wanna hear Ro sing,' Prisha says.

'Yeah!' one of Tanvi's uncles chimes in. 'I want to hear this famous voice we've heard all about.'

I throw Tanvi a panicked look, weak with relief when she interprets my reaction correctly.

'Maybe in a bit,' Tanvi says. 'Prish, Anish, you want to kick us off?'

Stupidly thankful to have escaped, I sink down on the floor and watch as Anish and Prisha peel themselves off the sofa and giggle their way through a song from a Bollywood film called 'Kabhi Alvida Naa Kehna'. They're followed by Tanvi's auntie Preti utterly mangling 'Rehab' by Amy Winehouse, Kamla and Krish hiding their faces in their hands from start to finish; Tanvi's parents tackling 'Don't Go Breaking My Heart', the two of them painfully out of tune; and Devin and one of his grandfathers honking their way through 'Hey, Jude'. Even though the singing is universally dreadful, watching everyone having such good fun is infectious, and I can't help but get swept up by it, laughing along with everyone else from the safety of my spot in the corner.

'OK, enough of this abuse!' Anish says, his hands over his ears. 'Ro? You're up.'

My eyes widen in alarm. Tucked away in the corner, I assumed I'd been forgotten.

'I'm fine just listening, thanks,' I say, hugging my knees to my chest in an attempt to make my body as small as possible.

Everyone roars with laughter as if I've just delivered a hilarious punchline.

'No, really,' I insist, pressing my back against the wall. Frantically, I look for Tanvi for backup, but she's on the other side of the living room, talking to one of her grandmothers, oblivious to my predicament.

'Sorry, Ro, you may be a guest tonight but you don't get off that easily,' Anish says. 'At least not where *Sing Star* is involved.'

He nods to Devin and one of Tanvi's uncles and between the three of them they haul me to my feet, their laughter drowning out my desperate protests.

Prisha thrusts a microphone into my hand. 'Please, Ro,' she says, her hands pressed together in prayer position. 'My ears can't take any more. We *need* you. Right, Tanvi?'

'What?' Tanvi asks, looking up from her conversation with her grandmother.

'We were just saying it's time for Ro to show us how it's done.'

I throw Tanvi another pleading glance, but this time she's not letting me off the hook. She grabs a controller and starts scrolling through the songs.

I sidle up next to her. 'But I don't sing solo,' I say, my voice wobbly with panic.

'I know,' Tanvi says, continuing to scroll. 'That's why I'm gonna sing with you.'

'*With* me?'

'Yeah. I'm putting it in competitive mode.'

'What does that mean?'

'It means we both sing the whole song – no solo lines.'

'Oh.'

Behind us, Devin has started to sing 'Why Are We Waiting'.

'We're picking a song!' Tanvi shoots back at him over her shoulder. 'OK, what do you reckon?' she asks, continuing to scroll through the songs. '"Someone Like You"? "Chandelier"? "Let It Go"?'

'"Let It Go"!' one of Tanvi's nephews cries, bouncing up and down on Prisha's lap, his sparkly green fairy wings flapping in her face.

'Yeah, "Let It Go"!' one of Tanvi's little cousins lisps, her words whistling through the gap where she had no front teeth. 'Please!'

Within seconds, every small person in the room is chanting 'Let It Go, Let It Go!'

'OK, OK!' Tanvi shouts over them. 'We get the message.' She turns to me. 'That's cool with you, right?' She doesn't exactly wait for my answer, the introduction kicking in just seconds later, turning my stomach to mush.

A hush falls over the room. My legs are shaking the way they did at the Birmingham audition and I'm grateful they're hidden from view under the sari. I turn my back on the sea of expectant faces and focus on the glowing lyrics on the TV above the fireplace. Maybe, if I keep my eyes glued on the screen and block everyone else out, I can convince myself this is just another practice session with Mr Milford.

With both hands, I lift the microphone to my lips and begin to sing, so quietly I can barely hear myself at first. Tanvi keeps looking at me but I daren't take my eyes off the screen.

We reach the chorus and the kids join in, their childish voices drowning us out, despite their parents' desperate shushing. As the noise mounts, I find myself relaxing a little, my grip on the microphone loosening ever so slightly, my legs now stable beneath the folds of Prisha's purple sari. Tanvi gives me a nudge with her elbow and I risk a glance in her direction. She shoots me a massive grin and I can't help but match it with a smile of my own.

That's when it dawns on me. I'm enjoying myself. I'm singing in front of people and I like it.

More than like it. I think I sort of love it.

As the song goes on, the children gradually stop singing and flop on the floor, exhausted by the big notes, and by the final chorus Tanvi has pretty much stopped singing too, her onscreen score plummeting as she steps aside and leaves me to complete the song alone. My initial panic melts away as everyone cheers me on, breaking into noisy applause as I deliver the final line.

'More, more!' Anish cries, dropping to his knees and bowing at my feet. 'We're not worthy, we're not worthy!'

My face is flaming with embarrassment, but I can't help but giggle at his reaction. It just seems so mad. Is all this fuss really for me?

'Anyone want to follow that?' Prisha asks.

'Hell, no!' Devin says and everyone laughs.

'Pardon the pun, but that seems a good note to end on,' Tanvi's dad says. 'Time for fireworks?'

Everyone happily agrees, pulling on coats and shoes and heading out into the garden.

As we huddle on the patio, I'm still buzzing, adrenaline continuing to pump its way around my body. Did I really just do that? While dressed like this? It feels like a weird dream.

I join in with the 'oohs' and 'aahs' as explosions of pink and silver and green and gold whizz and splutter above our heads, and as the last firework dissolves in the night sky, my heart wants to burst.

Tanvi's dad and uncles take a bow and we applaud their prowess. Everyone begins to drift inside apart from me and Tanvi. She produces a box of sweets and we eat them huddled on a bench, a blanket draped over our knees.

'If I tell you something, will you promise not to tell anyone else?' Tanvi asks after a bit, powdered sugar clinging to her lips.

'Of course,' I say. It's an easy enough answer to give. Who would I possibly tell?

'I like someone,' she says. 'Someone you know.'

'Emerson,' I say without missing a beat.

Tanvi's face falls. 'How did you know?' she cries.

'You flirt with him every day in registration.'

'No, I don't!'

'Er, yes, you do!' I say, laughing. Just today they had an

ultra-flirty debate about the best horror film ever made.

'Do I really?' Tanvi asks.

'Yes, Tanvi.'

'Do you think he knows?'

I pretend to think about it for a second.

'Yes, Tanvi.'

She covers her face with her hands and lets out a groan.

'He flirts back just as hard,' I add quickly.

She separates her fingers. 'He does?'

'Oh my God, totally.'

Tanvi lowers her hands. 'I swear I didn't even realize how much I liked him until he gave me half his Crunchie bar in maths last week. And now I can't stop thinking about him. Do you honestly think he might like me back?'

'He'd be really stupid not to.'

'That's not a proper answer.'

'Tanvi,' I say, turning to face her and trying to make my face look as serious as possible. 'Every time you walk into registration, he goes all giddy. You may as well just replace his head with a big fat heart eyes emoji.'

Tanvi's hands fly straight back up to her face. 'Really?' she squeaks through her fingers.

'Really. He's super into you.'

'Why didn't you say anything?'

'I don't know. I assumed you knew already.'

The whole time, I feel a bit like I'm delivering lines in a play. I'm not used to these sorts of chats – about boys and flirting and feelings. And yet there's something surprisingly nice about it – sort of warm and cosy.

'You're the best, Ro,' Tanvi says, resting her head on my shoulder.

'Just saying what I see,' I reply.

We sit in silence for a few moments, the firework smoke slowly clearing to reveal a brilliantly starry night.

'How about you?' Tanvi asks. 'Is there someone you like?'

I hesitate.

'Go on!' Tanvi says, sitting up straight.

'There is this one boy . . .' I begin experimentally.

'Who? It's Jamie Cannon, isn't it? I knew it!'

'No,' I say firmly. 'It's no one at school.'

Tanvi's brow furrows. 'Who then?' she asks.

I pause, surprised to discover just how much I want to tell Tanvi about Noah.

'He lives next door,' I say.

'Oh, how romantic!' Tanvi swoons, draping herself across my lap. 'Not to mention convenient.'

'Not exactly,' I say.

'How come?' she asks, sitting up again.

'He goes to boarding school so he's only there like once in a blue moon.'

'Does he know how you feel?'

'*I* don't even know how I feel,' I say. 'We've only really talked in person once. And that was ages ago.'

'Have you got his number?'

'Yeah. And we've texted and stuff, but it's not the same.'

'When will you next see him?'

'He'll be at his dad's for the second half of half term.'

We've arranged to meet on Wednesday afternoon. He

offered to come to mine but I quickly put him off, proposing we hang out at his place instead.

'But that's next week!' Tanvi squeaks.

'I know.' I've been trying not to fixate on it in case it falls through for some reason and I end up getting disappointed, but at the same time it's been difficult not to count down the days, my brain reeling off endless pages of scripted conversation.

'Oh my God, Ro, this is so cool!' Tanvi yelps.

'He might not even like me,' I say quickly.

'Don't be nuts! I bet he's well excited about seeing you again. What's his name?'

'Noah,' I admit.

Just saying his name out loud feels electrifying.

'Ro and Noah,' Tanvi says. 'Noah and Ro. Roah!'

'Ha! That would make you and Emerson, let's see, Tanvison.'

'Or Emi. Hey, maybe we can double date?'

'Um, aren't we getting a bit ahead of ourselves here?' I don't want to jinx things.

'Maybe,' Tanvi admits.

As we continue to talk, I wait for the inevitable regret and fear to kick in. I've never, ever confided in someone like this before. Five minutes pass, then ten, then another ten. And still nothing. Just the warm fuzzy glow of what I think might be friendship. Perhaps I *can* do this – protect Bonnie *and* have a best friend. Maybe they're not mutually exclusive after all. The prospect is both scary and exhilarating.

'Girls!' Tanvi's mum calls from the kitchen window. 'Can you come in now, please. It's nearly eleven.'

Reluctantly, we heave ourselves off the bench and return inside where people are starting to leave. Aunts and uncles and grandparents and cousins embrace me like I'm one of the family, congratulating me on my *Sing Star* performance and wishing me luck for my audition. It's overwhelming but really nice too.

'You girls ready?' Tanvi's dad asks.

'Aw!' Tanvi whines. 'Does Ro have to go?'

'It's gone eleven, *bachcha*. On a school night too.'

We head upstairs so I can change. Back in my normal clothes, I feel deflated, like a superhero stripped of their powers. As I'm pulling on my jeans, I can't help but look at the girl in the photos and once more find myself wondering why I was here tonight instead of her.

Tanvi insists I take the front seat in the car. As we turn into Arcadia Avenue, I feel the familiar sense of dread creep up my body. Passing number 48, I stare resolutely ahead. To my relief, Tanvi and her dad don't even look at it.

'It's just here, number fifty-six,' I say, stupidly happy to see the house in darkness.

Tanvi's dad turns off the engine.

'Thank you for the lift,' I say.

'You're very welcome, Ro.'

I get out of the car. Tanvi gets out too so she can transfer to the front seat.

'Did you have a good night?' she asks as we stand on the pavement.

'I really did,' I say.

'I'm sorry you had to sing in front of everyone.'

'That's OK,' I say lightly. 'It was probably good practice for the audition.'

'That's what *I* thought!'

Tanvi's dad winds down his window. '*Bachcha*,' he says. 'It's late.'

'OK, OK,' Tanvi says, rolling her eyes.

'Thanks again for coming,' she says, hugging me tightly. 'I had the best time.'

I hesitate before putting my arms around her and hugging her back.

'I'm really glad you told me about Noah,' she says into my hair.

'No big deal,' I murmur.

We separate.

'Well, see you tomorrow,' Tanvi says.

'Yeah, see you tomorrow,' I echo, hovering on the pavement as Tanvi climbs in the passenger seat.

I make my way up the path, pausing to wave before disappearing behind the side gate. I crouch down, and wait for them to drive away. I give it another few minutes before unlatching the gate and heading back down the path towards number 48.

The house is quiet. As I creep past the living-room door, I realize I haven't thought about the house or Bonnie all night.

And it has been lovely.

More than lovely.

In fact, it might just have been one of the nicest nights of my entire life.

26

My phone is missing. After my chat with Tanvi about Noah, I got the urge to text him when I got in but when I reached for my phone it wasn't there.

I'm not too worried. I must have left it at Tanvi's. I remember putting it on her bed when I was getting changed. I'll have forgotten to pick it up.

It turns out I was right. When I walk into registration the following morning it's sitting on the desk.

'I left it on your bed, right?' I say, scooping it up and dropping it my blazer pocket.

'Uh-huh,' Tanvi says. 'You haven't been too worried about it, have you? When I found it, I wanted to drop it off straightaway, but Dad said it was too late.'

We're interrupted by Emerson. 'You guys going to Jack's Halloween party next Friday?' he asks, his elbows resting on our desk. Even though he addresses the question to both of us, it's clear that Tanvi's is the response he's interested in.

'I don't know,' Tanvi says, twirling a piece of hair around her index finger. 'Why?'

'You should come,' Emerson says.

'Oh yeah?'

'Yeah.'

'How come?'

'Well, I'll be there for one,' he says, wiggling his eyebrows up and down.

I hide my smile behind my hand as Tanvi dissolves into giggles.

'Plus, Jack's parents are really cool,' Emerson adds. 'They let you drink and everything.'

'Hmmmm, let me think about it,' Tanvi says.

'You do that,' Emerson says, turning back to face the front of the class before Ms Cameron tells him off.

'Oh my God, oh my God,' Tanvi says the second the bell has rung for morning lessons and Emerson is out of earshot. 'We *have* to go to Jack's party, Ro, we have to!'

'But I thought you were going to Center Parcs next week.'

'I am. I'll be back by Friday though. You can come get ready at mine and we can go together!'

'What's all this "we" business?' I ask, pulling my backpack onto my shoulders.

'Well, I can hardly go alone. I need a wingwoman!'

'What about Marissa? I bet she's going.'

'Noooooo! It has to be you.'

'Why?'

'Because. We're a team.'

'But I'm no good at parties.'

'Er, excuse me, what about last night? Everyone *loved* you. Seriously, my parents won't stop going on about you.'

'That was different.'

It really was.

'Oh please, Ro,' Tanvi says, grabbing my hand and waggling it up and down. 'I'm nearly fifteen years old and I've never been to a party. This is beyond tragic.'

'What about last night?' I ask triumphantly.

Tanvi makes a face. 'You know what I mean. A proper party. Where actual stuff might happen, maybe even to me.'

I don't say anything.

'We don't have to go for long!' Tanvi continues. 'And if it's rubbish or boring or anything, we can leave and you can say "I told you so" until the end of time.'

'I don't know, Tanvi . . .' I begin.

Last night was brilliant and everything, but the idea of going to a party full of people from school is a completely different proposition and fills me with dread.

Tanvi plants herself in front of me with her hands on her hips. 'You give me no choice, Ro Snow,' she says.

I frown, unsure what she's getting at.

'Now,' she says. 'Are you seriously telling me that you'd deprive a girl who VERY NEARLY DIED, from attending her very first proper party?'

My mouth drops open. 'I can't believe you just went there, Shah,' I say.

Tanvi's stern expression melts into a mischievous grin. 'Well?' she demands. 'Are you?'

My insides twist. Every instinct is telling me to say no.

And yet the idea of Tanvi missing out because of me feels just as terrible, if not more.

I take a deep breath. 'You promise we can leave if it's awful?' I ask.

'It won't be.'

'But do you promise?'

'Cross my heart and hope to die,' Tanvi says solemnly, swiping her index finger across her chest.

27

I spend the early portion of the half-term week practising for my audition. Luckily, Bonnie has the TV and radio on so loud there's little danger of her hearing me.

I stand in front of the mirror on the back of my bedroom door and sing for hours on end, fascinated by the way my face and body transform into someone else entirely the moment I open my mouth.

My days are punctuated with flurries of messages from Tanvi. I'm treated to regular updates on her Center Parcs schedule – a dizzying timetable of swimming and badminton and archery and indoor climbing – interspersed with speculation about Jack's party.

It's funny, but after seeing Tanvi pretty much every day for nearly two months, I'm sort of missing her this week. It's not just that though; everything seems a bit easier lately. The state of the house is as bad as ever, but it's not quite getting to me in the way it used to. It's the same with Bonnie.

She went on another one of her shopping sprees the other day, and even though the sight of all those shopping bags most definitely upset me, I didn't fly off the handle the way I would have done a few months ago.

On Wednesday morning, I wake up to a text from Tanvi:

Have fun with Noah today!!!! Don't do anything I wouldn't do! Hahahahaha!

I can't believe I'm finally getting to see him. I don't know why but I keep worrying he's going to cancel on me, despite the fact he messaged me last night to ask what biscuits I like.

I spend the morning practising for my audition. I'm distracted though, jumpy and daydreamy. After lunch, I brush my teeth and replait my hair before planting myself on Noah's doorstep at two o'clock exactly, clutching the chess set to my chest. I ring the bell, nervous excitement pulsing through my body.

Mr Hornby answers. He's unshaven and has purply grey bags under his eyes. 'Can I help you?' he asks, his face exhibiting zero recognition.

I glance over his shoulder. The hallway looks nothing like it did when Terry lived there. The swirly carpet has been replaced with laminate flooring, the textured wallpaper with bland magnolia paint.

'It's for me, Dad,' a voice calls.

Mr Hornby drifts back to the living room as Noah comes galloping down the stairs.

'Hi,' he says, coming to an abrupt stop in front of me.

'Hi,' I reply.

There's a moment where we just look at each other, our eyes wide and unblinking. Noah's hair is longer and I swear he's taller.

'Er, do you want a drink or something?' he asks.

'Yes please,' I say.

I follow him through into the kitchen. In terms of layout, 46 Arcadia Avenue is the mirror of 48. Not that you'd ever guess. The dimensions may be the same but it feels like another world – clean and spacious, a blank canvas. It's like being in an alternate universe, one where Bonnie and I live together in peaceful magnolia-hued harmony.

The kitchen in particular is suspiciously bare, the counter tops empty apart from an expensive-looking coffee machine and a fruit bowl containing a single blackened banana.

'Coke?' Noah asks, opening the fridge.

'Please.'

He hands me a can, wedges an unopened packet of Jaffa Cakes under his arm and leads the way upstairs.

In keeping with the rest of the house, Noah's bedroom is sparse and impersonal, more like a guest room than a teenage boy's bedroom. The bed is unmade, a tangle of navy blue sheets.

'Most of my stuff is at my mum's,' he explains, tugging the duvet into place.

'Makes sense,' I say. 'I don't keep much at my dad's either.'

He turns to face me. 'Your parents are divorced too?'

'Yeah.'

'How often do you see your dad?'

'One weekend per month.'

'Your mum got full custody as well then?'

I realize I don't know, only that whatever arrangement they have seems to suit Dad just fine.

'It was kind of a long time ago,' I say. 'Chess?' I add, holding up the box. 'I wrote down where we were so we can finish that game.'

'Smart thinking.'

I kneel on the carpet, referring to my scribbled diagram as I place the pieces on the board, while Noah opens the Jaffa Cakes.

'Sorry my dad was so weird just then,' Noah says, offering me one. 'He's such a dick sometimes,' he adds, a fierce look in his eyes.

'It's fine, really,' I say.

When it comes to weird parents, I don't have a leg to stand on.

As we begin to play, the chat starts to flow. First of all, it's just general stuff – whether Jaffa Cakes are cakes or biscuits, summer versus winter, our favourite Harry Potter characters, the most annoying noise in the world, a documentary on sharks we've both happened to have seen. Gradually, though, we move on to more personal stuff. I find myself telling Noah about my audition tomorrow, my nerves and excitement fizzing over as I describe the day ahead. In return, Noah opens up about his parents' divorce. He's telling me about his mum's new boyfriend and how he can't decide if he's really nice or a complete phoney when my phone rings.

It's Jodie.

'Sorry, I need to get this,' I say, picking it up. I turn away. 'Hey, Jodie, everything OK?'

'Not exactly,' she says. 'I'm in A&E. I think I might have broken my ankle.'

'How?'

'Don't laugh, but I fell out of a tree. And I wasn't even drunk,' she wails. 'I was helping my mate Benny with his photography project.'

My heart sinks. I know what's coming next.

'I'm so, so sorry, Ro, but you're going to have to ask someone else to go with you tomorrow.'

'That's OK,' I say.

Because what else *can* I say?

'Really?' Jodie says. 'I feel so terrible letting you down but I literally can't walk right now. You'll be able to find someone else to fill in, right?'

'Course. It's fine, honestly.'

This is a lie but there's no point in making Jodie feel bad when she's stuck in A&E with a suspected broken ankle. At the same time, I'm so disappointed I could cry.

'Oh, babe, I've got to go,' Jodie says. 'They just called my name. Good luck tomorrow!'

I hang up.

'Everything OK?' Noah asks.

I tell him about needing an adult to come to the audition with me.

'Can't your mum go with you?' he asks.

'It's not that simple,' I say.

'How come? She's a singer, isn't she? Surely she's the perfect person.'

'She doesn't actually know about the audition.'

'You're kidding. Why not?'

I try to work out if there's a straightforward easy way to describe why I don't want Bonnie involved. I settle for, 'It's complicated.'

Noah is opening his mouth to ask me another question when the door bursts inwards. Even though there's an entire chessboard between us, we both jump a mile, making the chess pieces wobble violently.

Mr Hornby looks down at us wearily. 'Time for dinner, Noah,' he says.

I glance over my shoulder. It's dark out. How long have I been here? It feels like ten minutes.

'But we're midway through a game,' Noah says, pointing at the chessboard.

'You can finish it another day.'

'Can Ro stay and eat with us?'

'I didn't order enough pizzas.'

'She can share mine.'

'Not tonight, Noah.'

'But Dad—'

'I said, not tonight.'

'Told you he was a dick,' Noah says once Mr Hornby has gone.

'That's just parents for you, I reckon.'

He shoots me a grateful smile. 'What shall we do about the game?' he asks.

'Are you free on Friday afternoon?' I ask, mentally crossing my fingers. 'Maybe we could finish it then.'

'It's my dad's birthday so we're doing stuff for that all day,' Noah says, screwing up his face. 'Saturday?'

'I'll be at work in the morning but any time after one works.'

'Great,' Noah says. 'I'll leave the board set up. Unless you want to hang out at yours instead?'

'Here is good,' I say quickly.

I'm relieved when Noah doesn't push me on it.

'Noah! It's getting cold!' Mr Hornby's voice sails up the stairs.

'I should go,' I say.

Noah walks me to the door. 'Good luck tomorrow,' he says. 'If you're anywhere near as good as your mum, you'll smash it.'

'Thanks,' I reply.

'Saturday at one then?' he adds.

'Saturday at one,' I confirm, butterflies flapping in my chest and belly.

I sit down on my bed and scroll through the contacts on my phone in search for an adult to take Jodie's place.

Dad and Melanie are in France.

Eric has four kids and a full-time job.

Gran and Grandad are in Spain.

Tanvi and her family are at Center Parcs.

Noah and his dad have plans.

And I don't have any way of contacting Mr Milford.

Which leaves just one person.

The very last person I want to ask.

Bonnie.

I head downstairs and push open the living-room door. Bonnie is watching *Home and Away*. She's smoking. I pretend not to notice. Now isn't the time to start an argument.

'Everything OK?' she asks, glancing up at me.

I haven't seen her much this week.

'I need to ask you something,' I say.

'OK,' she says, turning down the volume slightly.

'Do you remember that letter you brought up to my room a few weeks ago?'

'Vaguely,' Bonnie says.

'The thing is, that letter was about a recall audition. For a choir.'

'A choir?' Bonnie says, suddenly alert. Her surprise seems genuine. Perhaps she didn't register the logo on the original letter after all.

'Yes,' I say. 'The National Youth Choir of Great Britain.'

'Never heard of it,' Bonnie says, her dismissive tone suggesting it therefore cannot possibly exist.

'I hadn't either. Auditioning was Mr Milford's idea. He runs the choir at school.'

'Wait, you're in the school choir?' Bonnie asks. 'You didn't say anything.'

'I know . . . Look, the thing is, the audition is in London and I need to take an adult with me.'

'London?' Bonnie says, her eyes lighting up.

'Yes. At the Royal Academy of Music.'

'Would we have time to do some shopping?'

'I don't know. Maybe. Does that mean you'll come?'

'Well, when is it?'

'That's the thing, it's tomorrow.'

'Tomorrow? Why didn't you ask me before now?'

I hesitate. I don't want Bonnie to know she's literally my last resort.

'I didn't realize until now. It was in the small print.'

She seems to buy it. 'Can we go to Harrods?' she asks eagerly.

'Er, sure,' I say, even though I have no idea if Harrods is anywhere near the audition venue.

'And Liberty's?'

'If we have time . . .'

'How exciting,' she says. 'I haven't been to London in ages.'

I smile faintly. I should be pleased. I was worried she'd say no, or make me grovel. Instead, though, all I feel a creeping sense of dread.

28

We are halfway to the station when Bonnie announces she's forgotten her purse. On returning to the house, it takes us a full fifteen minutes to find it, my anxiety doubling with every second that passes. I try to keep calm, to trick my body into thinking everything is under control, but by the time we leave the house for the second time, my carefully selected audition outfit is sticking to the fresh film of nervous sweat coating my skin.

We only just make the train. Finally in our seats, I put on my headphones in an effort to mask the squelching sound of Bonnie applying handcream and look out of the window, the countryside rushing past me in a blur of sludgy browns and dingy greens.

Bonnie keeps glancing over at me. I pretend not to notice, worried if I make eye contact she'll ignite my annoyance. After the stressful start, I'm more determined than ever for the rest of the day to go smoothly.

After a few minutes, Bonnie taps me on the arm. Reluctantly, I remove my headphones.

'I'm going to get a coffee from the buffet car. Want anything?'

'No thanks.'

Bonnie shrugs as if to say 'suit yourself' and pushes herself up out of her seat. She returns a few minutes later with a cup of coffee and a packet of shortbread. 'Want one?' she asks, removing the lid from her coffee and dipping in one of the biscuits.

I shake my head, put my headphones back on, close my eyes and try to focus on my audition material and the day ahead.

I'm murmuring the lyrics of my second piece under my breath when I feel hot liquid on my leg. My eyes fly open in shock as I yelp with pain. Next to me, what's left of Bonnie's coffee is dripping off the edge of her tray table.

'It wasn't my fault,' she cries, grabbing a napkin and dabbing uselessly at my coffee-soaked jeans. 'Some bloke knocked my arm. See, up ahead, the one with the denim jacket and the stupid big bag.'

'Why did you take the lid off in the first place?' I snap, snatching the napkin from her hand.

'You can't dunk with the lid on,' Bonnie says in a sulky voice. 'I mean, how was I to know he was about to come barging past? I bet once they're dry you won't even notice,' she adds.

I don't want to hear it. I put my headphones back on and turn towards the window. 'Don't talk to me until we get to

London,' I say.

I angle my body away from her, rest my head against the window and shut my eyes. Wide awake, I stay like that for the rest of the journey.

We arrive into St Pancras station at 1.30 p.m., a full hour and a half before my audition slot.

The audition venue is the Royal Academy of Music. 'We need to get the Hammersmith and City line to Baker Street,' I say once we've passed through the ticket barriers.

'What about lunch?' Bonnie asks.

'I made sandwiches, remember,' I say.

'Oh, it's too cold for sandwiches,' Bonnie says with a theatrical shiver. 'Let's get something hot here first. Your audition isn't for ages. Ooh, how about some pasta? That'll warm us up. I'll eat quickly, I promise.'

'No, Bonnie,' I say.

'It'll be my treat!'

'I said no.'

'But it's a special day.'

I don't say anything.

'Please, Ro,' she adds, pulling on my sleeve. 'I want to make up for this morning.'

'If you're that desperate for pasta, we can get some afterwards.'

'No! We're going to Harrods and Paperchase afterwards, remember? Oh, please, Ro. You can have anything you want, anything at all.'

'But I don't want anything.'

'Don't be daft, you must be starving! Now, come on,

you'll thank me for it, I promise.' She's tugging at my arm now, like a toddler begging for ice cream.

'Oh my God, OK!' I cry, shaking her off.

She beams.

'We'll have to be quick though. I mean it, Bonnie.'

'Of course we will!' she says happily.

The station's branch of Carluccio's is stupidly busy. The front of house manager greets us with a fixed smile and leads us to a table at the back of the restaurant where we're forgotten for a full ten minutes. But Bonnie is still dithering over the menu when our waiter finally appears, full of apologies for the delay.

Bonnie proceeds to ask him a series of questions about both the linguine *and* the lasagne before opting for the seafood spaghetti, one of the most expensive items on the menu. My nerves jangle with every word that falls out of her mouth. *What happened to her promise to be quick?*

'And for you?' the waiter asks, turning to me.

'Nothing, thank you,' I say, handing him my menu.

'What?' Bonnie cries.

'I'm not hungry. I'll just have a sandwich later.'

The stress of the morning combined with my growing audition nerves has tied my stomach in knots. The idea of adding a heaping bowl of pasta is unthinkable.

'Don't be so silly,' Bonnie says. She turns to the waiter. 'She'll have a margherita pizza.'

When it arrives, I manage to force down a single slice, my legs tremoring under the table as Bonnie lingers over her seafood spaghetti, taking at least twenty seconds to wind each mouthful around her fork, giggling every time the strands slip back into the bowl.

'I thought you were going to be quick,' I say, my voice shaking with mounting trepidation.

'Relax, we've still got plenty of time,' Bonnie replies.

I check my phone. Technically, she's right. The tube journey should only take five minutes and there's still an hour until my slot. But when I planned out the day, I'd imagined being at the audition venue by now, warming up in a quiet corner. Not in the world's noisiest branch of Carluccio's, my heart rate soaring with every minute that passes.

Bonnie finally declares herself full, resting her hands on her belly as the waiter collects our plates.

'Can we get the bill please?' I ask.

'No dessert? Coffee?'

'No,' I yelp before Bonnie gets any ideas.

The waiter returns in what feels like an eternity later with the card machine. I already have my coat on so we can make a swift getaway the second he gives us our receipt. Bonnie takes an age to find her bank card, handing it over with a girlish giggle that would make me want to crawl under the table were I not so stressed about the time.

When the waiter places the card on the sensor, it responds with a dull bleep.

'Ah, I'm afraid the payment didn't go through,' he says.

I throw Bonnie a panicked look but she doesn't appear to notice, humming as she pulls a second card from her bulging purse. It produces the same heart-stopping bleep.

'How odd,' Bonnie says. 'How much is the bill again?'

The waiter recites the total. 'Excluding service charge,' he adds with a tight smile.

I grab my purse, searching through it with trembling fingers.

'I have ten pounds,' I say. 'What cash do you have?'

Bonnie laughs. 'Oh, you know me, Ro, I never carry cash. I'm like the Queen!' She flashes the waiter one of her very best smiles. 'I'll just pop to the cashpoint. Be right back.'

As Bonnie makes her way out of the restaurant, I check the time. Fifty minutes to go. I do the maths. Even if we don't board the tube for another ten minutes, I'll still arrive over half an hour early. It does little to quell my growing ease though.

Nothing will until I'm there.

Another five minutes pass. Where on earth is she? The nearest cashpoint can't be that far away, surely.

My phone buzzes. It's a text from Bonnie. I leap on it.

I'm overdrawn! You're going to have a make a run for it. I'll see you in Paperchase xx

My eyes bulge. Is she actually serious? I call her number. No answer.

I scan the restaurant for the waiter. He's busy setting up a high chair for a family who have just arrived, his back to me. The rest of the staff members are equally preoccupied, taking orders or delivering food. My heart hammering, I pull up the furry hood on my coat and walk briskly through the restaurant.

The second I fall out onto the station concourse, I break into a run, dodging tourists and school groups and people recording videos of an elderly man playing 'The Entertainer' on one of the station's upright public pianos.

As promised, Bonnie is in Paperchase, looking at the greetings cards.

'Oh hello,' she says casually. 'I was wondering where you'd got to.'

'Are you actually kidding me?' I ask, my chest heaving up and down, partly from physical exertion, partly from red-hot anger.

Bonnie blinks, her eyes as wide as saucers. 'Excuse me?'

How dare she act the innocent right now? How dare *she?*

'I just ran out of a restaurant without paying and you're shopping?' I splutter.

Bonnie holds the clutch of cards in her hands to her chest. The one facing out has an image of two pretzels on it – one the knotted sort, the other a stick. There's a speech bubble floating above the pretzel stick's head – 'Why does everything have to be so complicated?' I want to throw it on the floor and stamp on it.

Instead, I snatch the lot from her hands and shove them back on the rack.

'Hey, I was going to buy those!' Bonnie says.

'What with? I thought you had no cash?' I snap. The sales assistant is looking at us. I grab Bonnie by the wrist and yank her towards the door.

'You're hurting me,' Bonnie cries.

I let go, and begin to march towards the Underground entrance, Bonnie's high-heeled boots clip-clopping against the tiled floor as she scurries to keep up.

'You're being daft,' she says. 'It's hardly the crime of the century!'

'What if they'd caught me leaving?' I demand. 'They could have called the police. They still might.'

'Over a seafood spaghetti and a margherita pizza? Don't be silly—'

Bonnie's words are suddenly drowned out by a fuzzy tannoy announcement:

'Due to a security alert, this station has been temporarily closed. No Underground trains will be stopping at King's Cross St Pancras. Please use alternative routes to complete your journey.'

There's a collective groan from everyone heading in our direction.

I swear under my breath. We're cutting it fine now. Too fine. Fresh panic forms in my belly.

'Come on,' I say, turning on my heel and heading for the exit.

Outside the station, the queues at the bus stops are epic.

'We're going to have to walk,' I say, pulling out the map included with the audition letter and tracing our route.

'But my boots are starting to rub,' Bonnie says.

'So why did you wear them?' I yell, losing my patience.

'Don't shout at me!' Bonnie cries, her hands over her ears.

'Oh, just come on,' I cry.

After the artificial lighting in the station, the daylight makes me squint. The roads are busy, cars and taxis and red buses and motorcycles roaring past, the heat from their engines warm against my cheeks, hordes of tourists and office workers clogging up the pavements. Bonnie hobbles behind me. I block out her complaints about her feet and try to focus.

We should cross over so we're on the right side of the road. I stop at a set of traffic lights and press the button before turning to make sure Bonnie has noticed I've stopped.

But Bonnie is nowhere to be seen.

My body swells with panic. The last time I looked, Bonnie was maybe ten paces behind me, fifteen at the most.

I retrace my steps, fighting against the flow of the pedestrians. The sun is in my eyes, flashes of white obscuring my vision.

No Bonnie. I feel sick. She couldn't have just vanished into thin air.

Could she?

I'm digging out my phone when I hear someone calling my name. I whirl around.

Bonnie is standing in the doorway of a fried chicken shop, one of her boots in her hand, a pained expression on her face.

'What's wrong?' I ask.

'It's my feet,' she wails. 'Look.' She balances on one leg and peels off her sock. The back of her heel is bright red, the exposed skin raw and shiny.

'I can't take another step,' she says. 'I'm in agony!'

'Maybe we could swap.'

The moment the suggestion leaves my mouth, I know it's ridiculous. My feet are at least two sizes bigger than Bonnie's. There's no way I can squeeze my feet into her ridiculous boots with their impossibly pointy toes.

'What if I get you some plasters?' I say, desperately trying not to get angry. 'Would that help?'

'I don't know. Maybe.'

'Wait here.'

And for the third time that day, I break into a run.

I'm at the front of the queue in Boots when I reach into my bag and realize my purse is missing.

'Just one second,' I say to the sales assistant, my heartbeat accelerating as I search.

No purse.

Panic building, I empty the contents of my bag on the floor to a chorus of tuts from the people queuing behind me. The sight of my sheet music for the audition I'm now bound to be late for makes my stomach clench.

I gather up my stuff, apologize, and dart out of the shop, leaving the box of plasters on the counter.

I must have left my purse in Carluccio's. As I run, I try to remember whether there was any ID inside it. Does my library card have my name on it? I can't remember. My brain feels like scrambled eggs.

Bonnie is where I left her, her foot back in her boot.

'Where are the plasters?' she asks when she realizes I'm empty-handed.

I let out an animalistic howl of frustration that shocks us both.

'What's wrong?' Bonnie asks.

'I left my purse in the restaurant.'

'Was there any ID in there?' Bonnie asks, genuine worry passing across her face for the first time that day.

'You're unbelievable,' I cry, pulling out my phone to check the time. It's nearly three o'clock and we're still over a mile away from the audition venue. 'I'm going to be late,' I say, tears of desperation brimming in my eyes.

All I want right now is for Bonnie to step up and take control of the situation; to make everything better, the way parents are supposed to.

But of course she doesn't.

She couldn't even if she wanted to.

A packed bus rushes past.

'Can you at least get to the bus stop?' I ask, pointing at the bus stop in the distance.

Bonnie takes an experimental step and yelps with pain.

'I'm going to have to go on my own,' I say.

'But I thought I had to be there?'

'I'll have to think of something, won't I? You wait here.'

I turn my back on Bonnie and break into a sprint.

By the time I reach the Royal Academy of Music, my calves and lungs are on fire and sweat mingled with tears is pouring down my face. I pound up the steps and into the foyer, flinging myself at the first official-looking person I see, a short woman with cropped blonde hair.

'Can I help you?' she asks, frowning at my dishevelled appearance.

'I've got an audition,' I say, panting. 'But I'm late.'

'What's your name?'

'Ro. Ro Snow.'

She consults her clipboard. 'I'm afraid the time slots are very strict,' she says. 'That's why we recommend you aim to arrive at least half an hour early.'

Do you think I don't know that? If it wasn't for my disaster of a mother I'd have been here with an hour to spare.

'Please,' I gasp. 'You don't understand what I've had to do to get here.'

She sighs. 'Let me see what I can do.'

I'm far too anxious to take in my impressive surroundings, shifting from foot to foot as I wait for the woman to come back. When she does, she has another woman with her, also holding a clipboard. She introduces herself as Gina, the choir's senior administrator.

'We're chock-a-block today,' Gina explains. 'But the panel have agreed to see you during their tea break. We'll have to be quick though. If you'll follow me.'

'You mean, now?' I say. 'But I haven't warmed up properly or anything.'

'I'm sorry,' Gina says with an apologetic tilt of the head. 'But, like I said, they're already giving up their tea break to squeeze you in.'

I follow Gina up a grand staircase and down a long corridor, our footsteps echoing off the tiled walls. I'm out of breath and I can feel the hair sticking to the back of my neck, the shirt clinging to my sweaty back. I try to block it all out, to ignore the voice inside my head telling me I'm not ready, but it's impossible: it's too loud, too insistent.

'Wait here one moment,' Gina says, coming to a sudden

stop outside an anonymous white door.

She slips inside, leaving me alone for a moment. I pull out my hairbrush, inspecting my reflection in the tiny mirror embedded into its handle. I look even worse than I feared – pale and tired and stressed and afraid. I pinch my cheeks in an attempt to look a little healthier but it does nothing to detract from the lavender semicircles under my eyes and the deep worry lines that look like they've been etched into my forehead with a scalpel.

I look like the oldest 14-year-old on the planet.

Gina reappears. 'Right, in you go.'

Before I have the chance to collect myself, I'm being ushered into the room, the door closing with a soft click behind me.

Despite the grandness of the building, the audition room is beige and unremarkable. I make my way to the centre of the room and face the panel – the same four people I met in Birmingham. Every muscle in my body feels tense and brittle.

'Ro, it's good to see you again,' the thin man says warmly.

'I'm so sorry I'm late,' I blurt.

The panel wave away my apologies and direct me towards the pianist. He's different to the guy I met in Birmingham. This one has floppy blond hair and looks grumpy and tired, not meeting my eye as I hand over my music.

'Seeing as we're pushed for time, we'll skip the sight-reading and go straight to the pieces, shall we?' one of the women says.

I swallow. I'd hoped I could use the sight-singing portion

of the audition to warm up my voice and calm down a little.

The pianist starts the introduction before I've even had the chance to make my way to the centre of the room.

'I'm not ready!' I want to yelp, but I know I can't.

My first few notes are wafer thin. It's like someone is squeezing me round the middle, forcing out the sound. I try to compensate with the next few notes but I push too hard, my voice cracking painfully. What is happening? I usually feel so in control when I sing, like I'm a braver, better version of myself. Today, I feel like the palest of copies – weak and wobbly and totally out of place. I try to disappear into the song, to lose myself in the lyrics, the way I usually do with so little effort, but I can't escape the stress of the last few hours – Jodie pulling out of coming, the coffee stain on my jeans, being forced to do a runner from the restaurant, Bonnie's stupid boots, my lost purse, and now, the knowledge I'm making a complete mess of this opportunity with every single breath. I was right all along. This choir isn't for me. Mr Milford got it wrong. Just look at me, I'm falling apart.

My voice cracks on another of the big notes, then another. I can feel tears building.

You cannot cry in front of them, Ro. No matter what happens, you cannot cry.

But at the same time, I can't ignore their disappointed faces, and a lone tear manages to escape, rolling determinedly down my cheek. I only hope they can't see it from where they're sitting.

The rest of the song is a blur of mangled lyrics and bumpy

vibrato, the notes falling clumsily from my mouth. When it comes to the end, there's an uncomfortable silence. I want to die. I want to shrivel to the ground, like the Wicked Witch at the end of *The Wizard of Oz*.

'Thank you, Ro,' the woman sitting closest to the door says. 'Just one moment.'

She bows her head towards the others. They lean in. While they aren't looking, I wipe away the path my tear has left on my cheek. In the corner, the pianist is yawning and checking his phone.

The panel looks up in unison, identical smiles of pity on their faces.

'Thanks for coming back to see us, Ro,' the woman says. 'We'll be letting everyone know in the next few weeks.'

'But I have another piece,' I say.

I hate how desperate I sound. I may as well just throw myself at their feet and beg.

The woman hesitates, clearly selecting her next few words with care. 'I think we've heard everything we need for now. But thank you, Ro.'

She says it nicely but you'd have to be an idiot not to understand the meaning. I've blown it and there's no need to prolong the agony, on either side. It's too late – their minds are made up. I, Ro Snow, am not good enough. That first audition was a blip; an anomaly; a one-off. The disappointment is so acute it takes all the strength I have to keep myself upright.

'Well, thank you for taking the time to see me,' I manage in a small voice, my eyes filling with tears.

They continue to smile their kind, bland smiles as I slip out of the room, my head down.

Gina is leaning against the clunky old-fashioned radiator. 'Everything all right?' she asks brightly.

'Yes, thank you,' I whisper.

'I'm so glad they were able to squeeze you in,' Gina says. 'It would have been such a shame to come all this way for nothing.'

29

It's only as the cold hits my cheeks on the steps outside that I realize no one ever asked where my parent or guardian was. I could have got away with coming alone, after all. I imagine an alternative version of the day, one where I arrived an hour early and had lots of time to warm up and the panel's smiles were warm and real. I walk for a few metres before sinking down on the pavement and bursting into hot fat tears of regret and frustration. People stare as they pass but I don't care any more.

After ten minutes, I get up and walk back to the fried chicken shop slowly, my feet dragging on the pavement, every step an effort. When I arrive, the doorway is empty. I look inside, but there are just a couple of teenage boys at the counter.

I check my phone.

In the café across the road! Bxx

The café is old-fashioned with wood panelling and big

glass cases containing elaborate cakes on polished wooden plinths.

Bonnie is sitting at a table at the back, a pair of bright pink crocs on her feet.

'Where did you get those?' I ask in a flat voice.

'The lovely lady who owns this place took pity on me and insisted I have them,' Bonnie says, extending her leg to show them off. 'Have you ever tried a pair? *So* comfy!'

My eyes fall on the empty mug and plate in front of her. The plate has cake crumbs on it. 'How did you pay for that?' I ask.

'I found a twenty in my coat pocket,' Bonnie says cheerfully.

I feel like I've been punched in the stomach.

'So, how was the audition?' Bonnie adds. 'You were very quick. Any good?'

I shake my head.

'Oh well, that's show business for you – you win some you lose some,' Bonnie says. 'Now, what time is the train back? Do we have time for another bit of cake before we pop to Harrods? The Black Forest gâteau was delicious.'

She licks her lips. I just stare at her. After a few seconds, her brow furrows as she finally appears to clock the upset carved into my face.

'Oh, no need to be glum,' she says, reaching over and waggling my hand. 'A piece of cake will make everything better. Now where did I put my change . . .' She begins rifling in her bag.

'It all worked out just the way you wanted, didn't it?' I say.

Bonnie glances up and tuts. 'Will you sit down, Ro. It's not very relaxing, you hovering over me like that.'

I stay where I am.

'You did it on purpose, didn't you?' I say.

'What *are* you talking about?' Bonnie asks with a nervous laugh.

'All of this. Being slow this morning, and making us go for pasta, and wearing those stupid boots. I think you wanted to mess today up for me. You made up your mind the second I told you about it and made it clear it was important to me.'

'Don't be silly,' Bonnie says, emptying her change out of her purse, coins rolling everywhere.

'I never ask you for anything, Bonnie,' I continue, brand-new tears streaming silently down my cheeks. 'And when I finally do, you do everything you can to ruin it.'

'Ro, please . . .'

I keep going, drowning her out. 'Because if it's not's about you, you're not interested. This *mattered* to me, Bonnie,' I say, stabbing my chest with my index finger, my voice shaking with anger. 'And you stamped all over it. And the worst bit is, I don't think you even realize how selfish you've been today. You're so used to playing the part of "Poor Bonnie", I don't think it even crosses your mind what it might be like to be her daughter. Well, I'll tell you. It's the worst thing on earth and I've had enough of it.'

I open up my bag and unzip the side pocket to retrieve our return train tickets. And there it is. My purse. I had it with me this entire time. My hands trembling with fresh fury, I slap one of the tickets down on the table and walk out of the café.

I don't sit in my reserved seat on the train home. It means I have to stand the whole way but I can't bear the thought of sitting next to Bonnie for two minutes, never mind two hours.

I try to read, but it's hard to turn the pages when I have to use my spare hand to hold onto the rail. I can't concentrate anyway, reading the same few paragraphs over and over. Every ten minutes or so, my phone buzzes in my pocket with a call from Bonnie. I cancel every one. There's nothing she can do or say to put this right.

Not this time.

30

Bonnie leaves the house while I'm still in bed, the back door banging shut to herald her departure.

Good.

When we got back to Ostborough last night, I refused to get in the car with her, catching the bus home instead. By the time I got home, she was already holed up in the living room with the TV on, and made no attempts to intercept me as I made my way through the house and up the stairs to bed.

I wonder how long we can go living in the same house without actually seeing each other? I'm fully prepared to find out.

I stay in bed most of the day, dozing and watching nature documentaries on my laptop. It's getting dark when I wake up from my latest nap. I reach for my phone. The screen is filled with text messages from Tanvi.

I told her last night that the audition didn't go very well (understatement of the year) but she refused to believe me, clearly under the impression I'm just being modest. I wish. Every time I think about it, I'm overcome with waves of nausea so strong I'm scared I might puke for real.

I skim the messages. They're all about the party tonight. My phone buzzes with yet another. I open it.

Tanvi: *Where are you??? I thought you were coming over to get ready for the party? I have snacks!!! Xxx*

Ro: *Sorry, I fell asleep.*

Tanvi: *No worries! I'm just glad you're OK (I was starting to worry!). What time are you coming over?*

I look at the time. The original plan was to go over to Tanvi's around five but I'm not sure I can handle all the inevitable questions about the audition and having to pretend I'm excited about the party. All I want to do is climb back under my duvet and forget yesterday ever happened.

R: *I've kind of got some stuff I need to do first. How about I meet you there?*

T: *WHAAAAAAAAT? I can't turn up alone!*

R: *I'll meet you outside then.*

T: *SAD TIMES :(:(. But I thought we were going to get ready together? I made a special playlist and everything!*

R: *Sorry, dude. Mum stuff, you know . . .*

I catch sight of myself in the mirror. I look awful, my face blotchy and creased from a day under the duvet.

T: *OMG, are you OK? Can I do anything to help? Can we pick you up at least?*

R: *No. I'll see you there at 7. Gotta go . . .*

I toss my phone on my bedside table and get back into bed.

*

Tanvi's dad's car is parked outside Jack's house when I arrive shortly after 7 p.m. The second Tanvi spots me, she leaps out and chucks her arms around me.

'OMG, I missed you so much!' she cries.

I know this is my cue to say I missed her too, but even though it's true (or at least it was), I can't quite bring myself to say it out loud.

'I like your make-up,' I say instead. 'Did Prisha do it?'

Tanvi looks exactly like she's from the musical *Cats*.

'Yes,' she says. 'If you'd come over, she would have probably done yours too.'

'Yeah, sorry about that.'

'Is everything OK? With your mum, I mean.' Her eyes are wide with concern.

'Yeah, fine,' I say, shifting from foot to foot. 'It was just hard for me to get away. Look, shall we go in? I'm freezing.'

Tanvi's dad honks his horn. 'I'll be back in this exact spot at ten thirty on the dot,' he says, poking his head out of the open window.

'But that's so early,' Tanvi whines. 'By the time we've gone in and taken our coats off, it'll be time to put them back on and come home again.'

'Ten thirty, *bachcha*, take it or leave it.'

'Fine,' Tanvi grumbles, kissing him on the cheek. 'I still can't get over the fact my dad rang Jack's mum up and asked how many adults would be "on duty",' she says as we make our way up the pumpkin-lined driveway. '*So* embarrassing.'

Neither Bonnie nor Dad has a clue where I am tonight. Bonnie was getting ready to go out when I left and Dad is still in France. Until I met Tanvi and her parents, it didn't bother me so much.

'Are you OK?' Tanvi asks. 'You don't quite seem yourself.'

'I'm fine.'

'Is it the audition?'

'No.'

'Are you *sure* it didn't go well?' Tanvi asks.

I sigh. 'I'm sure.'

'How do you know? What did they say?'

'I just know, OK?' I snap, irritation bubbling.

'Well, you don't know anything for sure until you get the results letter,' Tanvi says cheerfully.

Tonight, Tanvi's unfailing optimism feels almost unbearable. She's about to say something else but her words are swallowed by a sneeze.

'Bless you,' I say.

'Thanks,' Tanvi replies, wiggling her nose. 'I haven't messed up my make-up, have I? Prisha spent ages on it.'

'No. It's perfect,' I say truthfully.

Jack's front door is ajar. Inside, it's fully decked out for Halloween with black and orange balloons and streamers, cardboard skeletons dangling from the ceilings and fake cobwebs masking the doorways and winding up the bannister. A large doll dressed up as a witch is slumped at the top of the stairs. As we pass, it lets out a tinny cackle.

Tanvi shrieks in delight. 'This is so cool!' she squeals, clutching my arm.

We remove our coats and dump them on the bed in Jack's parents' bedroom.

'Ta-da!' Tanvi says, showing off her cat costume in full. With her fluffy tail and felt ears, she looks ridiculously cute.

'Where's your costume?' she asks.

'This is it,' I reply, gesturing down at my outfit. I'm dressed head to toe in black.

'But I thought you were coming as a witch?'

'I am a witch. A very discreet one.'

'Wait here,' she says, zipping out of the room.

She returns ten seconds later with a witch's hat and cloak. 'Borrowed from our little witchy friend on the landing,' she says, grinning.

'I'm fine like this,' I say, taking a step backwards. I'm not remotely in the mood for dressing up.

'But you'll literally be the only person not in costume.'

She makes a point. The last thing I want to do tonight is stand out.

'OK, fine,' I say with an impatient sigh. 'Witch me up.'

Tanvi grins and fastens the cloak around my neck, while I force the too-small hat on over my frizzy hair.

'Much better!' she declares.

I glance in the mirror. My stern face glares back at me. I need to snap out of it, but I don't know how.

'Do you think Emerson is already here?' Tanvi asks as we head out onto the landing.

'Who am I? A mind-reader?' I snap. Tanvi's eyes widen. 'Sorry,' I mutter. 'It was just a dumb question.'

'Are you *sure* you're OK?' Tanvi asks, tilting her head to one side.

Cue a whoosh of impatience. 'Oh my God, I told you I was, didn't I?'

Tanvi takes a tiny step backwards. 'OK, OK,' she says, holding up her hands in surrender. 'I was just asking.'

I tug at the cape. Tanvi has tied it too tightly around my neck.

'Come on, let's get a drink,' she says, taking my hand and gently leading me down the stairs.

'What can I get you?' Jack's mum asks as we enter the kitchen. Dressed as Morticia Addams in a slinky black dress and long black wig, she's standing guard over the alcohol supply. 'Beer? Cider? Fruity wine? Just one each now.'

'Do you have any Coke or lemonade or anything?' Tanvi asks.

'Of course,' Jack's mum replies, pointing to a selection of soft drinks further along the counter. 'Help yourself.'

As Tanvi reaches for a bottle of lemonade, I pick up a can of cider.

'I didn't know you drank,' Tanvi says, pouring a glug of lemonade into a flimsy plastic cup.

'You don't know everything about me,' I say, opening my can.

'OK,' Tanvi says uncertainly. 'Um, cheers then. To Halloween.'

'To Halloween,' I echo, pressing my can against Tanvi's cup and taking a sip. It's fizzier than I was anticipating, the bubbles tickling my nostrils.

Tanvi sneezes again, lemonade sloshing over the rim of her cup.

'Bless me,' she says, wiping her wet hand on her leggings. 'C'mon, let's go explore.'

I take another sip of cider and follow.

We've barely taken two steps when Tanvi is accosted by Georgia and Zahra. Like Tanvi, they're dressed as cats, but of the 'sexy' variety, their ears and tails teamed with fishnet tights and high heels that make them totter on the spot.

'Tanvi!' Georgia cries. 'You look sooooooo cute!'

Thanks!' Tanvi says happily.

She's stopped a further three times before we even reach the living room. Everyone seems delighted to see Tanvi, dishing out compliments for her costume and hair and make-up and telling her how 'cute' and 'adorable' she looks, like she's their plucky little mascot, to be praised and preened and patted on the head. And in return she grins and giggles and makes easy small talk. She manages to make it look so easy. The whole time, I keep waiting for her to sneak a conspiratorial eye roll in my direction, but I may as well be invisible for all the attention she's paying me. I take another gulp of cider. The first few mouthfuls were kind of gross, but I'm starting to get used to it now, the can quickly growing lighter in my hand.

We're about to enter the living room when Marissa bursts through the front door dressed as a zombie cheerleader, shrieking Tanvi's name at the top of her voice.

'I'm going to go to the loo,' I say, stepping aside just in time for Marissa to throw herself into Tanvi's arms.

I duck into the downstairs toilet and lock the door behind me. Sitting on the lowered toilet seat, I finish off my can of cider, and wonder how long I can realistically hide out here before anyone notices I'm missing. It's not like Tanvi needs me or anything – the past ten minutes have made that quite clear. I felt more like her grumpy bodyguard than her friend just now. I check the time. Still over three hours until my lift home.

The door handle starts to rattle.

'Hang on!' I call, standing up.

I leave the bathroom and head back to the kitchen. Jack's mum doesn't seem to recognize me, letting me help myself to a second can, no questions asked. I open it and go into the living room to look for Tanvi. 'Thriller' by Michael Jackson is blasting from the speakers and even though it's still early, almost everyone is dancing.

I make my way around the edge of the room, holding my cider close to my chest as I try to spot Tanvi in the crowd.

I clamber up on a chair for a better view. From my new vantage point, I zone in on Tanvi almost immediately. She's right in the middle of the throng, perfectly executing the dance moves from the 'Thriller' video, every step crisp and sharp. I suddenly understood why Tanvi had been so keen to play *Just Dance* on the PlayStation at the Diwali party – she's a really, really good dancer. A circle begins to form around her as people attempt to mirror her moves with varying degrees of success.

When the song comes to an end, the crowd bursts into wild applause. Someone starts chanting 'Go, Tanvi, go, Tanvi!' and within seconds the whole room has joined in. Tanvi laps it up, launching into the running man, pumping her arms and legs in time with the chanting, the noise building to a crescendo.

Tanvi spots me and waves. 'Come dance!' she yells over the delighted roar of the crowd as the introduction to 'Disturbia' by Rihanna kicks in.

I shake my head furiously. I don't dance and have no intention of starting now.

Tanvi presses her hands together in prayer position and flutters her eyelashes. The chorus saves me, kicking in before I can respond. I watch as Tanvi gets lost in the music, grinding and writhing in a way that manages to look both alien and totally natural at the exact same time. Various boys take it in turns to dance near her, their clumsy attempts to replicate her moves only emphasizing just how good a dancer she is.

I notice Emerson hovering by the fireplace, his eyes fixed on Tanvi. He puts down his drink and edges towards her, his face nervous yet determined. When he taps her on the shoulder, Tanvi whirls round and breaks into a smile so dazzling it could probably power the national grid.

Tanvi is the undisputed star of the party. She doesn't need a wingwoman; she doesn't need me to be here one bit.

As Tanvi and Emerson begin to dance, someone bangs into the chair I'm standing on. I choose to jump before I fall but misjudge the distance, my legs somehow managing to get tangled in the legs of the chair. I end up sprawled on the carpet, the chair wrapped round my ankles, my can of cider rolling out of reach, golden liquid fizzing on the carpet.

'You OK?'

I look up. Jamie's upside-down face is peering down at me, a blood-splattered surgical mask covering his mouth. He reaches out his hand. Reluctantly, I take it and let him pull me to my feet, dropping it the moment I'm vertical.

'I'll get you a new drink,' he says. 'Be right back.'

I wait until he's left the room before darting into the hallway. I try the door to the downstairs loo but it's locked and the main bathroom upstairs has been designated 'out of bounds'.

Out of hiding places, I huddle on the stairs, watching through the bannisters as the party unfolds below. Tanvi and Emerson have migrated to the sofa where they're deep in animated conversation.

God, I wish Noah was here. I wonder if he's having an OK time with his dad. I texted him earlier to ask how they were getting on, but he hasn't replied yet. I take out my phone and am in the middle of composing a message when a voice makes me jump.

'There you are.' Jamie is standing at the bottom of the stairs holding a drink in each fist. I swallow as he comes and sits down next to me, pressing one of the plastic cups into my hand.

'What is it?' I ask.

He lowers his mask. 'Voddy and coke,' he replies. 'Cheers.'

'Cheers,' I murmur.

Jamie downs his drink in one gulp. I sniff mine before taking a sip. It's horrible, like Coke gone rotten.

'I'm sorry, by the way,' Jamie says, wiping his mouth on his sleeve.

'Sorry?' I repeat.

'Yeah,' Jamie says, crushing his cup with his fist. 'The last time we talked, I think I acted like a bit of a dickhead.'

'It's fine,' I say. Because what else can I say? The last thing I want is for him to think it was a big deal.

'Honestly?' Jamie asks.

I'm surprised by how earnest he looks. 'Jamie, it was ages ago,' I say. 'I can't believe you even remember it.'

I'm shocked over how cool I sound. It's like I've been body-snatched.

'Oh, OK,' Jamie says. 'Well, that's good then.'

There's a pause. The fake blood on Jamie's hospital scrubs smells sweet and sugary. It makes me want to gag a little.

'You come on your own?' he asks.

'No, with Tanvi.'

'That girl who was dancing just now?'

'That's the one.'

'Why weren't you dancing too?'

'I don't dance.'

'What, ever?'

'Nope.'

'Not even if your life depended on it?'

'Even then.'

'Hardcore.'

We're interrupted by Ethan Beard yelling Jamie's name. 'You coming or what?' he calls from the bottom of the stairs.

'Just getting my stuff,' Jamie calls back, standing up.

'OK. Well, we'll be outside.'

'You want to come?' Jamie asks, standing up.

'Where?' I ask, taking another sip of my drink. Unlike the cider, it's not growing on me one bit and I have to force it down.

'Trick or treating,' Jamie replies.

'Isn't that for little kids?'

'Not the way we do it.'

'Nah, you're all right, thanks.'

'Oh, go on, it'll be a laugh. I mean, what you gonna do otherwise?' he says, nudging my calf with foot.

I glance through the bannisters. Tanvi and Emerson are still on the sofa. Tanvi's legs are draped over Emerson's and he's stroking her bare ankle. What was it she said? I had to come tonight because 'we're a team'? Some team. I could probably set myself on fire right now and Tanvi wouldn't notice.

I pick up my drink, down it in one and turn back to Jamie. 'Go on then.'

After all, what have I got to lose?

31

Five minutes later, Jamie and I join Ethan and six other kids from our year on the driveway – Ryan Attah, Max O'Brien, Jacob Shapiro, Andrew Seal, Sienna Blake and Cassie Harris.

Popular kids. The sort I usually go out of my way to avoid.

I'm surprised at how wobbly I feel. It can't be the drink, can it? All I've had is a bit of cider and that tiny cup of something and Coke.

'What's she doing here?' Ethan demands.

'I said she could come along,' Jamie says, puffing out his chest.

Ethan's eyes narrow as he looks me up and down. 'Fine,' he says. 'She'll have to share your supplies though.'

'No problem,' Jamie agrees.

'Supplies?' I ask.

Sienna makes a big show of rolling her eyes.

'Yeah,' Jamie says. 'You know, loo roll, flour, eggs . . .'

'Oh, right,' I murmur, trying to style it out. 'Course.' I've never been trick or treating before – yet another childhood rite of passage I missed out on.

'Right,' Ethan says. 'So, here's the plan.'

We huddle around him.

'We're gonna start at Bagshot's house—'

'Are you *sure* he's out?' Sienna interrupts. 'Because I'm not going anywhere near the place if there's a chance he's gonna be at home.'

'I told you,' Ethan says. 'He plays bridge on Friday nights. My gran belongs to the same club and she reckons he's not missed a session in like twenty years.'

'You better be right,' Sienna says darkly.

'Where after that?' Andrew asks.

'Paige's house,' Sienna says.

I frown. Paige is at the party. I saw her dancing a bit ago, dressed as an angel complete with white feathery wings and a silver tinsel halo. Why would Sienna want to egg and flour her house? They're mates.

'What did she do again?' Max asks.

'Are you joking me?' Sienna demands, her hands on her hips. 'She got off with Theo while I was at my great-nana's funeral.'

'*And* she tried to deny it,' Cassie chimes in. 'Even though half the year saw her sucking his face off at the ice rink.'

'Who's after that?' Andrew asks.

'Who do you think?' Sienna says. 'Theo, of course.'

Everyone creases up laughing. Apart from me. I'm still trying to figure out exactly what's going on.

'OK, everyone take one of these. I'll tell you when to put them on,' Ethan says, distributing a stack of cardboard masks. They're all of different celebrities – Simon Cowell and Prince Harry and Beyoncé. I'm given a Meghan Markle one.

We set off through the dark streets.

'Call me crazy,' I say, falling into step with Jamie. 'But this doesn't seem like traditional trick or treating. It sounds like we're just trashing people's houses.'

I hate how nervous I sound, the cool girl from earlier nowhere to be seen.

'Nah,' Jamie replies. 'It's just a bit of fun. And it's not like they don't deserve it. That's the whole point. Payback.'

'Oh, right,' I murmur, trying to block out the growing sense of unease in my belly.

'Here,' Jamie says, producing a two-litre plastic bottle from his backpack and passing it to me. 'You'll feel a bit better once you've had some of this.'

'What's in it?' I ask, peering at the brownish liquid sloshing around in the bottle, its label (Sprite Zero) bearing no resemblance to the sludgy contents.

'All the good stuff,' Jamie replies.

Desperate to let my inner cool girl out again, I murmur, 'Cool, my favourite,' and take a massive swig.

Mr Bagshot's is a large detached house near the leisure centre. We congregate on the pavement opposite and put on our masks. Mine is too big and keeps slipping down my face.

'The lights just came on!' Sienna shrieks, pointing up at the windows.

She's right. Mr Bagshot's house is suddenly lit up like a Christmas tree.

Ethan checks his watch. 'Nine o'clock, bang on,' he says. 'I bet the lights are on a timer.'

Sienna frowns.

Ethan sighs and grips her by the shoulders. 'Trust me, Senn,' he says.

'If you're wrong, I will literally kill you,' Sienna replies.

'Everyone know what they've got to do?' Ethan asks as I try to adjust the elastic on my mask.

The others nod.

'OK then. Let's do this. Time for 'ol Bagashit to finally get what's been coming to him.'

Five minutes later, we're running down the middle of the street, the soles of our shoes slapping against the tarmac. Ethan is hammering his fists against his chest like Tarzan, Jacob is riding on Jamie's shoulders, and Sienna and Cassie are skipping hand-in-hand, squealing at the tops of their voices. Everyone is hollering and whooping and laughing.

Including me.

I was hesitant at first, hanging back as the rest of the group started their assault on Mr Bagshot's house.

It was Jamie who intervened. 'Come on, Ro Snow,' he said. 'What you waiting for?'

The egg left my hand before I had time to think, smashing hard against Mr Bagshot's living-room window. As it exploded, instead of fear or nerves or guilt, I felt a weird rush of satisfaction I hadn't been expecting.

The same thing happens at Paige's house. I've spent so

long feeling scared, of hiding myself away – being on the other side for once feels good.

More than good.

It feels kind of great.

'Where next?' Ethan asks as Jamie's bottle is passed around the group. 'I reckon we've got enough supplies for one more house. We need to end on a high.'

I check the time. It's flown. Tanvi's dad is due to pick us up in just forty minutes.

'I thought we were doing Theo's?' Max says.

'Too far,' Ethan says. 'And way too obvious.'

'Ms Cameron's place?' Andrew suggests.

'Nah. If she recognized any of us we'd get crucified,' Cassie says. 'You know what she's like.'

A few more names are thrown into the mix, but every one is dismissed as being either too far away or too risky or not deserving enough to be the grand finale of the night.

'Hey, you,' Ethan says. 'Quiet girl. Any ideas?'

It takes me a moment to realize he's talking to me.

For a split second, I consider offering up Dad's house.

'No, sorry,' I say, swaying slightly and knocking into Sienna.

'Uh-oh, someone's wasted!' she says in a singsong voice.

Wait, is she talking about me?

'Maybe we should just quit while we're ahead,' Cassie says. 'My boots are killing me.'

As everyone begins to talk at once, I realize I desperately don't want to go back. Not yet. That's why I'm relieved when Jamie shouts, 'Hey, hey, I've got the perfect place.'

'Where?' Sienna demands.

He grins. 'Just you wait and see.'

'Are we nearly there yet?' Cassie whines roughly ten minutes later.

'Yeah, we've been walking for ages, Jamie,' Max adds.

I don't mind. I feel all sort of floppy and woozy, my feet almost moving of their own accord, my body lurching after them like I'm on strings.

'Just a bit further,' Jamie says. 'Right, Ro Snow?'

Is he talking to me?

'Right, Ro Snow,' he repeats.

'Huh?' I say.

'Is it the next left or the one after that?' he asks.

'Is what?'

He laughs. 'What do you think, drunkard? Your street.'

My heart plummets like a drop-tower ride at the funfair.

I cannot believe I've been such an idiot.

I know exactly where Jamie's taking us.

32

We're a few houses away when Ethan lets out a hoot of delight.

'Oh, mate,' he says, clasping Jamie's shoulders from behind. 'You have excelled yourself. This is perfect.'

'Now, that's what I'm talking about!' Ryan adds.

'Oh my God, talk about leaving the best until last!' Cassie chimes in. 'It looks like a freakin' haunted house!'

She and Sienna start jumping up and down like a pair of sugared-up toddlers while the boys slap Jamie on the back and start unloading the last of their supplies on to the pavement.

Jamie turns to face me. 'Amazing! It looks even worse than I remember,' he says, his eyes shining. He frowns. 'You OK?' he asks.

I nod wordlessly, hot with shame and panic as the others continue to crow over the state of the house. I've always known it looks bad, but forced to look at it afresh, through their eyes, I'm horrified by just how accustomed I've grown to its appearance over the years. Cassie was right – it looks *exactly* like a haunted house.

And I have to live there.

The unfairness of it all cuts like a knife.

I never asked to live like this.

This is all Bonnie's fault.

Just like everything is Bonnie's fault.

And as usual, there is nothing I can do about it.

A wave of anger surges through my body.

Jamie places an egg in my shaking hand.

'You wanna do the honours?' he asks. 'After all, I wouldn't have known about this place if it wasn't for you.'

I look down at the egg in my trembling palm, then back at the house.

Even though I know Bonnie is out with a friend tonight, I can't help but picture her inside, merrily 'sorting' through her never-ending piles of rubbish, totally oblivious to the scene unfolding outside. Just like she's totally oblivious to anything that affects me. Just like she was totally oblivious yesterday in London. Just like she was totally oblivious when she gave me scabies. Just like she's totally oblivious every time she hands over her credit card or refuses to part with a receipt or leaves her dirty clothes on the bathroom floor for me to take care of.

Another wave of anger. Bigger and stronger this time.

I throw the egg.

It hits the living-room window with a loud crack, the yolk exploding against the dingy glass.

Jamie lets out a cheer. Within seconds, the air is full of flying eggs and cascading flour. A toilet roll unfurls in a perfect arc. Max and Andrew grab another couple and attack the bushes and climbing ivy. Eggs splatter against the windows and walls. The close range makes them sound like bullets. *Bang, bang, bang.*

I tear about the garden, furious tears running down my face as I hurl anything I can get my hands on. I put my full force behind every throw, crying out with effort. The noises I'm making don't sound like they belong to me. They come from somewhere deep within, somewhere I'm not sure I've ever truly accessed before.

It takes several seconds to realize the others have stopped shouting. Another two or three to realize why.

Bonnie is standing at the corner of the house wearing a pink satin dressing gown and matching slippers, her face shiny with face oil, a mop in her hands. She holds it like a spear, the mop head facing outwards.

But she's not meant to be here. She's supposed to be out. She said she was going out.

'I said, get off my property!' Bonnie is yelling, jabbing the air with her mop.

She advances towards us.

'Are you deaf?' she shouts. 'Go away! The lot of you!'

She scans the group, the fury on her face melting into confusion when she gets to me.

'Ro?' Bonnie says, lowering the mop.

That's when I realize I'm not wearing my mask any more.

I'm dimly aware of the others pooling together on my

left, their frantic whispers full of scandal, indistinct and overlapping.

My body swells with anger and panic and fear all mushed up together.

Bonnie needs to shut up.

Now.

'Go back inside,' I say in a low voice.

Every nerve ending is fizzing, electrified.

'I will *not* go back inside,' Bonnie cries. 'What the hell is going on?'

I can't even begin to answer her.

'Ro, I asked you a question!'

'Please, Bonnie,' I whisper.

I'm desperate now, my eyes begging Bonnie to do as I've asked.

But Bonnie stays where she is.

Ruining everything.

Like she always does.

'Oh my God, just go inside!' I explode.

Bonnie's eyes widen in shock.

'Now!' I scream.

Bonnie flinches before dropping the mop with a clatter and slipping into the shadows.

The group has fallen silent behind me.

'Who *was* that?' Sienna asks. 'Jesus, she wasn't your *mum*, was she?'

I don't answer.

'Oh my God, is this your house?' Sienna cries.

I slowly turn to face them all. They've removed their

masks, their faces contorted with a cocktail of confusion and shock and delighted disgust.

'It is, isn't it?' Sienna continues, the sides of her mouth sagging with revulsion. 'You *live* here.'

I don't say anything.

'Oh my God!' she gasps, bouncing up and down on her toes. 'You just tricked your own house!'

There's an uncomfortable ripple of laughter.

Jamie doesn't join in. He just stares at me, utter bewilderment etched on his blandly good-looking face.

'Is Senn right?' he asks. 'Is this where you live, Ro?'

I feel dizzy. I want to scream, cry, throw up, run away, sink to the ground. Anything but answer his question.

'Of course it is!' Sienna cackles, answering for me. 'Just look at her face!'

Cassie tugs on Sienna's sleeve. 'Shut up now, Senn,' she says quietly.

I'm shaking.

'Go away,' I say, my voice shuddering to match, my breathing raggedy and uneven.

No one moves.

'I said, go away,' I scream, making the group flinch in unison. 'Now!'

By silent mutual agreement, they move away slowly, like motorists rubbernecking as they pass a car wreck. Some of them look away, mortified on my behalf. The rest stare at me, still in shock, apart from Sienna, who just looks disgusted, her lips curled into a sneer. Cassie's face is a little harder to read. As she meets my gaze, her eyes soften and she bites down hard on her lip. I look away. If it's sympathy Cassie is offering, I don't want it.

Jamie is the only one not to move. He blinks rapidly as he looks from me to the house and back again, like it's a riddle he needs to solve.

He takes a step towards me.

'You too, Jamie!' I shout, stopping him in his tracks.

He hesitates.

'I mean it! I want you to go away and never ever come back.'

He swallows hard before turning and jogging after the others.

I stay where I am, rooted to the spot, my head spinning. For a few seconds I can't move, can't think, can't do anything but stay upright.

I force myself to turn back towards the house. A light is shining at number 46.

The master bedroom.

There's a figure at the window. Watching me.

And then just like that, it's gone.

That's when I throw up.

My puke stinks of cider and whatever was in that bottle. Doubled over, I watch as it seeps between the paving slabs.

Coughing, I wipe my face on my sleeve, my eyes stinging with tears, my body throbbing with the shame and fear and shock of it all.

I've dedicated years to keeping my life with Bonnie a secret, and in less than ten minutes all that hard work and effort has become worthless. Because there's no way Sienna and co are going to keep this to themselves. By the end of the party, the whole of Year Ten will know the truth about me. And it won't stop there. It only takes one of them telling a well-meaning parent and . . .

I throw up again.

It's yellow and watery, its stench made worse by the accompanying whiff of eggs.

I try to straighten up but I can't, crouching on the ground instead. My throat is on fire and my breathing is all over the place. I think I'm having a panic attack. I try to calm down, but I can't. I'm such a mess I can't even count to ten.

Water. I need water.

I make it to the outside tap next to the back door. I turn it on and stick my head under the current. The water is icy cold and stings my lips and cheeks.

Once the taste of puke has gone, I struggle back to my feet, fumbling in my pocket for my keys.

I have my fingers on them when the door swings open to reveal Bonnie standing with her hands on her hips. She's wearing a fresh dressing gown. The one she was wearing, its hem soiled with egg, lies on the floor behind her in a silken puddle.

For me to take care of.

Because that's what happens in this house.

Bonnie makes a mess and I either clean it up or learn to tolerate it.

And tomorrow it will be *me* who deals with the mess outside, *me* who scrubs at the eggs and flour on the front door, *me* who wobbles atop a stepladder cleaning the windows and dragging lengths of toilet roll from the roof and bushes. *Me.*

Always *me.*

'What the hell was that?' Bonnie asks as I attempt to squeeze past her.

What? She's mad at me?

I whirl round to face her.

'I asked you a question,' she says. 'What the hell was that, Ro?'

She looks furious. How *dare* she look furious?

My phone buzzes in my pocket. I ignore it.

'Did you bring those people here on purpose?' she asks. 'What on earth is wrong with you, Ro?'

'What's wrong with *me*?' I splutter. 'What's wrong with *you*?'

'Me?' she cries, stabbing her chest with her index finger. 'I'm the victim here!'

Victim? Her? Don't make me laugh.

'You don't get it, do you?' I say, hot tears springing from my eyes. 'This is your fault!'

'My fault?' she cries. 'Our home being trashed is my fault now?'

'Yes! Our house is a joke, Bonnie, a disgusting, filthy joke. No wonder people want to throw stuff at it. It deserves it! *You* deserve it!'

Her mouth opens and closes like a goldfish.

'Do you have any idea how tiring it is?' I ask. 'Keeping this place vaguely liveable? Keeping it a secret? Protecting you?'

'I don't ask you to do it,' Bonnie cries, her face bright red. 'I don't ask you to do anything.'

I let out an angry howl of frustration. 'So, I'm supposed to sit back and leave you to it, am I? Bonnie, if it wasn't for me, this place probably wouldn't even be standing! If it wasn't for me, you'd probably be dead by now, buried under all your useless crap!'

'I'm not having this,' Bonnie says. 'Despite what you think, I'm the parent here, Ro, not you.'

'Then start acting like one!' I roar.

'I'm doing my best!' she shrieks back.

I look around the place – at the stacks of dirty dishes in the sink, the overflowing bin, the piles of crap covering the tables and chairs and floor.

'This is your best?' I say. 'Seriously, Bonnie? *This* is the best you can do?'

Her mouth trembles and for a split second I think she might cry. She catches herself just in time, rolling back her shoulders and jutting out her chin in defiance.

'I won't be spoken to like this,' she says in a tremulous low voice. 'Not in my own house.'

'It's my house too.'

'Well, I'm the one who pays for it.'

I snort. 'Barely, Bonnie.'

She slams her hand down on a pile of newspapers. 'That's it, I've had enough of this.'

'*You've* had enough? Well, now you know how I feel every second I'm stuck under this roof with you.'

We stare at each other, our chests heaving, eyes on fire.

She doesn't get it. She's never going to get it.

I leave the room, stamping over her abandoned dressing gown.

As I thunder up the stairs, I disturb the piles of paper on both sides of me. They teeter for a few seconds before slipping down the stairs, the worn carpet easing their journey – an avalanche of paper.

I let it fall.

33

I wake up before dawn. There are a blissful few seconds before my brain kicks into gear and the memories of last night hit. Unable to bear the assorted scenes flashing through my brain, I force myself out of bed and pull my tracksuit bottoms and hoodie on over my pyjamas.

I creep downstairs, stopping in the kitchen to collect a bucket, a bottle of washing-up liquid and a sponge, before heading out into the dark morning.

I spend the next few hours scrubbing at the doors and walls and windows and paths until I'm satisfied the main traces of the evening's events have been removed. It's cold and miserable work and by the time I'm finished my hands are red and numb. But at least I don't have an audience – my only witnesses, the postman and a couple of people out walking their dogs.

I crawl back into bed shortly after 8 a.m. and, for the first time ever, call in sick.

'God, you sound awful, Ro,' Eric says on the phone. 'You take care of yourself and we'll hopefully see you next week, yeah?'

His kindness only makes me feel worse, silent tears rolling down my cheeks as I hang up.

My phone is full of notifications from Tanvi – text messages and missed calls and voicemails – all of them begging me to get in contact and let her know I'm 'OK'. My stomach churns as I imagine Sienna and co returning to the party and gleefully describing the evening's events in all its gory detail. All my careful hard work, all those years of keeping myself to myself, and for what?

Absolutely nothing.

In the cold light of day, the anger I felt last night has been replaced with something far, far worse. At least anger has a purpose, some fire behind it. Right now, all I feel is numb. Like all I want to do is fall asleep and never wake up. Am I in shock? I don't know.

Amongst the dozens of messages from Tanvi, there's a single photo message from Dad – him, Melanie and Izzy grinning in front of Sleeping Beauty's castle. The caption reads: *Lots of love from the happiest place on Earth! Dad, Mel & Izz xxx*

I stare at it for ages, their happy faces blurring behind a film of tears before I delete it.

I delete all of Tanvi's messages too, then turn off my phone, shove it in the top drawer of my bedside chest and pull the duvet over my head.

When I next wake up, it's midday. Still groggy, I roll my

aching body out of bed. I'm due at Noah's in an hour's time. A big part of me wants to cancel, but I'm worried if I do, it might be Christmas before I see him again.

On autopilot, I shower and dress and venture downstairs, my heart clenching as I pause outside the slightly ajar living-room door. I peer through the gap.

No Bonnie.

My shoulders slump in relief.

I have zero interest in seeing her today.

Or tomorrow for that matter.

In fact, the way I'm feeling right now, I'm pretty certain I don't want to see Bonnie ever again.

At 1 p.m., I knock on Noah's door.

No answer.

I knock again.

Nothing.

I look through the living-room window. No signs of life.

I ring his number. It goes straight through to the answerphone.

I'm halfway through leaving a garbled message when I remember the figure at the window last night. Because it appeared at the master bedroom window, I'd assumed it was Mr Hornby, but what if it wasn't?

Dread creeps up my arms and legs and back as it dawns on me.

It wasn't Mr Hornby that saw me – it was Noah. And now he wants nothing more to do with me.

I realize I've stopped talking. I stab at the 'end call' button and shove it in my back pocket.

My eyes fill with tears. I blink them away.

I head back to the house.

Maybe I'm being silly. Maybe he's just gone out. Maybe he forgot we had plans.

I look frantically around the kitchen. I need a distraction – something, anything to keep my thoughts from consuming me. My eyes fall on the dirty dishes in the sink. I insert the plug and turn on the tap. As the sink fills up with steaming bubbles, I turn on the radio, blasting the volume up to maximum. It makes my brain ache but I don't care.

I'm almost finished when I look up and see a pink woolly hat with a huge pompom on the top passing under the window.

Tanvi.

First comes the disappointment – it's not Noah.

Followed by panic – Tanvi is here, at my back door.

My *actual* back door.

Shaking, I wipe my damp hands on my jogging bottoms and turn off the radio just in time for Tanvi to rap neatly on the glass. I duck down, my back pressed up against the cupboard under the sink, and remain as still as I can. My hands smell of dirty dishwater.

'Ro!' Tanvi calls in a croaky version of her usual singsong voice. 'It's me, Tanvi.'

I can make out her diminutive form, blurry through the frosted glass panel. My heart in my mouth, I begin to crawl towards the hallway. The lino is tacky, my palms sticking to the bubbled plastic.

Tanvi knocks again, more insistently this time. 'I know you're in there, Ro. I saw you washing up just now.'

I stop crawling.

'I'm going to keep knocking until you open up,' Tanvi adds.

I believe her too. After all, this is Tanvi Shah we're talking about. Persistence is her middle name.

Her fingers appear through the letter box, propping it open. 'Please open up, Ro,' she says. 'I'm worried about you.'

But I don't want Tanvi's worry or pity or sympathy. I want her to go away.

I leave the dirty dishes bobbing in the lukewarm water and keep crawling, not stopping until I'm at the foot of the stairs and firmly out of sight. Upstairs, I take out my maths homework and wait for Tanvi to give up and leave.

After about twenty minutes, curiosity gets the better of me and I peek through the gap in the curtains. For a second I think she's gone but then I spot her in the garden below, perched on the edge of Bonnie's rusty sunlounger, her arms clasped around her knees. Dressed in her electric blue duffel coat with its fat red toggles, she's the brightest thing in sight.

It's cold out, windy and damp, the sky grey, the air soupy. The back garden offers a little shelter but not much.

I dismiss the pinprick of guilt before it has the chance to burrow itself any deeper. I'm not forcing Tanvi to wait out there. And I'm certainly not going to invite her in.

If I wait long enough, she'll get bored. Or too cold. Or she'll be summoned home by her parents. Tanvi Shah may be determined, but I'm confident this is just a waiting game – one that I'm going to win.

Ten minutes later, I hear the sound of something being

thrown repeatedly against the wall. I return to the window. Tanvi has found an old tennis ball and is chucking it against the wall, letting it bounce on the patio each time.

Thwack, bounce, *thwack*, bounce.

I'm reaching for my headphones when I hear muffled voices outside, propelling me back to the window.

I press my face against the glass. In the garden below, Tanvi is talking to Bonnie.

No, no, no.

I dive off the bed and down the stairs, reaching the back door just as Bonnie is opening it. I squeeze through the gap, refusing to look at either of them, shame and fury battling for supremacy.

I need to get out of here. Now.

My arms folded across my chest, I stride down the path. My heart drops as Tanvi says a hurried 'goodbye' to Bonnie and scurries after me.

I hesitate on the pavement outside the house, my brain whirring as I try to come up with a plan.

'Where are you going?' Tanvi asks, reaching my side.

'None of your business,' I mutter, crossing the road.

'You're not wearing a coat,' she points out, scampering to keep up with my long strides.

'So?' I say.

'It's freezing.' As if on cue, she sneezes.

'I'm fine,' I say, trying to ignore the cold penetrating my baggy denim shirt.

'Look, can we talk?' she asks. 'I need to know you're OK.'

'I'm OK,' I snap.

'Don't believe you,' she hits back, not missing a beat.

I stop walking and let out a growl of impatience.

'Please, Ro,' Tanvi says, planting herself in front of me. 'Just hear me out. And after that, I promise I'll go away if you want me to.'

I look her in the eyes for the first time since she turned up. They're puffy and swollen, the whites rippled with blood.

'Go on then,' I say.

Tanvi hesitates. 'What, here? Don't you want to go back to yours, or to a café or something?'

What I want is for this to be over with. I look both ways down the street, my eyes resting on the unoccupied bus shelter about ten doors down.

'If you've got something to say, you can say it here,' I say, heading towards it.

She follows me, sitting down on the narrow metal bench, leaving a clear space so I can sit next to her. I ignore it and remain standing up, leaning against the side of the shelter.

She sneezes three times in quick succession. Her sneezes are high-pitched and delicate, like the sort you'd expect from an animated woodland animal.

'Gosh, excuse me,' she says.

I glance over at her as she digs into her pocket for a tissue. She really does look awful, her nose and upper lip area red raw.

A twinge of sympathy in my side.

I block it out.

If Tanvi felt *that* awful, she would be tucked up in bed right now, not here, sticking her nose in where it isn't wanted.

'So, what was it you wanted to say?' I ask as Tanvi stuffs her used tissue up her sleeve.

'Hang on a second,' she says, reaching into her backpack and pulling out a bulging plastic folder.

'What's that?' I ask, frowning. 'Coursework?'

'Uh-uh. I've been reading up,' she replies. 'On hoarding, I mean.'

I flinch at the word. 'What do you mean?' I ask.

'Well, that's what your mum does, isn't it? Hoards stuff?'

There's no point in denying it – Tanvi was literally just outside my back door – but I don't want to confirm it either.

'It's actually really common,' Tanvi says when I don't respond. 'Did you know that? Like, did you have any idea that in Australia over one third of *all* house fires are down to hoarding! *And* they reckon the only continent on earth where there's no hoarding at all is Antarctica and that's only because no one lives there apart from a few scientists and a whole lot of penguins.'

I stare at her. Does she honestly think I don't know this stuff already? That I've never thought to Google it?

'What I'm trying to say,' she continues, 'is that you're not alone. In fact, statistically speaking, there are probably other hoarders in Ostborough.'

She actually seems excited about this. What is she thinking? That we put out an advert? Form a support group? Because if she knew anything about what it's actually like to live with a hoarder, she'd know that people like Bonnie would never attend a support group in a zillion years.

'So other people hoard stuff?' I say. 'So what? That

doesn't help *me*, Tanvi. It doesn't change anything.'

'I'm getting to that,' she says. 'And the thing is, there *is* help out there. For you and your mum. Here, I printed off this list. One second.' She opens the folder and pulls out a sheaf of papers, sifting through them until she finds the one she's looking for.

She hands it to me. It's a list of helplines she's printed from a website called 'Help for Hoarders UK'. It's the same list I've presented to Bonnie more times than I can count: the same list she's happily ignored for years now.

'What's the rest of that stuff?' I ask, pointing at the other papers.

Tanvi hands the lot over. I flick through it. There are pages and pages of information and case studies and advice. She must have been up at the crack of dawn to read this.

Then my eyes fall to the date and time stamp at the bottom of the page. Friday 25 October. Over a week ago.

I can feel my temperature rising.

'I've spoken to my auntie Rina too,' Tanvi continues, oblivious to my discovery. 'Did I mention she's a psychologist? Anyway, she's going to have a chat with her colleagues and see if any of them have some suggestions.'

'You knew,' I say, cutting off the end of her sentence.

She blinks. 'Knew what?'

I point to the bottom of the page.

Tanvi leans in, her cheeks reddening as she realizes her slip-up.

'How long?' I demand.

She bites her lower lip. 'Since Diwali.'

'Diwali?'

'Remember you left your phone in the bedroom?'

I nod.

'Well, when I found it, I thought you might need it so we drove back and I knocked on your door, or at least what I thought was your door, and an old man answered.'

I tip my head backwards and focus on the bus shelter's translucent roof. It's covered with bird poo and head flies.

'He had no idea who I was talking about at first,' Tanvi continues. 'I thought I was going crazy! Then I described you and he told me I was in the wrong place; that I needed to try number 48. So I did.'

'You've known for a week and you didn't say anything?' I ask.

'I wanted to, I really did. But I didn't know how to bring it up without making you feel uncomfortable. I nearly did a few times, but it never felt quite right.'

'You let me lie to your face,' I say.

'I didn't want to embarrass you.'

'So you felt sorry for me?' I snap. 'Is that it?'

'No!' she cries. 'I just wanted you to talk to me about it when *you* were ready. That's why I did all this research, so that when you were up for it, I'd understand and be able to help.'

She's still not getting it.

'But it's not your problem to fix, Tanvi,' I say.

Her forehead crinkles in confusion. 'Of course it is,' she says, reaching for my hand. 'You're my best friend and you need me. We need each other.'

I think back to last night, when Tanvi was cocooned in

her own little world with Emerson. She certainly didn't need me then.

'Could have fooled me,' I say, shaking her off.

'What's that supposed to mean?'

'You literally begged me to go to the party with you and the second we got there, you abandoned me.'

Tanvi's eyes widen. 'Wait – I abandoned *you*? You're the one who full-on disappeared and didn't tell me where you were going. You were gone for hours!'

'The only reason I disappeared was because you went off with Emerson!'

'You disappeared before that too,' Tanvi says. 'When Marissa arrived. One minute you were right there and the next, you were gone.'

'And you were *so* heartbroken you headed straight for the dance floor.'

Tanvi's mouth opens then closes again. 'Look, I'm sorry if I got carried away,' she says. 'But last night was a big deal for me.'

'Well, I'm glad it all worked out for you.'

'Please, don't be like that, Ro. So, we both messed up a bit, there's no point in falling out over it.'

I don't say anything.

Tanvi responds by rifling through that stupid folder again. 'There's this one website that you should definitely look at because it's especially for children of parents who hoard,' she says. 'I only had a quick look, but some of the information looked really helpful.'

'Oh my God, can you just stop!' I cry.

She looks up in surprise.

'Has it not crossed your mind that I've tried all this stuff already?' I ask.

'I, I don't know,' she stammers. 'Listen, I didn't mean to upset you, I was just trying to understand.'

'Well, you can't, OK? You can read as much as you like but you're never ever going to know what it's like living with someone like my mum.'

'So tell me,' Tanvi says. '*Make* me understand.'

But I wouldn't even know where to start. And even if I had the words, I don't think I could say them out loud. It's all too raw, too messy, too shameful.

'I'm a good listener, I promise,' she adds.

'I'm sorry, Tanvi, but I can't.'

'Why not?' she asks, her voice tinged with frustration. 'We're best friends, aren't we?'

I wish she would stop calling us that. It was OK last week, before everything went wrong, but today it just feels suffocating, like I'm being forced into a hole I have no hope of ever fitting into.

'Well, best friends tell each other stuff,' Tanvi continues. 'There's nothing I wouldn't tell you.'

An image of the photo frame next to Tanvi's bed leaps into my head just in time. 'Yeah right,' I say.

'What's that supposed to mean?'

'The girl in the photos?'

'Photos? What photos?' Tanvi asks, blinking her big old bloodshot eyes.

She must think I'm a total idiot.

'The photos all over your bedroom! Don't pretend you don't know what I'm talking about, there's one right next to your bed.'

Tanvi's face falls. Caught red-handed.

'Anna,' she murmurs. 'You're talking about Anna.'

'How am I supposed to know what her name is? You've never even bothered to mention her.'

'If you wanted to know about her, Ro, then why didn't you just ask?'

'Because I'm not like you! I don't go sticking my nose in people's business all the time.'

Tanvi's lip begins to tremble and for a few horrible seconds, I'm scared she might start crying. 'Is that what you think?' she asks. 'That I'm just some kind of busybody?'

'Yes. No. I don't know.' I rub my face. I just want this conversation to be over.

'Well, come on, what is it?'

'You're just always *there*, Tanvi, you know?' I say. 'It's like I can't take a single breath without you popping up and offering me a plate of pancakes or something.'

'I was trying to be nice,' Tanvi rasps, her voice just about clinging on. 'Because that's how friendship works, Ro. You do nice things for each other; you make an effort. You're there when the other person needs you!'

'Well, I don't need you, OK? I don't *need* anyone. And if you're that bothered about *sharing*, then go hang out with your buddy Anna instead! Go make *her* some pancakes.'

'I can't!' Tanvi yells, the sudden fury on her face making her almost unrecognizable.

'Well, why not?' I yell back.

'Because she's dead!'

My mouth drops open.

What?

'What?' I whisper.

'She died just before Christmas. From thyroid cancer.'

Oh God, oh God.

'And the reason I don't mention her is because I still find it really painful to talk about,' Tanvi continues, spitting out her words, tears spilling down her cheeks. 'Maybe I'll be able to one day, but I'm not ready yet, and if you'd actually bothered to ask me about her instead of filling in the blanks for yourself, that's what I would have told you.'

I swallow hard. It didn't even cross my mind that Anna could be a friend Tanvi met in hospital. I feel so stupid.

'But you didn't ask, did you?' Tanvi adds. 'You made up your mind all by yourself.'

My entire body is quivering.

'You're not the only one who has a hard time, you know?' Tanvi says. 'You don't have the monopoly on misery.'

'I never said I did,' I hit back weakly.

'You didn't have to!' Tanvi snaps, her eyes on fire, her anger making her look like a stranger. 'You spend so much time protecting yourself, it doesn't even cross your mind that other people might be struggling too.'

My mouth hangs open uselessly. I have no idea what to say.

'I can't do this any more,' Tanvi says, wiping away her tears with a mittened hand.

'What do you mean?' I ask.

'This,' she says, gesturing at me. 'With you. I'm too tired.'

I open my mouth to say something but no words come out. Tanvi holds my gaze for a couple of seconds, then shakes her head, her eyes full of water and sadness. She puts the folder in her bag and walks away, the pompom on her hat wobbling with every step.

Go after her, a voice inside my head whispers as Tanvi's form grows smaller and smaller.

Apologize.

Explain.

Fix this.

I don't, though.

I just let her go.

34

I spend the rest of Saturday and the whole of Sunday cooped up in my room. Apart from coming upstairs for a shower, Bonnie sticks to the living room, the door firmly shut. My only contact with the outside world is a text from Dad letting me know he's back in the country and that he, Melanie and Izzy had a 'magical time'.

I replay my fight with Tanvi over and over and agonize about all the things I should have said and done. I compose dozens of apologetic messages but fail to press send on any of them. My head feels like a bowl of spaghetti, my thoughts all tangled up. Beyond saying I'm sorry for what I said, I have no idea how to put any of this right. I don't even know if I want to. Perhaps it's better this way, to sever our friendship sooner rather than later. I'm clearly not the person Tanvi thought I was, so maybe there's no point in even trying to salvage it.

*

I knew school was going to be bad, but nothing could have prepared me for the reaction on Monday morning. As I walk to registration, the whispers and nudges race down the corridor like falling dominoes. I can't make out the exact words being uttered, but I can take a pretty good guess at the content – that I'm disgusting, dirty, crazy, messed up. I try to keep my head up high and pretend I'm not rattled, but inside I'm crumbling with every step. I knew there was no way Sienna and the others would keep what happened at my house to themselves, but from what I can work out, the news has spread well beyond Year Ten, kids from Year Seven right up to sixth form openly gawping at me as I make my way to class. And if that many people know, it's only a matter of time before Social Services are sticking their noses in.

I take a sudden right and stumble into the toilets, barging past a bunch of Year Eights trowelling on make-up in front the mirrors, and lock myself in the furthest away cubicle.

I drop to my knees and flush the loo in an attempt to disguise the sound of my retching but nothing comes up. I wish it would – anything to ease the tangle of panic and fear buried deep inside me.

I yank off a wad of toilet paper and use it to soak up the sweat on my face and under my arms. Within seconds, it's a soggy mess in my hands. Using the toilet-paper dispenser as leverage, I pull myself up into standing position and open the cubicle door.

I recoil at my reflection in the mirrors above the sinks. I look exhausted. The concealer I applied less than an hour ago has sweated away, exposing the grey circles under my eyes.

As I wash my hands, I can feel the clown-faced girls watching me.

'Yes?' I snarl. 'Can I help you?'

They all shake their heads frantically, the two-year age gap guaranteeing I have the upper hand. Just.

I shake my wet hands over the sink and leave the room, my stomach still churning despite the fact I've barely eaten a thing since Friday afternoon.

In registration, I'm thrown to discover Tanvi's seat empty. Apart from that first day when she got lost, Tanvi is always early, grinning and waving the moment I enter the room, brimming with news and gossip and silly little anecdotes and a full rundown of what she ate for breakfast.

As I make my way up the aisle, my classmates don't even bother to hide their stares. I do my best to ignore them, fixing my gaze on a spot on the wall and trying to look as blank as possible. It's all an act. By the time I reach my seat, I'm sweating like mad.

As I sit down, Emerson twists round in his seat.

'You haven't seen Tanvi, have you?' he asks, licking his lips nervously.

I shake my head.

'Oh,' he says, looking disappointed. 'Do you reckon she's poorly?'

'How should I know?' I snap.

He frowns. 'You're best mates, aren't you?'

I don't answer him, pulling my backpack onto my lap and pretending to sort through its contents until he gets the message and leaves me alone.

The first lesson of the day is art and I'm dreading it. Jamie, Sienna *and* Cassie are all in my class, and even though Mrs Skinner insists on silence, my insides twist at the thought of being stuck in the same room as them for an hour.

I walk into the classroom to discover a man with a bushy brown beard sitting on Mrs Skinner's desk.

'Where's Miss?' Alice asks.

'She's unwell,' the man replies. 'My name's Mr Bute and I'll be taking the class today.'

As I sit down, Jamie strides into the classroom. I turn away and pretend to be engrossed with the view of the car park, fixing my gaze on a robin hopping from car bonnet to car bonnet.

'Oh hi, Ro,' Sienna says as she squeezes past. 'How's your mum?' She doesn't wait for an answer, bursting into peals of laughter.

'Don't be such a bitch, Senn,' Cassie mutters, pushing after her.

'I want you all to work in pairs,' Mr Bute says once everyone has sat down. 'One of you will draw a portrait of your partner during the first half of the lesson, then on my say-so, you'll swap over. The medium is up to you but no paints, please. I don't want to be here until six cleaning up your mess.' He claps his hands. 'Off you go then, sort yourselves out.'

I glance around the classroom, trying not to look desperate as I attempt to identify someone to work with.

'Anyone without a partner?' Mr Bute asks after a few minutes.

As I raise my hand, I know the entire class is watching.

'And what's your name?' Mr Bute asks.

'Ro,' I say quietly.

'Anyone else?' Mr Bute asks.

No one replies.

'There must be an odd number. You'll have to make a three. Anyone happy for Ro to join their group?'

A suffocating silence falls over the classroom like a vast cloak.

Mr Bute sighs. 'Anyone?'

'As if,' Sienna says from over the other side of the room. 'We don't want to catch something.'

Anger bubbles in my belly, my hands instinctively balling into fists.

'What was that?' Mr Bute asks, frowning.

'Nothing, sir,' Sienna says in a singsong voice. I can practically hear her fluttering her eyelashes.

'Anyone?' Mr Bute says in a bored voice. 'Come along now, before I have to pick.'

'She can join our group, sir.'

I blink, turning with the rest of the class to look in the direction of the volunteer.

Jamie lowers his hand. 'I mean, if she wants to,' he adds, his face turning red.

I stare at him. Is this some kind of joke? Was Friday's

humiliation not enough for him? My fists grow tighter, my fingernails digging into my palms.

Next to Jamie, his partner, a pretty redhead called Alana, doesn't even bother to hide her disgust, her jaw jutting out in silent protest.

'Excellent,' Mr Bute says, totally oblivious. 'Ro, if you'd like to join that group.'

I get up and carry my chair over to where Jamie and Alana are sitting. It's only a few steps, but it feels like a marathon.

'Seeing as there're three of you,' Mr Bute continues. 'One of you is going to have to forego being the subject.'

'I don't mind,' I say quickly.

'Whatever,' Alana mutters, tossing her *Little Mermaid* hair over her shoulder.

She volunteers to sit first, arranging herself sideways on her chair and pouting her lips.

I pick up a piece of charcoal and begin to draw, starting with Alana's eyes. Within seconds, it's clear they're going to be far too big but I don't care, sketching in enormous eyebrows to match. Next to me, I can sense Jamie gearing up to say something, his mouth opening then closing again.

'If you've got something to say, then just say it,' I hiss.

'Sorry?'

I hesitate. His surprise seems genuine.

'I was just going to say that I didn't know,' he says in a low voice.

'About what?'

'About you living, you know, where you live. What I mean is, I didn't go there on purpose.'

'Oh,' I say, my brain aching as I try to decide if this makes things any less hideous.

'Can we cut the chat please?' Mr Bute calls. He's lounging in Mrs Skinner's chair, his feet on her desk, a phone cradled in his palm.

'I just wanted you to know that,' Jamie whispers, the tips of his ears turning pink.

'OK,' I whisper back. 'Thank you.'

We continue to draw in silence. I wish I hadn't used charcoal. My fingertips and the side of my hand are filthy.

Mr Bute's phone begins to ring. 'I'll be back shortly, class,' he says, jumping up from his chair and ducking out into the corridor.

The second the door falls shut behind him, the volume in the classroom rises by at least five notches. Alana drops her pose, turning to talk to a girl behind her. I continue to draw her stupid pouty face from memory. I still can't figure out whether Jamie's words have made me feel any better.

'Hey, Jamie! You sure you wanna sit that close to her?' Sienna's voice cuts through the chatter, reigniting the heat in my belly.

Jamie ignores her, continuing to apply broad confident strokes to the page.

'Hey, Jamie, are you listening to me or what?'

Jamie lets out a tired sigh. He lowers his pencil and twists round in his seat to face Sienna's direction. 'What?' he asks.

'Aw, don't be like that,' Sienna says in a baby voice. 'I thought we were mates. Or is there only room for one girl in your life?'

'What are you talking about?' he demands, his voice suddenly all spikes and sharp angles.

I silently will him to turn back round, to ignore the bait, to keep drawing.

'Your new girlfriend,' Sienna says.

'She's not my girlfriend,' Jamie growls.

'Oh really? Then why did you spend half of Jack's party with her? And bring her trick or treating? And team up with her today? Hmmmmm?'

I still can't see Sienna, but I can picture her smug expression perfectly.

Jamie stands up, the legs of his chair scraping against the floor with a high-pitched squeal.

'Look, she's not my girlfriend, OK?'

The entire class is listening in now. I press against my paper so hard the piece of charcoal goes through to the page beneath.

'Where do you do it?' Sienna asks. 'Like, in the rubbish?'

Giggles ripple across the classroom.

The anger in my belly continues to bubble furiously.

'It must stink,' Sienna crows, soaking up the nervous laughter. 'Or maybe that turns you on.'

The bubbling is right under my skin now, threatening to spill, to send me over the edge.

'Senn,' Cassie says quietly. 'Stop it now.'

'I'm not judging,' Sienna says, ignoring her. 'I mean, if that's what you're into, go for it, by all means.'

'I mean it, Senn,' Cassie says.

'Oh, wait, hang on, maybe it's her mum you're into,'

Sienna continues. 'Is that it? Or maybe you're into both at the same time. Like mother, like daughter . . .'

I stand up, my chair flying from beneath me. My piece of charcoal falls to the ground.

35

'One last time, Ro,' Mr Modi, the head of Year Ten says. 'Why did you physically attack Sienna?'

'I only pushed her,' I say quietly.

It wasn't my fault Sienna made such a meal out of falling over, knocking over a load of paintbrushes on her way down and howling like a Premier League footballer trying to get a penalty.

Mr Modi sighs. 'Fine, then why did you *push* Sienna?'

'I don't know, sir,' I say.

He sighs again. 'So, you just pushed her for no reason? She did absolutely nothing to provoke you?'

I'm grappling for a plausible answer when his phone rings.

'Excuse me, Ro,' he says, turning his back on me to answer it.

While Mr Modi is talking, I take an inventory of his wastepaper basket and conclude he has a thing for chunky KitKats.

'Right,' he says, replacing the receiver. 'If you'd like to come with me, Ro. We're wanted in Mrs Hibbert's office.'

Mrs Hibbert is not alone.

'Welcome, Ro,' she says in her husky Liverpudlian accent. 'Take a seat. Now, have you met Ms Habib? She's our head of pastoral support.'

'Hi, Ro,' Ms Habib says, smiling.

'Hi,' I say faintly, a fresh helping of dread pinning me to my chair.

'How are you doing today, Ro?' Mrs Hibbert asks, her tone uncharacteristically gentle.

'Er, OK,' I say, trapping my sweaty hands under the backs of my thighs. The upholstery is rough and scratchy against my damp palms.

'Just to reassure you, Ro, you're not in trouble. OK? No one is.'

That's when I know for sure this has nothing to do with me pushing Sienna.

'We just want to have a bit of a chat,' Mrs Hibbert continues, nodding at Ms Habib.

Ms Habib angles her chair towards me and smiles. Her teeth are very white. 'We just have a few questions, Ro, about things at home.'

The word 'home' makes my blood run cold.

'Nothing to worry about,' Ms Habib adds. 'All very straightforward.'

Then why is my heart beating so fast? And why is sweat dripping down my back, pooling at the waistband of my skirt? And why are my ears ringing? And why do I feel like my brain has been freshly stuffed with cotton wool?

Ms Habib looks down at the notebook on her lap, flipping back through the pages. They're filled with handwritten notes.

I wonder who told. It could be anyone. Practically the whole of Year Ten was at Jack's party.

Ms Habib looks up, smiling another toothpaste-ad smile. 'Now, let's start with the basics, shall we? You live the majority of the time with your mum, is that correct?'

They keep referring to it as a 'chat'. It doesn't feel like a chat, though; it feels like an interrogation. They think they can throw me off the scent with their smiles and kind voices and assurances that everything would be OK, but I knew the score the second Ms Habib got her notebook out. I downplay or deny every single suggestion that there's an issue at home, feigning confusion at every step, stretching my acting skills to the absolute limit.

'So, would you say you and your mum have quite a normal mother-daughter relationship?' Ms Habib asks.

'Yes, of course,' I say, blocking out pretty much every memory of Bonnie from the last ten years. 'Totally normal.'

I have no idea if they're buying it but I have no idea how else to play it.

Half an hour later, it's all over.

'If you'd like to wait outside, Ro,' Mrs Hibbert says.

After ten minutes Ms Habib and Mr Modi leave and I'm called back in to speak to Mrs Hibbert alone.

'Mr Modi filled me in on what happened this morning,' Mrs Hibbert says. 'Has it got anything to do with what we discussed just now?'

I shake my head hard. 'No, miss.'

'We have a very strict policy on physical violence here at Ostborough Academy.'

'Yes, miss.'

'Having said that, I get the feeling the circumstances around what happened this morning are not that black and white.'

I don't say anything even though I can tell she wants me to.

'I think the best option for all parties is to suspend you for the rest of the day and start tomorrow afresh. Does that sound fair?'

'Yes, miss. Thank you.'

She's being generous. She could have easily just stuck me in the exclusion centre for the rest of the week.

'Now,' she continues. 'Miss Tavistock in the office couldn't get hold of your mother. But she's managed to track down your stepmother. She'll be here to collect you shortly.'

Melanie.

Great.

'We'll discuss this properly when we get home,' Melanie says briskly as we walk towards her car. I spot Izzy in the passenger seat, playing on her iPad.

'Why isn't she at school?' I ask.

'She's poorly. She thinks we've come to pick you up

because you have a tummy ache by the way. I don't want her to know you've been fighting.'

Of course not, for precious little Izzy must be protected at all costs.

'I haven't been fighting,' I say. 'I barely even pushed the girl. And what makes you think I'm coming back with you anyway?'

'For one thing, I'm pretty certain your father is going to want to talk to you about this.'

'Then he can wait until it's my weekend at yours.'

Melanie stops walking and puts her hands on her hips. 'Rosie, considering the circumstances, I don't think you're in any position to be calling the shots right now. We'll drop you back at your mother's later, but until then, you're in my care and you'll do as I ask.'

A fresh jolt of anger shoots up my spine. 'No,' I say.

Melanie's perfectly plucked eyebrows leap halfway up her forehead. 'Excuse me, young lady?'

'No,' I repeat. 'You and Dad don't just get to simply pick and choose when I'm "in your care". What about the rest of the time? Where are you then? Do you know what my life is like when you're not around?' The words fall out of me in an angry torrent. 'Of course you don't!' I say when she doesn't answer. 'You probably don't even give me a second thought when I'm not shoved under your nose.'

'You're exaggerating!'

'Am I though? My boss at work checks in with me more than Dad does!'

'You're just being silly now. Your dad is an incredible father!'

'Wrong, Melanie. He's an incredible father to *Izzy*. Me? His *actual* daughter? Not so great.'

'Well, it's not like you make it very easy for him, skulking round the place with a face like a smacked bottom. It's a two-way street, Rosie!'

God, I hate her. I used to think I'd done OK in the step-mother stakes, that at least I hadn't ended up with someone downright evil, but over the years it's become obvious that Melanie's breed, with her plastered-on smile and fake concern, is just as dangerous.

'Ever wondered why I might look pissed off?' I ask.

She hesitates.

'Thought not. Because all you care about is yourself and your mini-me over there. You don't give a toss about me. You never have.'

'How dare you!' Melanie cries, her face tomato red. 'I've bent over backwards to welcome you into our family!'

'He was my family first!' I scream.

'Well, he chose us, didn't he?' she says, smiling smugly. 'Me and Izzy. I'm sorry if that hurts to hear, Ro, but it's true, and no amount of kicking and screaming is going to change that.'

Izzy has stopped playing on her iPad and is watching us with interest through the front windscreen.

Melanie notices her, rearranging her features and waving. 'Now, get in the car,' she says to me through gritted teeth.

She actually thinks she's won.

I stay where I am.

'I said, get in the car,' she repeats.

As if I'm going to go anywhere with her.

'No,' I say.

'No?' she repeats. 'You're walking on thin, thin ice, young lady.'

'You can tell Dad that if he wants to talk to me, he knows where to find me. Bye, Melanie.' I turn on my heel and start walking.

'Rosie Snow!' Melanie yells after me, her voice verging on hysterical. 'Come back here this instant!'

I ignore her and keep going.

36

I'm watching videos on YouTube when there's a knock at the back door. I look out of my window. Emerson is standing on the patio. What on earth does he want?

I drag myself off my bed and head downstairs, opening the door a crack so Emerson can't see inside.

'What?' I ask.

'I was just wondering if you'd heard from Tanvi?'

'You came all the way here to ask me that? Why don't you just ring her?'

'I have. She didn't answer.'

'So try again and leave a message.'

I go to close the door but Emerson jams his toe in the gap. 'I have,' he says. 'Three times. And before you ask, I've texted and sent her messages on Facebook, Instagram and Snapchat too. I haven't heard a thing from her since Saturday.'

I frown. When I last saw Tanvi and Emerson, they were

totally wrapped up in each other. I get Tanvi not messaging me, but why would she ghost Emerson?

'When did you last see her?' I ask.

'At the party.'

'And how did she seem?'

'Worried about you mostly. When she found out about what happened at your house, all she wanted to do was get hold of you and make sure you were OK.'

'But before that? Were you getting on OK then?'

Emerson blushes. 'Yeah, I think so.'

'You didn't try anything weird, did you?' I ask, my body seized with a fierce and unexpected protectiveness over Tanvi.

'No!' Emerson yelps. 'Of course not! We were messaging back and forth loads on Saturday morning and then she went totally quiet.'

'When on Saturday?' I ask sharply.

'Hang on, I can tell you.' He takes out his phone. 'I last heard from her at one forty-four.'

What time did Tanvi turn up at Arcadia Avenue? Two p.m.-ish?

My stomach turns over. What if Tanvi never got home? But if that were the case, her parents would have contacted me by now. Unless she didn't tell them where she was going . . .

'Do you think something's wrong?' Emerson asks.

His question makes my heart beat faster. 'I don't know,' I admit.

'I'm worried,' Emerson says. 'Do you know where she lives?'

I nod.

'Will you take me there?' he asks.

I hesitate.

'Please, Ro.'

'Hang on a second. I'll just get my coat.'

The lights are on at Tanvi's house. Emerson and I arrange ourselves neatly on the front doorstep and ring the bell.

It's Bonfire Night in two days' time and, as we wait for what seems like for ever, fireworks glitter in the sky. The explosions remind me of standing in the Shahs' back garden on Diwali, Tanvi's arm linked with mine. And for a few seconds, I'm catapulted back there – a beautiful purple sari swishing around my legs, my tummy full of food, my cheeks hurting from smiling so much. Was that really only a week and a half ago? It feels like another life.

Footsteps. Then the sound of a key in the lock. In unison, Emerson and I stand up that little bit straighter. The door swings inwards to reveal Devin. He's wearing tracksuit bottoms and a Rolling Stones T-shirt, and his hair, perfectly styled when I last saw him, is flat on one side, sticking up on end on the other.

'Ro,' he says, rubbing his right eye with his fist. 'Hi.'

'Hey,' I mumble. 'Um, this is Emerson. He's in mine and Tanvi's form at school. This is Tanvi's big brother, Devin. Can we see her?'

Devin's face crumples like a crisp packet. 'Shit, you don't know. Of course you don't.'

'Know what?' I ask, suddenly very afraid.

Devin hesitates. 'You'd better come in.'

Emerson and I step into the hallway. The house is uncharacteristically quiet. No radio, no conversation, no cooking noises coming from the kitchen.

'Tanvi's in hospital,' Devin says as the door falls shut behind us.

'What? Why? Is she OK? Has the cancer come back?' The words tumble out of my mouth in a clumsy stream, tripping over one another to be heard. They're overlapped with a similar set of questions from Emerson.

'She has pneumonia,' Devin says.

'But I didn't think pneumonia was that serious,' Emerson says. 'My dad had it once and he just took some tablets for a bit and he was fine.'

'Tanvi's immunity is still pretty weak from the cancer,' Devin explains gently. 'The pneumonia came out of nowhere and kind of knocked her sideways.'

I remember Tanvi's appearance at my back door on Saturday – her puffy eyes, her runny nose, the croaky voice. I assumed it was just a cold.

'How long has she been in hospital?' I ask.

'Since Saturday afternoon. She kept saying she was OK, then she collapsed in the bathroom.'

It's all my fault. How long had Tanvi been forced to sit outside in the cold while I sulked inside? Half an hour? An hour?

'Will she be OK?' I whisper.

'They think so,' Devin says. 'She's still pretty weak though. They need to make sure her lungs are strong enough before they can discharge her.'

'Can we visit her?' Emerson asks.

'I'm afraid it's family only at the moment,' Devin says. 'But as soon as she's feeling a bit more with it, I bet she'd love to see you. Here, why don't you write down your numbers so I can give you a ring when she's up and about?'

Emerson and I write our numbers on the pad of paper next to the phone.

Devin checks his watch. 'I'd better get going. I'm due at the hospital with a change of clothes for Mum.'

'OK,' we mumble, shuffling towards the door.

Emerson and I are at the bottom of the driveway when I stop abruptly.

'Just one second,' I say.

I sprint back and knock on the door.

'Can you do me a favour?' I ask breathlessly when Devin answers.

'Sure,' he says.

'Can you tell Tanvi I'm sorry?'

'Sorry?'

'Yes.'

'Can I ask what for?'

'She'll know,' I say.

I say goodbye to Emerson and walk home alone. With every step, I can't stop picturing Tanvi in the hospital, lying in a stark white room, her black hair fanned out on a crisp white pillow, her tiny body wired up to a load of machines that flash and beep, a nurse with a clipboard standing at the end of her bed frowning and taking notes.

Number 46 Arcadia Avenue is in darkness. Noah must be back at school by now. Despite several text messages, I still haven't heard from him. It shouldn't hurt so much. After all, it was just a few games of chess. It does though. I thought there was something between us – an understanding. I hate the fact I was wrong.

Bonnie's home. All the lights are on and the usual racket of music versus television is blaring from the living room.

I'm making my way up the stairs, dragging one exhausted foot after another when she appears in the doorway, a cigarette between her fingers.

It's the first time I've seen her face to face since our row on Friday night.

'Your dad just called me,' she says.

Bonnie and Dad rarely communicate. If they have anything to say to each other, they use me as the messenger.

'What about?' I ask.

'He wouldn't say, only that he's been trying to get hold of you.'

'Oh.'

I take out my phone. Eleven missed calls and three (no doubt furious) voicemails – all from Dad.

'What's going on, Ro?'

'They're on to us,' I say.

'Who are?'

'I was hauled into the head's office today. They were asking questions. It's only a matter of time before they speak to Social Services. In fact, they probably already have.'

'What kind of questions?'

I fill her in.

'And what did you say?' she asks, panic finally registering on her face.

'I denied it all.'

She has the nerve to look relieved. 'Well, that's OK then,' she says.

Does she really think it's that simple? That easy?

'It's not OK, Bonnie,' I say. '*Nothing* is OK.'

She covers her ears like a little kid. 'Oh, please, Ro, not another lecture.'

I'm speechless. Has *nothing* I've said to her over the past week gone in? What more of a wake-up call does she need?

'What?' she says, lowering her hands. 'Why are you looking at me like that?'

'Have you ever heard of the Collyer Brothers?' I ask.

She frowns and shakes her head.

'They're this pair of brothers who lived in this massive mansion in New York in the nineteen thirties and forties. Homer and Langley.'

And just like that, I'm back on the lumpy sofa bed at Dad's old flat, the one he lived in for a few months after he left Arcadia Avenue, before he moved in with Melanie, flicking through the TV channels because I couldn't sleep.

'When I was little, I watched a documentary about them,' I continue. 'They lived in this big old house together and filled it with junk.'

Something small but unmistakeable flickers across Bonnie's face.

'Anyway, one day, the police got a tip-off from a neighbour

that they hadn't seen either of the brothers in a while. They broke in and found Homer's body.'

'I don't know what you're getting at here, Ro,' Bonnie says. 'I really don't.'

I ignore her and keep going.

'It took them another two whole weeks to find Langley. He'd been literally suffocated by his own stuff. And the thing is, Homer was blind and relied on Langley to bring him his food, so with Langley rotting under a load of old crap, poor Homer starved to death.'

'Ro, stop this.'

'I made the mistake of typing their names into Google images,' I say. '*Not* a good idea.'

The grainy image of Langley's decomposing, rat-nibbled body, haunted my dreams for weeks.

'Why are you telling me this?' Bonnie asks, visibly flustered.

'I couldn't get the story out of my head,' I say. 'Even though their house was a load worse than ours, I knew something like that could happen to us if things got out of control. So I made a promise to myself – that I would look after you, no matter what.'

I remember getting Dad to drop me back at Arcadia Avenue the next day and my distress when I couldn't find Bonnie straightaway, convinced she'd befallen the same fate as Homer and Langley. When I finally did find her, dozing on a narrow strip of mattress in her bedroom, piles of black plastic bags looming over her, I had frantic, hot panicky tears running down my cheeks. That was when I knew. It was going to be my job to prevent what happened to the Collyer brothers from happening to my mum.

'How old were you?' Bonnie whispers.

'Eight,' I reply.

Her mouth falls open. 'Ro, I—'

'What?' I ask.

There's a long pause.

'I . . . I didn't realize,' she says eventually.

I sigh. 'Do you think I don't know that, Bonnie?'

I continue up the stairs, locking my door behind me.

I'm so shattered I don't even brush my teeth or wash my face. I just pull on my pyjamas and crawl under the duvet.

37

Smoke.

Heat.

A bonfire?

No. Closer than that.

Light. Turn on the light.

Smoke everywhere.

Fire.

Need to get out.

Stumble out of bed.

Ro! Ro! Ro!

Someone is shouting my name.

Bonnie?

Head pounding.

Throat burning.

Can't stop coughing.

Legs all floppy.

Door won't open.

Locked.
Reach for key.
It falls.
Drop to my knees.
Can't get up again.
Sirens.
Ro! Ro! Ro!
Fire.
Need to get out.
Can't get out.
Ro! Ro! Ro!

38

The first thing I see when I wake up is a Winnie the Pooh mural. The colours are overly bright – Piglet too pink, Tigger too orange, Pooh himself as yellow as tinned custard.

My eyes are gluey and sore, my eyelids feel tender. Every blink hurts. My gaze drifts to the bedside table, which holds a jug of water and two plastic beakers. The sight makes me realize just how thirsty I am.

I try to sit up, but my body won't let me. I manage to lift my head a couple of centimetres before my strength fails me and I sink back onto the pillows.

The lighting is bright and I'm aware of people moving about and the hum of voices, which suggests it's daytime, but there's no window within view so I can't know for sure.

As my eyes adjust to the brightness, every blink an effort, the events of the night before begin to come back to me in a series of hazy fragments, the pictures and sounds overlapping, like a film and its soundtrack being played out of sync. I try to put them in order, moving them around like Post-it notes in my head. I remember very little about the fire itself. The first concrete thing I'm able to cling onto is being in the back of the ambulance – with Bonnie's scared eyes peeking out at me over the top of her oxygen mask as we rode to the hospital, the siren wailing, blue lights flashing, the paramedics speaking in loud, steady voices.

The next few hours were a blur of machines and tubes and doctors and nurses and bright lights and efficiency. A nurse with kind brown eyes stayed with me the entire time, explaining exactly what was happening and why in a low, melodic voice, her thumb massaging my palm during all the uncomfortable bits. Once my breathing had been stabilized, a doctor inserted a short thin tube with a camera in its tip into my mouth in order to examine my airways. I remained awake throughout but I was groggy, my brain fuzzy and slow, the voices of the doctors and nurses loud one second, faraway the next, like someone was fiddling with the volume button inside my head, sliding it up and down on a whim.

I don't remember arriving on the ward or falling asleep. Or changing into the pale pink standard issue hospital nightie I'm now wearing. I wonder where my pyjamas are.

Perhaps Bonnie will know.

Bonnie.

I haven't seen her since arriving at the hospital.

I try to call out but the only sound I produce is a filthy wheeze that burns the back of my throat.

I groan inwardly and slowly turn my head. It takes more

effort than I was anticipating, every muscle in my neck throbbing.

Bonnie is slumped in the leather-backed chair to the right of my bed, her head lolling forward on her chest, her face streaked with what looks like soot or ash.

Flooded with relief, I summon up the strength to extend one arm out of the bed, my fingertips just managing to graze Bonnie's knee.

She wakes with a start. 'Ro,' she rasps. 'You're awake.' She throws her arms around my neck, covering my face and neck with kisses, her dry lips dragging against my skin. Her breath smells stale – of cigarettes and no sleep.

'Water,' I croak. 'I need water.'

Every word stings.

Bonnie leaps up, splashing water on the floor as she fills a plastic beaker to the brim, holding it to my lips.

I'm on my second when a tall nurse wearing pale blue scrubs, her hair braided in immaculate cornrows, appears at the end of the bed. 'Well, look who's up,' she says, smiling. 'I'm Nurse Karen. OK if I check you over?'

After Karen's checks and several more beakers of water, I drift back off to sleep.

When I wake up, Bonnie is sitting on the edge of her seat, her hands sandwiching my left one. She must have washed her face because the smudge on her cheek has gone.

'How did it start?' I ask.

Bonnie blinks, as if surprised by the question.

'Th-they're not entirely sure yet,' she stammers.

It gives her away.

'It was a cigarette, wasn't it?' I say.

Bonnie opens her mouth and closes it again.

'Wasn't it?' I repeat.

Bonnie hesitates before nodding. 'I tried to put it out,' she says. 'But there was nothing I could do. It spread so quickly.'

Of course it did.

There's a pause.

'Go on then,' Bonnie says, her lower lip trembling. 'Say it.'

'Say what?'

'You know.'

I shake my head.

'*I told you so*,' Bonnie says, her eyes glistening. 'Go on, I deserve it.'

That may be true, but I still can't quite bring myself to say it out loud.

'Please, Ro, just say it.'

'Why? Would it help? Would it fix things?'

'No,' she admits. 'I'm sorry,' she adds. 'I'm so sorry, Ro.'

I don't respond. I can't.

We're interrupted by Karen. 'Mrs Snow?' she says. 'There are some people at Reception who'd like to talk to you.'

Bonnie's face pales. 'Who?' she asks, her eyes darting over Karen's shoulder. 'I'm not expecting anyone.'

'If you'd like to come with me, I can introduce you,' Karen says, neatly sidestepping Bonnie's answer.

Bonnie looks both ways as if assessing her possible escape routes before standing up, resigned to what lies beyond the double doors at the end of the ward.

'This way,' Karen says.

Bonnie gives me a tight smile and follows Karen. Next to her, she looks tiny. Tiny and scared.

I manage to push myself up onto my elbows. As the double doors swing open, I glimpse two people standing at the nurses' station – a man and a woman. They're both dressed reasonably smartly with lanyards around their necks.

I know where they're from immediately.

After all these years, Social Services have finally caught up with us.

I've feared this moment all my life. And now that it's here, it's nothing like I imagined.

Instead of terror, all I feel is exhausted relief.

39

'Ro, Ro! Wake up!'

If it wasn't for the fact my throat is still incredibly sore and incapable of volume unless warmed up and well lubricated, I would have screamed. As it is, the best I'm able to manage is a sort of squeak, a bit like a mouse in distress.

'Oh, shit, sorry!' Tanvi says, her face centimetres away from mine. 'I didn't mean to scare you.'

Her breath is warm and sweet and smells of Lucozade.

'What time is it?' I rasp, struggling to prop myself up on my pillows. The rest of the ward is still.

'I dunno,' Tanvi replies. 'Two? Three?'

I reach for a glass of water, gulping it down. 'How did you know I was here?' I ask, setting down my empty beaker. I'm still not entirely convinced I'm actually awake and Tanvi Shah is actually sitting in a wheelchair next to my bed wearing a furry dressing gown with teddy bear ears stitched onto the hood.

'OK,' Tanvi says in a noisy whisper. 'So last night, Devin told me that you and Emerson had come round and that you'd asked him to tell me that you were sorry. Which he did. Anyway, I asked to borrow his phone – mine is broken cos when I collapsed the other day, I managed to drop it in my bath water and no one realized until the next day – duh! So, I tried calling you, but you didn't answer, so I wrote you a note – old school, huh? – and asked Devin to drop it through your door. Which he tried to do this morning and couldn't because your house is all cordoned off at the moment. So he put two and two together and asked the nurses if you were here, and they said yes and that you were going to be OK, and basically, I would have come sooner but he literally only told me this afternoon.'

Tanvi says all of this very quickly, barely pausing to take a breath.

'Which is why,' she continues, panting slightly, 'I hijacked this baby from the kid in the bed next to mine.' She thumps the arms of her wheelchair.

'You *stole* someone's wheelchair?' I say.

'No!' Tanvi gasps in mock outrage. 'I *borrowed* someone's wheelchair.'

'Where is your ward anyway?'

'Literally next door.'

'What if the nurses realize your bed is empty?'

'Not to worry. I've left them a very comprehensive note.'

'But should you even be out of bed? Aren't you really ill? You collapsed!'

Tanvi pauses. 'OK, I'm perhaps not feeling one hundred

per cent right now, but I'm basically fine. They're just being uber-careful because of my history.'

'Did you get poorly because of me?' I ask. It's the question that's been haunting me ever since I spoke to Devin.

'What do you mean?'

'I made you sit outside.'

'When?'

'On Saturday,' I say, wincing at the memory of Tanvi perched on the edge of Bonnie's sunlounger in the back garden.

'Don't be a ninny! I was already ill by then. Don't you remember me coughing and sneezing at the party?'

I nod uncertainly.

'Is that what you were sorry for?' Tanvi asks.

I bite my lip. 'Not just that.' I want to expand, but as usual I don't know where to start.

'Anyway,' Tanvi says breaking the silence, 'enough about me and my boring old pneumonia. How on earth are you?'

'Oh, I'm OK, I think. My throat feels kind of shredded from the smoke inhalation, but they reckon there'll be no long-lasting damage.'

'So you'll still be able to sing?'

Oh God, that hadn't even crossed my mind.

'I think so, yes.'

'Oh, that's such good news!'

The child in the next bed stirs. Tanvi pulls a 'whoops' face and lowers her voice back down to a whisper.

'Fancy a li'l field trip?' she asks.

*

'OK, in here,' Tanvi says, prodding me through a door.

We haven't ventured all that far from the ward, but the journey was far from straightforward – dodging members of staff and hiding behind pillars and vending machines in order to escape detection.

My eyes adjust to the darkness a little. We're standing in the entrance to what looks like a miniature soft-play centre.

'Follow me,' Tanvi says, abandoning her wheelchair by the door and wading into the darkness.

I do as I'm told.

The dirty white moon spills light through the windows, illuminating a pile of plastic-coated beanbags in the far corner of the space. Tanvi flops onto one and indicates I should do the same.

'This used to be my favourite spot,' she says, turning on her back and stretching out her legs. She glances across at me. 'What's up? You've gone all quiet.'

'Sorry,' I say. 'I just didn't properly twig until now.'

'Twig what?'

'That this was the hospital where you were treated for your cancer. You must know it inside out.'

'You could say that, yeah.'

We sit in silence for a little while, our breathing slowing down until we're in sync with one another.

'I'm really glad you're OK, Ro,' Tanvi says.

'Why are you being so nice to me?' I ask.

'Nice?' she asks, tilting her head to one side.

'Yeah. When I last saw you, you said you didn't want to talk to me ever again.'

She frowns. 'I didn't say that.'

'Yeah you did. You said that you couldn't "do this any more".'

'And you interpreted that as me never wanting to talk to you ever again?'

'Well, yeah.'

'When I said I couldn't do this, I meant I couldn't keep having that conversation.'

'Oh.'

'I'm not going to lie, the stuff you said about Anna really upset me, but once I'd calmed down a bit, all I wanted to do was come straight back and talk to you about it properly. Alas, my stupid pneumonia had other ideas . . .'

I feel really stupid.

'Did you honestly think I was going to be that easy to shake off?' she adds, laughing.

'Good point,' I admit.

She reaches across and punches me on the arm.

'I'm really sorry,' I say.

'I know. I'm sorry too.'

'What are *you* sorry for?'

'Not telling you straightaway when I found out where you lived. And not saying anything about Anna.'

'Don't be stupid. You don't have to tell me anything you don't want to.'

'That's the thing though – I almost told you about her loads of time. But every time I stopped myself because I knew I'd only get upset if I did.'

'What would be wrong with that?'

'I didn't want you to see me like that.'

'Why not?'

Tanvi takes a deep breath. 'OK, so for three years, pretty much every single person I met automatically felt sorry for me. When I came back to school, I was determined not to have people see me that way, like a victim, or someone to be pitied. And you didn't. That was a big part of why I liked you straightaway. You didn't wrap me up in cotton wool, you just treated me like a normal human being.'

'I don't know. I think I was probably pretty rude.'

'I liked that though!'

'Weirdo.'

She grins and sticks out her tongue. 'I know you don't like loads of people,' she adds. 'But you'd have liked her, I think. Anna, I mean.'

'Yeah?'

'Yeah.'

'What was she like?'

Tanvi shifts on her beanbag so she's lying on it sideways. I do the same so our bodies are facing each other.

'She was . . . the best,' Tanvi says, her face softening. A single tear escapes and trickles down her cheek. 'See!' she says. 'Instant tears!'

'We don't have to talk about her,' I say quickly.

'No, no. I want to,' she says. 'It feels like the right time.'

So I lie back and let her talk.

She tells me everything – meeting Anna in chemo where they bonded over their shared crush on a hot nurse called Lachlan; the silly games they made up together; their midnight excursions to the vending machine; the slow painful acknowledgment that as Tanvi was getting better, Anna was only getting worse; the multiple goodbyes, never knowing for sure which one was going to be the actual one – the definitive goodbye.

The entire time, tears roll down Tanvi's cheeks.

After she finishes describing Anna's funeral in January, we lapse into silence. For a few seconds I think Tanvi has fallen asleep, until she says, 'I've just thought of another thing I'm sorry about.'

'What's that?'

'The folder. That was dumb of me. Of course you'd looked into all that stuff before.'

'That's OK,' I say. 'You were just trying to help. And to be fair, I haven't tried any of that stuff in a while.'

'Has your mum always, you know, kept things?'

I swallow hard before answering her question. 'Pretty much,' I say. 'Even though it's a lot worse now, the house has never looked normal. Well, apart from this one time, when I was seven. Bonnie went away for the weekend and while she was gone, my dad got a cleaning team in.'

There were six of them, all dressed in white overalls. For two days straight they trooped in and out of the house, removing bag after bag of rubbish. When they left, I remember walking from room to room, marvelling over corners and skirting boards and power sockets I never knew existed.

'I was so sure she would be pleased, but she went mad, shouting and screaming and crying,' I say.

'But why?' Tanvi whispers.

'I don't know,' I say. 'She couldn't even explain it. She just started filling the place up all over again. By Christmas it looked exactly the same as it did before.'

'Wow,' Tanvi says softly.

With gentle prompting, I tell her more about life at 48 Arcadia Avenue – the Christmas dinners eaten in empty Chinese restaurants; the Saturday nights spent sitting in the wings of dingy social clubs, eating endless bags of Mini Cheddars as Bonnie performed on stage; the terrible audition in London; Halloween; this afternoon's visit from Social Services.

'What do you think will happen?' Tanvi asks.

After speaking to Bonnie, the two social workers came to talk to me. The first thing they did was reassure me they would do their best to keep Bonnie and I under the same roof.

'Our principal aim is to keep families together,' the woman, Carina, explained. 'Not tear them apart.'

At the same time, Carina made it clear that Bonnie had some work to do before she and her team would be happy for me to return to Arcadia Avenue.

As she spoke, I couldn't help but wonder what might have happened if I'd known this sooner. How would my life have looked? I quickly realized there was no point. I'm tired of looking back. I only want to look forward now.

'What happens in the meantime?' Tanvi asks once I've explained all this. 'Where will you stay?'

'I guess I'll have to live with my dad.'

I shudder at the thought. We spoke on the phone earlier

but he seemed way more upset about the way I spoke to Melanie the day before than the fact I was in hospital.

'You don't look too happy about that,' Tanvi observes.

'No,' I admit.

There's a pause. Then Tanvi sits up suddenly. 'I've just had *the* most amazing idea,' she says. 'Why don't you come stay at my house?'

'Your house?'

'Yeah! We have the space – you can have Anish's old room. And just think of the fun we'll have.'

'You think your parents would be OK with it?'

'Course they will! They think the sun shines out of your bum!'

'What about Social Services? Would they let me, do you think?'

'Well, I don't know. It's worth asking though, isn't it?'

There's a pause and I'm flooded with gratitude for my pint-sized friend.

'Thank you, Tanvi,' I say. 'That's probably the nicest thing anyone's offered to do for me.'

'Anytime, Ro Snow,' she replies.

We continue to talk, our voices becoming slow and sleepy as we drift from one subject to another. Tanvi's hand finds mine in the darkness. For once, I don't feel the urge to shake her off or wriggle from her grip. Instead, I give it a gentle squeeze and don't let go until the sun is coming up.

40

I'm finishing my breakfast when a smiley nurse called Tim informs me I have a visitor.

'Who?' I ask.

'A rather handsome young gentleman,' Tim says, wiggling his eyebrows up and down. 'Noah?'

My eyes widen. 'Noah. Are you sure?'

Tim laughs. 'Yes, I think so . . . Well, am I all right to let him in? I can send him away if you don't feel up to it.'

'No!' I say. 'It's, er, it's fine . . .'

'Righty-oh,' Tim says. 'Be right back.'

As Tim walks away, my heart begins to gallop.

Noah is here.

To see me.

I comb through my hair with my fingers and check I don't have egg down my nightie. I don't need to look in a mirror to know I'm probably not looking my best. I didn't crawl back into bed until 7 a.m., and have no doubt the lack of sleep is plastered all over my face right now.

I shove two Polo mints in my mouth and grab the magazine Bonnie left on my nightstand. I spread it open on my lap and pretend to be engrossed in a story about two celebrities who met on a reality TV show and are getting married. My sweaty palms stick to the pages as I hear footsteps on the lino, not quite daring to look up.

'Hi.'

I raise my head.

Noah is standing at the bottom of my bed, wearing an expression that straddles relief and wonder.

'You're OK,' he says, his lips quivering into a smile.

'Aren't you supposed to be at school?' I blurt in response.

'Oh,' Noah replies, looking down at his fancy school uniform. 'Yes.'

'You're bunking?' I ask.

'I suppose so, yeah.'

'How?'

'I crept out of prayers this morning and caught the first train out of York.'

'Won't you be in loads of trouble?'

'Probably. Who cares.'

I swallow. 'Um, would you like to sit down?' I ask, indicating the chair next to my bed.

Noah sits down. It's surreal having him so close. I have to resist the urge to reach out and touch him, to check he's really here.

'How did you know where to find me?' I ask.

'My dad texted me about the fire last night. I didn't know

you'd be here for definite, but I thought it was worth a try. How are you feeling?'

'OK, I think. I inhaled a fair bit of smoke but they don't think it's going to cause any lasting damage.'

'That's good,' Noah says.

There's a pause.

'Oh, I got you something,' he says, pulling a plastic bag onto his lap. 'I was going to get flowers. But then I remembered reading somewhere that lots of hospitals ban flowers so I went for chocolates instead. Is that OK?' He hands over a plastic tub of Quality Street.

'It's more than OK,' I reply. 'Thank you.'

'I got you this too,' Noah says, producing a flat square box wrapped in Thomas the Tank Engine paper. 'Sorry about the wrapping paper,' he adds. 'It was all I could get my hands on.'

I open the package to reveal a travel chess set.

'It's magnetic,' Noah explains. 'It might be a while before we can finish our game from the other day, but in the meantime, maybe we can start a new one?'

My heart lifts.

'I'm sorry, by the way,' Noah adds. 'About Saturday. My dad and I had a massive bust-up at family therapy on Saturday morning so I ended up going back to my mum's. I would have texted, but my phone's been out of action all week . . .' His voice trails off. 'He didn't tell you, did he?' he says.

'Tell me what?'

He discreetly punches the mattress. 'I asked my dad to

knock on your door and tell you I couldn't come over.'

'You don't hate me,' I murmur.

Noah frowns. 'Hate you? What are you talking about?'

'Halloween. I saw you at the window.'

Noah winces. 'I didn't mean to spy on you, I swear. I didn't even realize it was you I was watching until the very last minute. Wait, why did you think that'd make me hate you?'

'I don't know,' I admit.

'I thought it was kind of badass. If I could do something like that to get through to my dad, I'd totally do it.'

'Noah, why do you hate him so much?' I ask.

Noah blinks. 'You mean you don't know? I thought everyone round here did.'

I shake my head.

He takes a very large breath. 'Six months ago my dad was sacked from his job for sexually harassing five members of staff.'

I wasn't sure what I'd been expecting him to come out with, but that definitely wasn't it.

'The company settled out of court in an attempt to keep the whole thing under wraps,' he continues. 'But it ended up all over the local papers anyway. "The Harvey Weinstein of Ostborough" they were calling him.' He shudders slightly.

Now that I think about it, the story rings a bell.

'It was awful. Pretty much overnight, I went from being the kid who flew under the radar to the most hated person at school. It was like I was guilty of all the shitty stuff my dad had done, just by extension of being his son.'

I'm quiet. From the very first moment I clapped eyes on Noah I've been trying to work out why I feel this weird affinity towards him. And finally I do. He knows what it feels like to be ashamed of something you have no control over.

'I'm really sorry,' I say.

Noah shrugs. 'It is what it is.'

'Are things still hard at school?'

'It's a lot better this term,' Noah says. 'People have short memories, luckily.'

I hope he's right.

There's a pause.

'I meant what I said,' Noah says. 'It must have taken proper balls to do what you did at Halloween.'

'I'm not sure it *felt* very ballsy,' I admit.

'Well, it looked it. *You* looked it.'

'Thanks,' I say, heat creeping up my neck. My eyes fall on the travel chess. 'Got time for a game?' I ask. 'Or will the boarding school police be after you?'

Noah smiles. 'Let 'em.'

I smile back and begin to set up the pieces.

About an hour later, Tanvi joins us in a wheelchair she didn't steal, a huge grin spreading across her face the second I introduce Noah.

We swap chess for Uno and play game after game, drinking gallons of syrupy orange squash and ploughing our way through the tub of Quality Street until the bed is littered with shiny rainbow-coloured wrappers. As we giggle and crack jokes like we've all known each other for years, it dawns on me that this is what friendship feels like. I've been so afraid of it, so certain it wasn't for me.

Part of me is gutted I spent so long resisting it.

Another, much bigger part of me just can't wait to make up for lost time.

41

'Ready?' Tanvi asks as the car pulls up outside the school gates.

It's less than two weeks since I was last here, but it feels like longer.

'As I'll ever be,' I reply.

'Have a good day, girls,' Tanvi's mum says. 'Now, are you absolutely sure you're OK getting the bus home?'

'Sure,' we say in unison.

As Tanvi and I make our way to registration, people whisper and stare.

'Is it true you tried to burn your house down?' Sienna asks, falling into step with us.

'Oh, shut up, Sienna,' I say, and keep walking.

'You OK?' Tanvi whispers, scampering to keep up.

'I'm good,' I reply.

And I am.

With everything out in the open, there's nothing left to fear now. At least, not from them.

I am a duck and their opinions are water off my back.

It's only now I realize that they always were.

WINTER

42

I stick my head around Tanvi's bedroom door.

'You off?' she asks. She's sitting on the floor painting her nails Father Christmas red.

'Yep,' I reply.

'How you feeling?'

'Weird.'

'Ring me if you need me.'

'I won't, but thank you.'

She grins and salutes. I salute back and leave her to it.

Downstairs, I yell goodbye to her parents and head out into the fading December daylight.

After all those Saturday mornings leafleting here, I'm still getting my head around the fact Hopewood Gardens is my temporary home. I've been living with the Shahs for nearly six weeks now and it's been pretty great. Despite my monthly visits to Dad's over the years, I'd forgotten what it was like to feel like part of a family. I relish every bit of it, from the chaotic breakfasts and noisy dinners, to the squabbles over whose turn it is to wash up and what to watch on TV.

There's a bus due, but I decide to head on foot into town instead. As I walk, I murmur 'O Holy Night' under my breath. I'm singing it in the school concert next week, and even though I know it inside out I'm not taking any chances, practising any chance I can get.

By the time I reach the high street, it's almost dark and the Christmas lights are on.

I pause outside the café where Bonnie and I have arranged to meet and peer through the snow-sprayed window. She's sitting at the table in the corner of the café, stirring her tea. She looks nervous.

It's been six whole weeks since I last saw her. She's been staying with Danielle, a singer friend of hers over one hundred miles away. We've texted and talked on the phone, but this is our first face-to-face meeting.

I take a deep breath and push open the door.

Noticing me, she stands up, her mouth twisting into a timid smile. She holds out her arms, but I can't quite bring myself to step into them. She realizes, swallowing and dropping them to her sides.

'Hi,' she says.

'Hi,' I murmur.

'It's nice to see you.'

'You too.'

There's a pause. Kylie's version of 'Santa Baby' is playing in the background.

'Er, would you like something to drink?' she asks.

I glance up at the chalkboard menu on the wall. 'Hot chocolate please.'

She nods and heads up to the counter, returning a few minutes later with my drink plus a slice of Yule log on a small china plate.

'I thought we could share,' she says, slicing it in half, transferring the smaller half onto a napkin and pushing the rest across the table towards me.

'You got a gig tonight?' I ask, nodding at Bonnie's battered hot-pink suitcase, the one she takes to gigs, at the side of her chair. One corner of it is shrivelled from where the plastic casing melted in the heat of the fire.

'Yes. Corporate jobbie at that big hotel on the ring road.'

'Nice.' A pause. 'How's life at Danielle's?' I ask, blowing on my hot chocolate.

'Oh, you know. All right,' Bonnie says, wrapping her hands around her mug of tea. 'Bit cramped, and in the middle of bloody nowhere, but it could be worse.'

I wonder how Bonnie's coping there, with only a suitcase of belongings for company, or whether she's already started rebuilding her hoard within the four walls of Danielle's spare room, albeit on a slightly smaller scale. My stomach turns over at the thought.

'I'd prefer not to be there for Christmas, but what can you do?' Bonnie adds. 'Beggars can't be choosers.'

'Any news on the house?' I ask.

'They're saying after Christmas now. I keep pushing for earlier but I'm not holding out hope . . .'

'Right,' I murmur.

'How about you?' Bonnie asks. 'How are you getting on at Tanvi's?'

'Good,' I say. 'The Shahs have been really nice to me.'

Understatement of the year. They've been incredible.

'Remind me to add them to my Christmas card list,' Bonnie says.

I smile faintly.

'I saw Yvette again yesterday,' she adds.

It was Social Services who put Bonnie in touch with Yvette, a psychologist with specialist experience in treating people with compulsive hoarding disorder.

'And?' I say.

'It was hard work,' Bonnie says.

I frown.

'No, no, that's a good thing,' she insists. 'Apparently it means I'm putting in the work.' She smiles a smile that manages to be look both proud and sad at the same time. 'And I am,' she says. 'Working hard, I mean. I want you to know that, Ro, that I'm taking it seriously.'

I nod, unsure what to say. I want to believe Bonnie but there's still a glimmer of fear (more than a glimmer) that all the progress could unravel at any moment and we'll end up back at square one.

'She suggested I share some of the stuff I've been talking about with you,' Bonnie continues tentatively. 'Yvette, I mean. If that's OK with you, of course.'

'OK,' I say slowly.

'OK, super.'

There's a pause.

Bonnie looks down at her hands then back up again. 'You've probably already worked out that I don't get on all that well with my parents,' she says.

'The fact I've never met them is kind of a giveaway.'

She smiles tightly.

'How come?' I ask. 'Did you fall out?'

'It's not quite as straightforward as that.'

'What were they like?'

She thinks for a moment. 'Cold,' she says. 'You've heard the saying "children should be seen and not heard"?'

I nod.

'Well, that was my parents to a tee.'

As I listen to Bonnie telling the story of her lonely childhood rattling around a big empty house, for perhaps the very first time I feel like there might actually be a day when the massive join-the-dots puzzle that is my mother stops being a collection of random dots with no numbers and starts to form some sort of picture.

'Yvette thinks that's why I started singing,' she says. 'For the attention. You've got to admit, it sort of makes sense . . .' She pauses and plucks a shard of chocolate off her slice of Yule log.

'So what happened?' I asked. 'How come you don't see them any more?'

'There was no big showdown as such, just the gradual realization I was never going to be the daughter they wanted, and they were never going to be the parents I needed. I moved out the second I was old enough and that was that.

'What are you thinking?' Bonnie asks, tilting her head to one side.

'Just that that sounds really sad,' I say.

She smiles and shrugs. 'Oh, I'm sure there are *much* sadder tales . . . They just never should have become parents. Then again, you could probably say the same for me . . .'

Her voice trails off and there's a moment of almost complete silence before the next song kicks in.

'Before I forget,' Bonnie says, producing a red envelope from her handbag and pushing it across the table towards me.

'Do you want me to open it now?' I ask.

'It's Christmas time, isn't it?'

I open the envelope. The front of the card features a picture of three penguins, each of them wearing a red Rudolph nose and a pair of antlers. Inside, in her distinctive slanted handwriting, Bonnie has written: *To Ro, I found this card when I was going through the house the other day and I don't know why, but I thought the picture might make you smile. Love, Mum xxx*

Not Bonnie.

Mum.

'Thank you,' I say, sliding it into my bag. 'It did.'

'What?'

'Make me smile.'

Bonnie's face melts into a grin.

What time's your gig?' I ask.

'Seven.' She checks her watch. 'In fact I should probably get going in a bit if I'm going to fit in a proper sound check.'

I nod.

'You could, er, come along if you fancied,' she adds

casually as she checks her reflection in her compact mirror.

'To your gig?' I ask, blinking in surprise.

Bonnie's face flushes a little. 'Yes. You could sit at the back, I'm sure they wouldn't mind.'

I consider her proposition. I haven't seen Bonnie sing in ages. Years. I'm tempted. But not enough. The bottom line is, I'm not ready to pretend everything is OK between us. Not yet.

'I don't think so, Bonnie.'

Her face falls slightly.

'But ask me again,' I add.

'I will,' she promises.

Bonnie insists on giving me a lift back to Tanvi's.

'Sorry about the mess,' she says, clearing the passenger seat so I can sit down.

'That's OK,' I say, pulling on my seat belt. Although the car looks just as awful as it did when I last saw it, this is the first time Bonnie has acknowledged it or looked even remotely embarrassed. It's only a small change, but it feels enormous somehow.

'Anything exciting on this week?' Bonnie asks we turn into Hopewood Gardens.

'Nothing special. Just end of term stuff,' I reply.

This isn't strictly true. Friday is the Christmas concert.

'How about you?' I ask.

'Back-to-back gigs,' Bonnie says. ''Tis the season and all that.'

'It's this one,' I say, pointing out Tanvi's house.

All the lights are on, making it look extra warm and welcoming.

'Nice digs,' Bonnie says, letting out a low whistle of appreciation as she pulls up outside.

'Yeah, I kind of lucked out.'

The engine's purr dies out, plunging into silence.

'Have you heard from your dad?' she asks.

'A few times, yeah.'

'Everything OK there?'

'As OK as it can be.'

I'm just sorry it took the house burning down for me to finally accept Dad was never going to step up and be the person I needed him to be.

There's a pause.

'I'm going to get better, Ro,' Bonnie says, her fingers gripping the steering wheel, her eyes fixed on an invisible point beyond the windscreen. 'I've been doing lots of thinking, not just with Yvette but on my own too, and I'm serious about sorting myself out, I really am.'

I bite my lip. I want to believe her. More than anything.

'I'm going to go in now,' I say.

'OK,' Bonnie whispers.

I plant a dry kiss on her cheek. She smells of hairspray and her favourite perfume. I'm shocked to realize just how much I've missed it. How much I've missed her.

'Night, Bonnie,' I say.

'Night night,' she murmurs in reply.

I slam the door behind me and make my way up the driveway. Bonnie waits until I'm inside before driving away.

Tanvi is waiting for me on the stairs. 'So? How was it?' she asks as I take off my shoes.

'It was . . . OK,' I say.

'Good OK or bad OK?'

'Let's go with interesting OK.'

'Wanna talk about it?'

'Yes. But maybe not right away if that's all right.'

'Want some of my mum's dhal in the meantime?'

'Definitely.'

That night, as I lie in Anish's old bed, staring at the ceiling that still looks strange, even though I've been sleeping beneath it for over a month now, I'm overcome by a wave of sadness and longing that ties my stomach in a series of impenetrable knots.

Because as much as I'm enjoying living with Tanvi and her impossibly kind family, I'm homesick.

I'm homesick for Arcadia Avenue.

For Bonnie.

For the place, for better or for worse, I call home.

43

I think I'm going to throw up, a situation not helped by the fact Tanvi keeps peering through the gap in the curtains and reporting just how many people are in the audience.

'Oh my God, it's almost full!' she gasps. 'Come see!'

I shake my head hard. Having spent dozens of hours up in the lighting box, I can easily imagine the scene – the school hall dark and dim as the audience file in and take their seats, the sense of anticipation in the air as they flip through their paper programmes and open their sweets. The Christmas concert is always popular, people forced to stand at the back once all the seats have been taken.

'Positions, everyone,' Mr Milford says. 'Tanvi, how many times do I have to tell you, come away from the curtain.'

Tanvi reluctantly shrinks into line, grinning sheepishly.

The choir is opening the concert with a medley of festive hits, before returning to perform a more traditional selection to close the second half.

Including my solo.

Yesterday's dress rehearsal actually went pretty well. My voice, still tender if not fully warmed up, felt strong and healthy as I lost myself in the soaring music. But that had been singing to an empty, brightly lit hall. With the choir standing behind me, out of sight, it was easy to convince myself that it was just another rehearsal with Mr Milford. Even though the memory of the London audition no longer hurts in the way it once did, I still can't forget the way the nerves attacked my weak defenceless body like limpets, clinging on until I crumbled. Successful dress rehearsal or not, there is no guarantee it won't happen again tonight.

I take my place in line next to Tanvi. As the red velvet curtains swing open, a hush falls over the waiting audience. Mr Milford steps forward and welcomes them before striding over to the piano. As he starts the introduction to 'Sleigh Ride', I allow my eyes to adjust to the strange version of darkness in front of me. Although I can only make out the first few rows, I can sense just how full the room is. I wonder where Jodie and the poor mate she's dragged along are sitting.

And Noah.

Over the past month we've played eleven games of chess, watched three films at the cinema, and shared two large portions of fish and chips.

Oh, and one kiss.

The kiss happened on Sunday night, the last time we saw each other. It was gentle and soft and made my tummy turn over and I've replayed it in my head at least a thousand times, counting down the minutes until I can do it again.

The opening medley goes well. The songs are natural crowd-pleasers and the audience is clearly in a festive mood, many of them draped with tinsel or wearing flashing Santa hats as they clap along with the familiar tunes.

As the choir troops off stage to make way for the school band, the nerves that more or less behaved themselves in the group numbers just now, are back, creeping up my legs like the climbing ivy that covers 48 Arcadia Avenue.

I remove myself from the group and walk over to the corner of the room, my back to everyone. A few seconds later, Tanvi is at my side, waggling my arm.

'Ro?' she says sternly. 'What are you doing?'

'Freaking out,' I reply.

'Why? You're going to kill it out there.'

I whirl round to face her, gripping her elbows. 'But what if I don't? What if I miss all the big notes or forget the words or I open my mouth and nothing comes out?'

'None of those things are going to happen, Ro.'

'But what if they do?'

'Then they happen.'

'Tanvi!' I cry. 'You're supposed to be helping!'

'I mean, it'll be shit and everything,' Tanvi continues. 'Painful and humiliating and frustrating, but do you know what would be even worse?'

'I don't know – being buried alive? Burnt at the stake? Eaten by a bear?'

'No! *Not* singing the solo at all and regretting it your entire life. Worst comes to worst,' she adds, 'just imagine everyone in the audience totally naked. Or even better, on the loo. Having a really painful poo.'

I can't help but laugh.

'Thank you,' I say. 'For that delightful image.'

'What are best friends for?' Tanvi says, taking a small bow.

The rest of the concert passes in a flash and it's soon time to reassemble on the stage. 'O Holy Night' is the penultimate number. During 'Carol of the Bells', I can feel my heart thumping inside my chest so loudly I can hear it over the rest of the choir. It gets faster and faster, until the individual heartbeats are almost indistinguishable from each other. And then the audience is applauding and I'm putting one foot in front of the other and making my way to the centre of the stage. The applause dies out and there's a pause as Mr Milford adjusts his position at the piano stool. The audience follows his lead, taking the opportunity to cough and shift in their seats and rustle in their packets of sweets. Unsure quite where to look, I find my gaze drifting up towards the lighting box. My old domain.

I glance back at Mr Milford.

'You got this,' he mouths. 'Ready?'

I nod before I can change my mind.

The first few notes that come out of my mouth are quiet and hesitant. My heart begins to quicken. I can't fall apart. Not here, not now.

Then I remember that Tanvi is just behind me, rooting for me, and so is Mr Milford, and the rest of the choir, and

Jodie, and Noah, and this strange sense of calm washes over me, melting my anxiety away and my voice begins to soar, fierce and powerful and passionate, as I sing like my life depends on it.

The applause is like nothing I've ever heard – clapping and stamping and cheering combined. I'm so thrown I forget to take a proper bow, managing a sort of nod before floating back to my place in a daze. My choir mates are all clapping too, Tanvi the loudest of all, grinning madly as she pounds her hands together.

It's only as the introduction for the final song of the night, 'Ding Dong Merrily on High', kicks in that I realize my face is wet with happy tears I didn't even know had fallen.

There's just one thing stopping the moment from being perfect. And I know it's a stupid thing, because I even didn't tell Bonnie about the concert and even if I had she wouldn't have been able to come, but in this moment, there's only one more thing I want, and that's for my mum to be in the audience right now.

44

It takes me a full ten minutes to make it across the foyer, random parents and people I barely know stopping me and congratulating me on my performance. I'm accosted by Jodie (on tinselly crutches) and her friend Benny, both of them looking festive in equally hideous Christmas jumpers.

'OMG!' Jodie squeals. You can *sing*, Ro!'

'Have you thought about going on *X Factor*?' Benny, a skinny boy with a bleached-blond afro, asks. 'Cos you totally should.'

'I don't think so,' I say, laughing.

'What?' he cries. 'You crazy, girl!'

Benny is still trying to persuade me to apply for next year's auditions when I spot Noah in my peripheral vision. Luckily, Jodie notices him too, a smile spreading across her face.

'Come on, Benny,' she says, pulling at her Benny's sleeve and winking at me. 'Let's make tracks, I'm gasping for a pint.'

I wave them off before turning to face Noah. He's wearing his school uniform. Today is his last day of term too.

'Hi,' I say.

'Hi,' he replies.

He hesitates before leaning in to kiss me on the cheek. He aims a little off and gets my ear. It still feels nice though.

'You were really good,' he says.

'Thank you.'

'No, you don't get it – you were really, really, *really* good, Ro.'

'Thank you,' I say again, laughing.

There's a pause.

'Er, what are you doing on Sunday?' he asks.

'No plans, I don't think.'

'Um, do you want to come over to my mum's place? She's taking Finn to this football tournament in Sheffield so we'll be able to watch what we want on TV and stuff, and not have Finn interrupting all the time . . .' He trails off, his olive cheeks turning pinker by the second.

'OK,' I say, my heart fluttering a little.

'OK, great,' he says, smiling shyly. 'Hang on a second, my phone's ringing.' He pulls it out of his pocket. 'It's my irritatingly punctual mum. She's outside. Sorry.'

'No worries. See you Sunday then?'

'Yeah. We'll come pick you up from Tanvi's. Is around ten OK?'

'Great.'

There's another pause. Noah leans in for a second kiss. This time his aim is perfect.

*

I find Tanvi's family by the exit. When I approach, they break into noisy cheers. It's lovely but I can't help but feel sad too. Because no matter how kind and welcoming they are, the Shahs can't help but act as a reminder that my actual family is nowhere to be seen.

I sent Dad a text about the concert last week. His reply came two days later:

Sorry, but it's Izzy's dance recital that night. Hope it goes well. Dad x

I wasn't exactly surprised, but it still hurt. I have a feeling it always will a bit.

I'm chatting to Prisha when Tanvi interrupts us. 'Sorry to butt in,' she says. 'But can I borrow Ro for a second?'

'Sure,' Prisha says, standing aside.

'What's up?' I ask.

'There's someone here to see you.'

'Who?' I ask, frowning.

Please not my dad.

She points.

The foyer is so crowded, it takes me a few seconds to work out what I'm supposed to be looking at.

Then I see her.

Standing over by the Christmas tree, a backpack at her feet.

Bonnie.

Her hair is freshly dyed a deep cherry red for the winter. It suits her.

'I invited her,' Tanvi says. 'I hope you don't mind.'

I shake my head wordlessly and push my way through the crowd. I'm a couple of metres away when Bonnie notices me, her face springing into a smile.

'You're here,' I say, stopping in front of her.

I don't know why, but I sound out of breath.

'I'm here,' she confirms.

'But I thought you had a gig.'

'I got Danielle to cover it for me.'

There's a pause as I process the fact that Bonnie was in the audience just now, that she heard me sing after all.

'Your voice, Ro,' Bonnie says. 'It's . . . it's outstanding.'

My heart swells. I never knew how much I wanted to hear her say that until she did.

'Thank you,' I say.

'I mean it, Ro. It's beautiful. I had no idea . . .' She takes hold of my hands. 'I'm so sorry,' she says, her eyes filling with tears. 'About the audition. I behaved badly and it cost you a place with that choir, I can see that now. Can you try again? Please tell me you'll get another chance.'

'I, I suppose so,' I say. 'Next year maybe.'

'Good,' Bonnie says, pumping my arms, her face almost as red as her hair. 'Promise me you'll try again, won't you? Please.'

'OK,' I say.

'Promise?'

'Promise.'

And in that moment, I know I'll keep my word, that I'll definitely try again.

'Good girl.'

She lets go of my hands. We look at our feet in unison, suddenly slightly shy with each other.

Bonnie clears her throat. 'Look, I don't suppose you fancy coming home with me tonight?'

I look up. 'But I thought the house wasn't going to be ready until way after Christmas?'

'I managed to move things along a bit.'

I hesitate. I wasn't expecting this. Any of it.

'It's not perfect,' Bonnie continues. 'I mean, there's still a lot of stuff and I don't know how long it's going to take me to sort it all. It's early days and I've got a lot of progress still to make but I'm getting there, I am . . .

'Carina says it's OK, if that's what you're worried about,' she adds. 'That can we can review things after Christmas. I've got some overnight things for you. A toothbrush, pyjamas, a towel . . .' She points down at the backpack.

When I don't say anything, her face droops with disappointment.

'Perhaps I shouldn't have sprung it on you,' she says. 'I wanted it to be a surprise, that's all. Silly of me . . .'

'No, no,' I say. 'It's not that. It's just that me and Tanvi had plans to go to Shake It Off.'

'Oh, well, I won't keep you then. How about I give you a ring tomorrow instead?' She bends down to pick up the backpack.

'Wait,' I say. My eyes search the crowd for Tanvi. She spots me and smiles and waves. I turn back to Bonnie. 'What if Tanvi came with us instead?'

Bonnie straightens up. 'To the house?'

'Yes. I mean, if that's OK with you.'

Bonnie's face relaxes into a smile. 'I'd really like that, Ro.'

Bonnie, Tanvi and I catch the bus home, getting off a couple of stops early to buy fish and chips. We walk the rest of the way, holding our individually wrapped portions in our hands to keep our fingers warm, Bonnie and Tanvi getting on like old friends, just like I would have predicted, had it ever crossed my mind that one day we'd all be heading home together like this.

I haven't been back to Arcadia Avenue since the night of the fire and it feels strange to walk down the street for the first time in six weeks. Stripped of its climbing ivy, the house looks naked and vulnerable, a bit like Bonnie without her make-up.

Instinctively, I make my way down the path leading to the back door, Tanvi automatically following.

'I thought we could go through the front,' Bonnie calls after us, a set of shiny keys dangling from her index finger.

I swallow hard. The last time I went through the front door I was barely tall enough to peep through the letter box. In the darkness, Tanvi finds my hand and gives it a squeeze.

'Remember what I said before,' Bonnie says in a low voice as I retrace my steps towards her, Tanvi just behind me. 'It's not perfect.'

'I remember, Bonnie,' I say.

Bonnie smiles a nervous smile and inserts the key into the lock. For a moment it seems to stick, but with a gentle wiggle it turns and the door creaks open. I'm greeted with the smell of fresh paint, a scent so incongruous with this house it makes my brain ache with confusion.

Bonnie reaches inside and turns on the light. As I peer into the illuminated hallway, I realize that I've never seen it from this angle before.

Bonnie's right – it isn't perfect. There's still stuff piled up against the walls, but substantially less than before, and there's a defined path leading to the kitchen straight ahead. My eyes fall to the carpet.

'It's green,' I say softly.

'What?' Bonnie asks.

I shake my head and smile. 'It doesn't matter.'

Miracles come in all different shapes and forms. Some are big and dramatic, others small and quiet.

To the outside world, it's probably a very ordinary scene – a mother, her daughter and her daughter's best friend sitting at the kitchen table eating fish and chips straight from the paper.

But Ro Snow knows differently.

Acknowledgements

This book would not exist were it not for the patience and enthusiasm of my wonderful publisher, David Fickling Books. The entire team is such a pleasure to work with and I thank my lucky stars every day that I get to call myself a DFB author. Special thanks go to my editor, Bella Pearson. You always push me to make my books the best they can possibly be with your probing questions; fiendishly clever suggestions and almost forensic attention to detail. It goes without saying, but I'm going to miss you terribly. I'd also love to thank Rosie Fickling for being an invaluable second pair of eyes and championing Ro's story from the very beginning; the design team (especially Alice Todd) for another smasher of a cover; Carolyn McGlone for being calm and kind and brilliant at all times; Phil Earle for his continued passion and generosity, and David Fickling for making every moment a joy.

Massive thanks to my agent, Catherine Clarke, for

making me feel safe and sane every step of the way! Your support and guidance means the world.

A big shout-out to the authors, bloggers, booksellers and publishing folk that make up the UK YA community – you make it a very special place to be. In particular, I'd like to thank Non Pratt for being such a wonderful friend (and Aldi, for supplying the cheap champagne).

Thanks to Gregory Ashton for the title, too many brilliant ideas to count and some solid gold friendship; Matt Phillips for reading an early draft and persuading me to stick with it; Anne Murphy for answering my questions about social work procedures and Kath Nolan and Helen Williamson for answering my questions about hospital procedures (in both cases, any errors are entirely my own).

A special thank you to Emerson Milford Dickson for bidding so generously in the Authors for Grenfell auction. Thank you for letting me use not one, but two of your names in the book.

I started writing this book in 2014, abandoning it twice before deciding to resurrect it (with serious intent!) in January 2017. My Monday night writing group colleagues have been valued readers from the very beginning. Chris, Maria, Sara-Mae, Fiona and James, thank you for your ongoing patience and support.

As always, thanks to my family (Mum, Dad, Helen, Jake and Isla) for supporting me in their own unique down-to-earth way, and my dear friends Nikki Dibley, Katherine Jackson, Winnie Tang and Dave Whitfield for letting me rabbit on about plot holes and titles and deadlines. That's

About the Author

Lisa was born and grew up in Nottingham. Following a degree in drama, she worked as an actor for over a decade. Lisa also spent two years working at the Gender Identity Development Service of the NHS, which inspired her to write her Waterstones Children's Book Prize-winning debut novel, *The Art of Being Normal*. She has also written *All About Mia* and *Malala (Yousafzai – First Names)* and was one of the seven authors for the collaborative YA novel, *Floored*.

When she's not writing, Lisa loves long walks, long talks, dessert, good books and bad TV. She lives in London.

true friendship, right there.

Finally, I'd like to thank Dylan Bray. On top of being my biggest cheerleader, our conversations had a genuine impact on the shape of the finished book. The free haircuts are just a bonus, honest.